HUNTINGTOWER

JOHN BUCHAN led a truly extraordinary life: he was a diplomat, soldier, barrister, journalist, historian, politician, publisher, poet and novelist. He was born in Perth in 1875, the eldest son of a Free Church of Scotland minister, and educated at Hutcheson's Grammar School in Glasgow. He graduated from Glasgow University then took a scholarship to Oxford. During his time there – 'spent peacefully in an enclave like a monastery' – he wrote two historical novels, one of them being *A Lost Lady of Old Years*.

In 1901 he became a barrister of the Middle Temple and a private secretary to the High Commissioner for South Africa. In 1907 he married Susan Charlotte Grosvenor; they had three sons and a daughter. After spells as a war correspondent, Lloyd George's Director of Information and a Conservative MP, Buchan moved to Canada in 1935 where he became the first Baron Tweedsmuir of Elsfield.

Despite poor health throughout his life, Buchan's literary output was remarkable – thirty novels, over sixty non-fiction books, including biographies of Sir Walter Scott and Oliver Cromwell, and seven collections of short stories. His distinctive thrillers – 'shockers' as he called them – were characterised by suspenseful atmosphere, conspiracy theories and romantic heroes, notably Richard Hannay (based on the real-life military spy William Ironside) and Sir Edward Leithen. Buchan was a favourite writer of Alfred Hitchcock, whose screen adaptation of *The Thirty-Nine Steps* was phenomenally successful.

John Buchan served as Governor-General of Canada from 1935 until his death in 1940, the year his autobiography *Memory Hold-the-door* was published.

ANN WIDDECOMBE was born in 1947 in Bath, Somerset. She was educated at the Royal Naval School, Singapore, La Sainte Union Convent, Bath, Birmingham University (BA Hons Latin) and Oxford University (BA Hons Politics, Philosophy and Economics) LMH MA 1976. From 1973 to 1975 she worked in marketing at Unilever and then as Senior Administrator at London University from 1975 to 1987. From 1987 to 2010 she was the Member of Parliament for Maidstone (and The Weald). Her writing career began in 2000 with *The Clematis Tree* (which reached number eight in *The Times* Bestseller List) and is now engaged in writing her fifth novel, *An Act of Brotherhood*.

JOHN BUCHAN

Huntingtower

Introduced by Ann Widdecombe

First published in 1922 by Hodder & Stoughton
This edition published in Great Britain in 2012
by Polygon, an imprint of Birlinn Ltd

West Newington House
10 Newington Road
Edinburgh
EH9 1QS

www.polygonbooks.co.uk

ISBN 978 1 84697 223 2

British Library Cataloguing-in-Publication Data
A catalogue record for this book is available
on request from the British Library.

Typeset by Hewer Text UK Ltd, Edinburgh
Printed and bound by CPI Group (UK) Ltd, Croydon, CR0 4YY

Introduction

Huntingtower was my introduction to John Buchan. I was nearly nine when I came home from Singapore and saw television for the first time in my life. A year later the BBC serialised *Huntingtower* and the grown-ups were glued to it. I was a bit less enchanted but thought that if I kept quiet and looked interested I might stay up a bit longer.

The humour was rather too subtle for me, but I became engrossed in the story and that of course is what John Buchan is all about: a gripping tale or, as he would have put it, a rattling good yarn. I graduated from Dickson McCunn to Hannay and then to Leithen but the retired grocer is different from those two because he is not Buchan by any other name; he is not autobiographical. Buchan may have met a dozen McCunns but he himself is not the model.

One feels Buchan created McCunn for some light relief. By the time *Huntingtower* was written both Hannay and Leithen were established and much liked by the public, but, with the exception of Leithen in *John Macnab*, neither could be assigned much comic value. Leithen is a dry lawyer, Hannay a general. Yet the author could not entirely abandon the cast of his previous works and he has Archie Roylance playing a distinguished part.

Buchan did not return to McCunn as often as he reintroduced his other heroes. It was eight years between *Huntingtower* and *Castle Gay* and another five till *The House of the Four Winds*.

One intriguing facet of *Huntingtower* is the way that Dickson McCunn unfolds as a character in the course of this tale of revolution, a princess, jewels, kidnap and intrigue. When we first meet him he is a fussy sort of fellow and a bit lost as he faces retirement but by the end he is a man of true valour. The

Gorbals Die-Hards make a wonderful band of helpers but so sturdy and steadfast are they that it is not altogether easy to see them as McCunn does: 'so tiny, so poor, so pitifully handicapped . . . their few years have been spent in kennels and closes, always hungry and hunted with none to care for them'.

As with so many of Buchan's works you can almost smell the heather as the adventure is set in his beloved Scotland. The backdrop is all hills, coastline and impenetrable accents. 'Govey Dick! But yon was a fecht,' says Dougal, and one almost feels the princess might be more easily understood were she speaking her native Russian. Hilariously Dougal decides the princess is 'either foreign or English for she couldn't understand what I said'. Readers may well sympathise with the lady.

The Buchan recipe is simple and consistent: mix lofty ideals, usually of a patriotic nature, with high adventure, plenty of setbacks for the hero, lots of physical exertion and all the goodies living happily ever after. Stir in a stalwart of the underprivileged (Dougal in *Huntingtower*, Fish Benjie in *John Macnab*) and allow to set in Scotland.

It is a formula which works, for, despite language which appears sometimes casually racist and an outmoded paternalism, the works of Buchan have an enduring appeal. His characters never seem to change and nor do the surroundings in which they operate. They age in years but not in vigour. Until *Sick Heart River*, written as the author's own death was approaching, they appear immortal.

The first Leithen novel appeared in 1916, the last twenty-five years later; the first Hannay appeared in 1915, the last in 1936. Yet, despite the tumultuous social changes which happened between those years, the world of Buchan's characters seems to stand still. Dickson McCunn changes more in the space of *Huntingtower* than Buchan's other heroes change in a lifetime but in the later McCunn novels – *Castle Gay* and *The House of the Four Winds* – he appears much as he did at the end of *Huntingtower*. Once his character is established, he too becomes frozen in time.

Unlike Hannay and Leithen who occasionally find themselves ranged against paganism or dark superstition or the subverting of religion, McCunn takes on enemies who are very practical if often politically motivated and reliant on cunning. It is perhaps the main role of the Die-Hards to counter them with equal cunning, with the ways learned by boys who have survived by their wits all their short lives. McCunn is a pillar of the bourgeoisie while the Die-Hards are its challenge.

More than half a century since I first saw *Huntingtower* on television it retains its appeal as a story, a yarn, a tale of mystery, intrigue and derring-do. I watched it in black and white. Twenty years later it was remade in colour, which certainly improved the appearance of the heather but added nothing to the central characters who have always been colourful enough. I am glad Dickson McCunn set out on his great adventure and glad that Buchan took me along too.

For those who have never read *Huntingtower* this could be the introduction to hours of discovering Buchan. For those who are already devotees of the works but who have not yet met Dickson McCunn, a whole new cast of characters is about to be unveiled. For those like me, who are returning after a prolonged absence, you will find it hasn't much changed; McCunn has waited for you.

Ann Widdecombe
July 2012

Contents

If the Professor of Poetry in the University of Oxford has not
forgotten the rock whence he was hewn, this simple story may
give an hour of entertainment. I offer it to you because I think
you have met my friend Dickson McCunn, and I dare to hope
that you may even in your many sojournings in the Westlands
have encountered one or other of the Gorbals Die-Hards. If you
share my kindly feeling for Dickson, you will be interested in
some facts which I have lately ascertained about his ancestry. In
his veins there flows a portion of the redoubtable blood of Nicol
Jarvies. When the Bailie, you remember, returned from his
journey to Rob Roy beyond the Highland Line, he espoused his
housekeeper Mattie, 'an honest man's daughter and near cousin
o' the Laird o' Limmerfield'. The union was blessed with a son,
who succeeded to the Bailie's business and in due course begat
daughters, one of whom married a certain Ebenezer McCunn,
of whom there is a record in the archives of the Hammermen of
Glasgow. Ebenezer's grandson, Peter by name, was Provost of
Kirkintilloch, and his second son was the father of my hero by
his marriage with Robina Dickson, eldest daughter of one
Robert Dickson, a tenant-farmer in the Lennox. So there are
coloured threads in Mr McCunn's pedigree, and, like the Bailie,
he can count kin, should he wish, with Rob Roy himself through
'the auld wife ayont the fire at Stuckavrallachan'.

Such as it is, I dedicate to you the story, and ask for no better
verdict on it than that of that profound critic of life and literature,
Mr Huckleberry Finn, who observed of the *Pilgrim's Progress* that
he 'considered the statements interesting, but tough'.

J. B.

Prologue

THE girl came into the room with a darting movement like a swallow, looked round her with the same birdlike quickness, and then ran across the polished floor to where a young man sat on a sofa with one leg laid along it.

'I have saved you this dance, Quentin,' she said, pronouncing the name with a pretty staccato. 'You must be lonely not dancing, so I will sit with you. What shall we talk about?'

The young man did not answer at once, for his gaze was held by her face. He had never dreamed that the gawky and rather plain little girl whom he had romped with long ago in Paris would grow into such a being. The clean delicate lines of her figure, the exquisite pure colouring of hair and skin, the charming young arrogance of the eyes – this was beauty, he reflected, a miracle, a revelation. Her virginal fineness and her dress, which was the tint of pale fire, gave her the air of a creature of ice and flame.

'About yourself, please, Saskia,' he said. 'Are you happy now that you are a grown-up lady?'

'Happy!' Her voice had a thrill in it like music, frosty music. 'The days are far too short. I grudge the hours when I must sleep. They say it is sad for me to make my début in a time of war. But the world is very kind to me, and after all it is a victorious war for our Russia. And listen to me, Quentin. Tomorrow I am to be allowed to begin nursing at the Alexander Hospital. What do you think of that?'

The time was January 1916, and the place a room in the great Nirski Palace. No hint of war, no breath from the snowy streets, entered that curious chamber where Prince Peter Nirski kept some of the chief of his famous treasures. It was notable for its lack of drapery and upholstering – only a sofa or two and a few fine rugs on the cedar floor. The walls were of a green marble veined like malachite, the ceiling was of darker marble inlaid with white intaglios. Scattered everywhere were tables and cabinets laded with celadon china, and carved jade, and ivories, and shimmering Persian and Rhodian vessels. In all the room there was scarcely anything of metal and no touch of gilding or bright colour. The light came from green alabaster censers, and the place swam in a cold green radiance like some cavern below the sea. The air was warm and scented, and though it was very quiet there, a hum of voices and the strains of dance music drifted to it from the pillared corridor in which could be seen the glare of lights from the great ballroom beyond.

The young man had a thin face with lines of suffering round the mouth and eyes. The warm room had given him a high colour, which increased his air of fragility. He felt a little choked by the place, which seemed to him for both body and mind a hot-house, though he knew very well that the Nirski Palace on this gala evening was in no way typical of the land or its masters. Only a week ago he had been eating black bread with its owner in a hut on the Volhynian front.

'You have become amazing, Saskia,' he said. 'I won't pay my old playfellow compliments; besides, you must be tired of them. I wish you happiness all the day long like a fairy-tale Princess. But a crock like me can't do much to help you to it. The service seems to be the wrong way round, for here you are wasting your time talking to me.'

She put her hand on his. 'Poor Quentin! Is the leg very bad?'

He laughed. 'Oh, no. It's mending famously. I'll be able to get about without a stick in another month, and then you've got to teach me all the new dances.'

The jigging music of a two-step floated down the corridor. It made the young man's brow contract, for it brought to him a vision of dead faces in the gloom of a November dusk. He had once had a friend who used to whistle that air, and he had seen him die in the Hollebeke mud. There was something macabre in the tune . . . He was surely morbid this evening, for there seemed something macabre about the house, the room, the dancing, all Russia . . . These last days he had suffered from a sense of calamity impending, of a dark curtain drawing down upon a splendid world. They didn't agree with him at the Embassy, but he could not get rid of the notion.

The girl saw his sudden abstraction.

'What are you thinking about?' she asked. It had been her favourite question as a child.

'I was thinking that I rather wished you were still in Paris.'

'But why?'

'Because I think you would be safer.'

'Oh, what nonsense, Quentin dear! Where should I be safe if not in my own Russia, where I have friends – oh, so many, and tribes and tribes of relations? It is France and England that are unsafe with the German guns grumbling at their doors . . . My complaint is that my life is too cosseted and padded. I am too secure, and I do not want to be secure.'

The young man lifted a heavy casket from a table at his elbow. It was of dark green imperial jade, with a wonderfully carved lid. He took off the lid and picked up three small oddments of ivory – a priest with a beard, a tiny soldier, and a draught-ox. Putting the three in a triangle, he balanced the jade box on them.

'Look, Saskia! If you were living inside that box you would think it very secure. You would note the thickness of the walls and the hardness of the stone, and you would dream away in a peaceful green dusk. But all the time it would be held up by trifles – brittle trifles.'

She shook her head. 'You do not understand. You cannot understand. We are a very old and strong people with roots deep, deep in the earth.'

'Please God you are right,' he said. 'But, Saskia, you know that if I can ever serve you, you have only to command me. Now I can do no more for you than the mouse for the lion – at the beginning of the story. But the story had an end, you remember, and some day it may be in my power to help you. Promise to send for me.'

The girl laughed merrily. 'The King of Spain's daughter,' she quoted,

> *Came to visit me*
> *And all for the love*
> *Of my little nut-tree.*

The other laughed also, as a young man in the uniform of the Preobrajenski Guards approached to claim the girl. 'Even a nut-tree may be a shelter in a storm,' he said.

'Of course I promise, Quentin,' she said. '*Au revoir.* Soon I will come and take you to supper, and we will talk of nothing but nut-trees.'

He watched the two leave the room, her gown glowing like a tongue of fire in the shadowy archway. Then he slowly rose to his feet, for he thought that for a little he would watch the dancing. Something moved beside him, and he turned in time to prevent the jade casket from crashing to the floor. Two of the supports had slipped.

He replaced the thing on its proper table and stood silent for a moment.

'The priest and the soldier gone, and only the beast of burden left . . . If I were inclined to be superstitious, I should call that a dashed bad omen.'

ONE

How a Retired Provision Merchant Felt the Impulse of Spring

MR DICKSON McCUNN completed the polishing of his smooth cheeks with the towel, glanced appreciatively at their reflexion in the looking-glass, and then permitted his eyes to stray out of the window. In the little garden lilacs were budding, and there was a gold line of daffodils beside the tiny greenhouse. Beyond the sooty wall a birch flaunted its new tassels, and the jackdaws were circling about the steeple of the Guthrie Memorial Kirk. A blackbird whistled from a thornbush, and Mr McCunn was inspired to follow its example. He began a tolerable version of 'Roy's Wife of Aldivalloch'.

He felt singularly light-hearted, and the immediate cause was his safety razor. A week ago he had bought the thing in a sudden fit of enterprise, and now he shaved in five minutes, where before he had taken twenty, and no longer confronted his fellows, at least one day in three, with a countenance ludicrously mottled by sticking-plaster. Calculation revealed to him the fact that in his fifty-five years, having begun to shave at eighteen, he had wasted three thousand three hundred and seventy hours – or one hundred and forty days – or between four and five months – by his neglect of this admirable invention. Now he felt that he had stolen a march on Time. He had fallen heir, thus late, to a fortune in unpurchasable leisure.

He began to dress himself in the sombre clothes in which he had been accustomed for thirty-five years and more to go down to the shop in Mearns Street. And then a thought came to him which made him discard the grey-striped trousers, sit down on the edge of his bed, and muse.

Since Saturday the shop was a thing of the past. On Saturday at half-past eleven, to the accompaniment of a glass of dubious sherry, he had completed the arrangements by which the provision shop in Mearns Street, which had borne so long the legend of D. McCunn, together with the branches in Crossmyloof and the Shaws, became the property of a company, yclept the United Supply Stores, Limited. He had received in payment cash, debentures, and preference shares, and his lawyers and his own acumen had acclaimed the bargain. But all the weekend he had been a little sad. It was the end of so old a song, and he knew no other tune to sing. He was comfortably off, healthy, free from any particular cares in life, but free too from any particular duties. 'Will I be going to turn into a useless old man?' he asked himself.

But he had woke up this Monday to the sound of the blackbird, and the world, which had seemed rather empty twelve hours before, was now brisk and alluring. His prowess in quick shaving assured him of his youth. 'I'm no' that dead old,' he observed, as he sat on the edge of the bed, to his reflexion in the big looking-glass.

It was not an old face. The sandy hair was a little thin on the top and a little grey at the temples, the figure was perhaps a little too full for youthful elegance, and an athlete would have censured the neck as too fleshy for perfect health. But the cheeks were rosy, the skin clear, and the pale eyes singularly childlike. They were a little weak, those eyes, and had some difficulty in looking for long at the same object, so that Mr McCunn did not stare people in the face, and had, in consequence, at one time in his career acquired a perfectly undeserved reputation for cunning. He shaved clean, and looked uncommonly like a wise, plump schoolboy. As he gazed at his simulacrum he stopped whistling 'Roy's Wife' and let his countenance harden into a noble sternness. Then he laughed, and observed in the language of his youth that there was 'life in the auld dowg yet'. In that moment the soul of Mr McCunn conceived the Great Plan.

The first sign of it was that he swept all his business garments unceremoniously on to the floor. The next that he rootled at the bottom of a deep drawer and extracted a most disreputable tweed suit. It had once been what I believe is called a Lovat mixture, but was now a nondescript sub-fusc, with bright patches of colour like moss on whinstone. He regarded it lovingly, for it had been for twenty years his holiday wear, emerging annually for a hallowed month to be stained with salt and bleached with sun. He put it on, and stood shrouded in an odour of camphor. A pair of thick nailed boots and a flannel shirt and collar completed the equipment of the sportsman. He had another long look at himself in the glass, and then descended whistling to breakfast. This time the tune was 'Macgregors' Gathering', and the sound of it stirred the grimy lips of a man outside who was delivering coals – himself a Macgregor – to follow suit. Mr McCunn was a very fountain of music that morning.

Tibby, the aged maid, had his newspaper and letters waiting by his plate, and a dish of ham and eggs frizzling near the fire. He fell to ravenously but still musingly, and he had reached the stage of scones and jam before he glanced at his correspondence. There was a letter from his wife now holidaying at the Neuk Hydropathic. She reported that her health was improving, and that she had met various people who had known somebody who had known somebody else whom she had once known herself. Mr McCunn read the dutiful pages and smiled. 'Mamma's enjoying herself fine,' he observed to the teapot. He knew that for his wife the earthly paradise was a hydropathic, where she put on her afternoon dress and every jewel she possessed when she rose in the morning, ate large meals of which the novelty atoned for the nastiness, and collected an immense casual acquaintance, with whom she discussed ailments, ministers, sudden deaths, and the intricate genealogies of her class. For his part he rancorously hated hydropathics, having once spent a black week under the roof of one in his wife's company. He detested the food, the Turkish baths (he had a passionate aversion to baring his body before strangers), the inability to find anything to do, and the compulsion to endless small talk. A thought flitted over his mind which he was too loyal to formulate. Once he and his wife had had similar likings, but they had taken different roads since their child died. Janet! He saw again – he was never quite free from the sight – the solemn little white-frocked girl who had died long ago in the spring.

It may have been the thought of the Neuk Hydropathic, or more likely the thin clean scent of the daffodils with which Tibby had decked the table, but long ere breakfast was finished the Great Plan had ceased to be an airy vision and become a sober well-masoned structure. Mr McCunn – I may confess it at the start – was an incurable romantic.

He had had a humdrum life since the day when he had first entered his uncle's shop with the hope of some day succeeding that honest grocer; and his feet had never strayed a yard from his sober rut. But his mind, like the Dying Gladiator's, had been far away. As a boy he had voyaged among books, and they had given him a world where he could shape his career according to his whimsical fancy. Not that Mr McCunn was what is known as a great reader. He read slowly and fastidiously, and sought in literature for one thing alone. Sir Walter Scott had been his first guide, but he read the novels not for their insight into human character or for their historical pageantry, but because they gave him material wherewith to construct fantastic journeys. It was the same with Dickens. A lit tavern, a stage-coach, post-horses, the clack of hoofs on a frosty road, went to his head like wine. He was a Jacobite not because he had any views on Divine Right, but because he had always before his eyes a picture of a knot of adventurers in cloaks, new landed from France among the western heather.

On this select basis he had built up his small library – Defoe, Hakluyt, Hazlitt and the essayists, Boswell, some indifferent romances, and a shelf of spirited poetry. His tastes became known, and he acquired a reputation for a scholarly habit. He was president of the Literary Society of the Guthrie Memorial Kirk, and read to its members a variety of papers full of a gusto which rarely became critical. He had been three times chairman at Burns Anniversary dinners, and had delivered orations in eulogy of the national Bard; not because he greatly admired him – he thought him rather vulgar – but because he took Burns as an emblem of the un-Burns-like literature which he loved. Mr McCunn was no scholar and was sublimely unconscious of background. He grew his flowers in his small garden-plot oblivious of their origin so long as they gave him the colour and scent he sought. Scent, I say, for he appreciated more than the mere picturesque. He had a passion for words and cadences, and would be haunted for weeks by a cunning phrase, savouring it as a connoisseur savours a vintage. Wherefore long ago, when he could ill afford it, he had purchased the Edinburgh *Stevenson*. They were the only large books on his shelves, for he had a liking for small volumes – things he could stuff into his pocket in that sudden journey which he loved to contemplate.

Only he had never taken it. The shop had tied him up for eleven months in the year, and the twelfth had always found him settled decorously with his wife in some seaside villa. He had not fretted, for he was content with dreams. He was always a little tired, too, when the holidays came, and his wife told him he was growing old. He consoled himself with tags from the more philosophic of his authors, but he scarcely needed consolation. For he had large stores of modest contentment.

But now something had happened. A spring morning and a safety razor had convinced him that he was still young. Since yesterday he was a man of a large leisure. Providence had done for him what he would never have done for himself. The rut in which he had travelled so long had given place to open country. He repeated to himself one of the quotations with which he had been wont to stir the literary young men at the Guthrie Memorial Kirk:

> *What's a man's age? He must hurry more, that's all;*
> *Cram in a day, what his youth took a year to hold:*
> *When we mind labour, then only, we're too old—*
> *What age had Methusalem when he begat Saul?*

He would go journeying – who but he? – pleasantly.

It sounds a trivial resolve, but it quickened Mr McCunn to the depths of his being. A holiday, and alone! On foot, of course, for he must travel light. He would buckle on a pack after the approved fashion. He had the very thing in a drawer upstairs, which he had bought some years ago at a sale. That and a waterproof and a stick, and his outfit was complete. A book, too, and, as he lit his first pipe, he considered what it should be. Poetry, clearly, for it was the spring, and besides poetry could be got in pleasantly small bulk. He stood before his bookshelves trying to select a volume, rejecting one after another as inapposite. Browning – Keats, Shelley – they seemed more suited for the hearth than for the roadside. He did not want anything Scots, for he was of opinion that spring came more richly in England and that English people had a better notion of it. He was tempted by the Oxford Anthology, but was deterred by its thickness, for he did not possess the thin-paper edition. Finally he selected Izaak Walton. He had never fished in his life, but *The Compleat Angler* seemed to fit his mood. It was old and curious and learned and fragrant with the youth of things. He remembered its falling cadences, its country songs and wise meditations. Decidedly it was the right scrip for his pilgrimage.

Characteristically he thought last of where he was to go. Every bit of the world beyond his front door had its charms to the seeing eye. There seemed nothing common or unclean that fresh morning. Even a walk among coal-pits had its attractions. . . . But since he had the right to choose, he lingered over it like an epicure. Not the Highlands, for spring came late among their sour mosses. Some place where there were fields and woods and inns, somewhere, too, within call of the sea. It must not be too remote, for he had no time to waste on train journeys; nor too near, for he wanted a countryside untainted. Presently he thought of Carrick. A good, green land, as he remembered it, with purposeful white roads and public-houses sacred to the memory of Burns; near the hills but yet lowland, and with a bright sea chafing on its shores. He decided on Carrick, found a map, and planned his journey.

Then he routed out his knapsack, packed it with a modest change of raiment, and sent out Tibby to buy chocolate and tobacco and to cash a cheque at the Strathclyde Bank. Till Tibby returned he occupied himself with delicious dreams . . . He saw himself daily growing browner and leaner, swinging along broad highways or wandering in bypaths. He pictured his seasons of ease, when he unslung his pack and smoked in some clump of lilacs by a burnside – he remembered a phrase of Stevenson's somewhat like that. He would meet and talk with all sorts of folk; an exhilarating prospect, for Mr McCunn loved his kind. There would be the evening hour before he reached his inn, when, pleasantly tired, he would top some ridge and see the welcoming lights of a little town. There would be the lamp-lit after-supper time when he would read and reflect, and the start in the gay morning, when tobacco tastes sweetest and even fifty-five seems young. It would be holiday of the purest, for no business now tugged at his coat-tails. He was beginning a new life, he told himself, when he could cultivate the seedling interests which had withered beneath the far-reaching shade of the shop. Was ever a man more fortunate or more free?

Tibby was told that he was going off for a week or two. No letters need be forwarded, for he would be constantly moving, but Mrs McCunn at the Neuk Hydropathic would be kept informed of his whereabouts. Presently he stood on his doorstep, a stocky figure in ancient tweeds, with a bulging pack slung on his arm, and a stout hazel stick in his hand. A passer-by would have remarked an elderly shopkeeper bent apparently on a day in the country, a common little man on a prosaic errand. But the passer-by would have been wrong, for he could not see into the heart. The plump citizen was the eternal pilgrim; he was Jason, Ulysses, Eric the Red, Albuquerque, Cortez – starting out to discover new worlds.

Before he left Mr McCunn had given Tibby a letter to post. That morning he had received an epistle from a benevolent acquaintance, one Mackintosh, regarding a group of urchins who called themselves the 'Gorbals Die-Hards'. Behind the premises in Mearns Street lay a tract of slums, full of mischievous boys, with whom his staff waged truceless war. But lately there had started among them a kind of unauthorized and unofficial Boy Scouts, who, without uniform or badge or any kind of paraphernalia, followed the banner of Sir Robert Baden-Powell and subjected themselves to a rude discipline. They were far too poor to join an orthodox troop, but they faithfully copied what they believed to be the practices of more fortunate boys. Mr McCunn had witnessed their pathetic parades, and had even passed the time of day with their leader, a red-haired savage called Dougal. The philanthropic Mackintosh had taken an interest in the gang and now desired subscriptions to send them to camp in the country.

Mr McCunn, in his new exhilaration, felt that he could not deny to others what he proposed for himself. His last act before leaving was to send Mackintosh ten pounds.

TWO

Of Mr John Heritage and
the Difference in Points of View

DICKSON McCUNN was never to forget the first stage in that pilgrimage. A little after midday he descended from a grimy third-class carriage at a little station whose name I have forgotten. In the village near-by he purchased some new-baked buns and ginger biscuits, to which he was partial, and followed by the shouts of urchins, who admired his pack – 'Look at the auld man gaun to the schule' – he emerged into open country. The late April noon gleamed like a frosty morning, but the air, though tonic, was kind. The road ran over sweeps of moorland where curlews wailed, and into lowland pastures dotted with very white, very vocal lambs. The young grass had the warm fragrance of new milk. As he went he munched his buns, for he had resolved to have no plethoric midday meal, and presently he found the burnside nook of his fancy, and halted to smoke. On a patch of turf close to a grey stone bridge he had out his Walton and read the chapter on 'The Chavender or Chub'. The collocation of words delighted him and inspired him to verse. 'Lavender or Lub' – 'Pavender or Pub' – 'Gravender or Grub' – but the monosyllables proved too vulgar for poetry. Regretfully he desisted.

The rest of the road was as idyllic as the start. He would tramp steadily for a mile or so and then saunter, leaning over bridges to watch the trout in the pools, admiring from a drystone dyke the unsteady gambols of new-born lambs, kicking up dust from strips of moor-burn on the heather. Once by a fir-wood he was privileged to surprise three lunatic hares waltzing. His cheeks glowed with the sun; he moved in an atmosphere of pastoral, serene and contented. When the shadows began to lengthen he arrived at the village of Cloncae, where he proposed to lie. The inn looked dirty, but he found a decent widow, above whose door ran the legend in home-made lettering, 'Mrs brockie tea and Coffee', and who was willing to give him quarters. There he supped handsomely off ham and eggs, and dipped into a work called *Covenanting Worthies*, which garnished a table decorated with sea-shells. At half-past nine precisely he retired to bed and unhesitating sleep.

Next morning he awoke to a changed world. The sky was grey and so low that his outlook was bounded by a cabbage garden, while a surly wind prophesied rain. It was chilly, too, and he had his breakfast beside the kitchen fire. Mrs Brockie could not spare a capital letter for her surname on the signboard, but she exalted it in her talk. He heard of a multitude of Brockies, ascendant, descendant, and collateral, who seemed to be in a fair way to inherit the earth. Dickson listened sympathetically, and lingered by the fire. He felt stiff from yesterday's exercise, and the edge was off his spirit.

The start was not quite what he had pictured. His pack seemed heavier, his boots tighter, and his pipe drew badly. The first miles were all uphill, with a wind tingling his ears, and no colours in the landscape but brown and grey. Suddenly he awoke to the fact that he was dismal, and thrust the notion behind him. He expanded his chest and drew in long draughts of air. He told himself that this sharp weather was better than sunshine. He remembered that all travellers in romances battled with mist and rain. Presently his body recovered comfort and vigour, and his mind worked itself into cheerfulness.

He overtook a party of tramps and fell into talk with them. He had always had a fancy for the class, though he had never known anything nearer it than city beggars. He pictured them as philosophic vagabonds, full of quaint turns of speech, unconscious Borrovians. With these samples his disillusionment was speedy. The party was made up of a ferret-faced man with a red nose, a draggle-tailed woman, and a child in a crazy perambulator.

Their conversation was one-sided, for it immediately resolved itself into a whining chronicle of misfortunes and petitions for relief. It cost him half a crown to be rid of them.

The road was alive with tramps that day. The next one did the accosting. Hailing Mr McCunn as 'Guv'nor', he asked to be told the way to Manchester. The objective seemed so enterprising that Dickson was impelled to ask questions, and heard, in what appeared to be in the accents of the Colonies, the tale of a career of unvarying calamity. There was nothing merry or philosophic about this adventurer. Nay, there was something menacing. He eyed his companion's waterproof covetously, and declared that he had had one like it which had been stolen from him the day before. Had the place been lonely he might have contemplated highway robbery, but they were at the entrance to a village, and the sight of a public-house awoke his thirst. Dickson parted with him at the cost of sixpence for a drink.

He had no more company that morning except an aged stone-breaker whom he convoyed for half a mile. The stone-breaker also was soured with the world. He walked with a limp, which, he said, was due to an accident years before, when he had been run into by 'ane o' thae damned velocipeeds'. The word revived in Dickson memories of his youth, and he was prepared to be friendly. But the ancient would have none of it. He inquired morosely what he was after, and, on being told, remarked that he might have learned more sense. 'It's a daft-like thing for an auld man like you to be traivellin' the roads. Ye maun be ill-off for a job.' Questioned as to himself, he became, as the newspapers say, 'reticent', and having reached his bing of stones, turned rudely to his duties. 'Awa' hame wi' ye,' were his parting words. 'It's idle scoondrels like you that maks wark for honest folk like me.'

The morning was not a success, but the strong air had given Dickson such an appetite that he resolved to break his rule, and, on reaching the little town of Kilchrist, he sought luncheon at the chief hotel. There he found that which revived his spirits. A solitary bagman shared the meal, who revealed the fact that he was in the grocery line. There followed a well-in-formed and most technical conversation. He was drawn to speak of the United Supply Stores, Limited, of their prospects and of their predecessor, Mr McCunn, whom he knew well by repute but had never met. 'Yon's the clever one,' he observed. 'I've always said there's no longer head in the city of Glasgow than McCunn. An old-fashioned firm, but it has aye managed to keep up with the times. He's just retired, they tell me, and in my opinion it's a big loss to the provision trade. . . .' Dickson's heart glowed within him. Here was Romance; to be praised incognito; to enter a casual inn and find that fame had preceded him. He warmed to the bagman, insisted on giving him a liqueur and a cigar, and finally revealed himself. 'I'm Dickson McCunn,' he said, 'taking a bit holiday. If there's anything I can do for you when I get back, just let me know.' With mutual esteem they parted.

He had need of all his good spirits, for he emerged into an unrelenting drizzle. The environs of Kilchrist are at the best unlovely, and in the wet they were as melancholy as a graveyard. But the encounter with the bagman had worked wonders with Dickson, and he strode lustily into the weather, his waterproof collar buttoned round his chin. The road climbed to a bare moor, where lagoons had formed in the ruts, and the mist showed on each side only a yard or two of soaking heather. Soon he was wet; presently every part of him – boots, body, and pack – was one vast sponge. The waterproof was not water-proof, and the rain penetrated to his most intimate garments. Little he cared. He felt lighter, younger, than on the idyllic previous day. He enjoyed the buffets of the storm, and one wet mile succeeded another to the accompaniment of Dickson's shouts and laughter. There was no one abroad that afternoon, so he could talk aloud to himself and repeat his favourite poems. About five in the evening there presented himself at the Black Bull Inn at Kirkmichael a soaked, disreputable, but most cheerful traveller.

Now the Black Bull at Kirkmichael is one of the few very good inns left in the world. It is an old place and an hospitable, for it has been for generations a haunt of anglers, who above all other men understand comfort. There are always bright fires there, and hot water, and old soft leather arm-chairs, and an aroma of good food and good tobacco, and giant trout in glass cases, and pictures of Captain Barclay of Urie walking to London, and Mr Ramsay of Barnton winning a horse-race, and the three-volume edition of the Waverley Novels with many volumes missing, and indeed all those things which an inn should have. Also there used to be – there may still be – sound vintage claret in the cellars. The Black Bull expects its guests to arrive in every stage of dishevelment, and Dickson was received by a cordial landlord, who offered dry garments as a matter of course. The pack proved to have resisted the elements, and a suit of clothes and slippers were provided by the house. Dickson, after a glass of toddy, wallowed in a hot bath, which washed all the stiffness out of him. He had a fire in his bedroom, beside which he wrote the opening passages of that diary he had vowed to keep, descanting lyrically upon the joys of ill weather. At seven o'clock, warm and satisfied in soul, and with his body clad in raiment several sizes too large for it, he descended to dinner.

At one end of the long table in the dining-room sat a group of anglers. They looked jovial fellows, and Dickson would fain have joined them; but, having been fishing all day in the Loch o' the Threshes, they were talking their own talk, and he feared that his admiration for Izaak Walton did not qualify him to butt into the erudite discussions of fishermen. The landlord seemed to think likewise, for he drew back a chair for him at the other end, where sat a young man absorbed in a book. Dickson gave him good evening, and got an abstracted reply. The young man supped the Black Bull's excellent broth with one hand, and with the other turned the pages of his volume. A glance convinced Dickson that the work was French, a literature which did not interest him. He knew little of the tongue and suspected it of impropriety.

Another guest entered and took the chair opposite the bookish young man. He was also young – not more than thirty-three – and to Dickson's eye was the kind of person he would have liked to resemble. He was tall and free from any superfluous flesh; his face was lean, fine-drawn, and deeply sunburnt, so that the hair above showed oddly pale; the hands were brown and beautifully shaped, but the forearm revealed by the loose cuffs of his shirt was as brawny as a blacksmith's. He had rather pale blue eyes, which seemed to have looked much at the sun, and a small moustache the colour of ripe hay. His voice was low and pleasant, and he pronounced his words precisely, like a foreigner.

He was very ready to talk, but in defiance of Dr Johnson's warning, his talk was all questions. He wanted to know everything about the neighbourhood – who lived in what houses, what were the distances between the towns, what harbours would admit what class of vessel. Smiling agreeably, he put Dickson through a catechism to which he knew none of the answers. The landlord was called in, and proved more helpful. But on one matter he was fairly at a loss. The catechist asked about a house called Darkwater, and was met with a shake of the head. 'I know no sic-like name in this countryside, sir,' and the catechist looked disappointed.

The literary young man said nothing, but ate trout abstractedly, one eye on his book. The fish had been caught by the anglers in the Loch o' the Threshes, and phrases describing their capture floated from the other end of the table. The young man had a second helping, and then refused the excellent hill mutton that followed, contenting himself with cheese. Not so Dickson and the catechist. They ate everything that was set before them, topping up with a glass of port. Then the latter, who had been talking illuminatingly about Spain, rose, bowed, and left the table, leaving Dickson, who liked to linger over his meals, to the society of the ichthyophagous student.

He nodded towards the book. 'Interesting?' he asked.

The young man shook his head and displayed the name on the cover. 'Anatole France. I used to be crazy about him, but now he seems rather a back number.' Then he glanced towards the just-vacated chair. 'Australian,' he said.

'How d'you know?'

'Can't mistake them. There's nothing else so lean and fine produced on the globe today. I was next door to them at Pozières and saw them fight. Lord! Such men! Now and then you had a freak, but most looked like Phoebus Apollo.'

Dickson gazed with a new respect at his neighbour, for he had not associated him with battlefields. During the war he had been a fervent patriot, but, though he had never heard a shot himself, so many of his friends' sons and nephews, not to mention cousins of his own, had seen service, that he had come to regard the experience as commonplace. Lions in Africa and bandits in Mexico seemed to him novel and romantic things, but not trenches and aeroplanes which were the whole world's property. But he could scarcely fit his neighbour into even his haziest picture of war. The young man was tall and a little round-shouldered; he had short-sighted, rather prominent brown eyes, untidy black hair, and dark eyebrows which came near to meeting. He wore a knickerbocker suit of bluish-grey tweed, a pale blue shirt, a pale blue collar, and a dark blue tie – a symphony of colour which seemed too elaborately considered to be quite natural. Dickson had set him down as an artist or a newspaper correspondent, objects to him of lively interest. But now the classification must be reconsidered.

'So you were in the war,' he said encouragingly.

'Four blasted years,' was the savage reply. 'And I never want to hear the name of the beastly thing again.'

'You said he was an Australian,' said Dickson, casting back. 'But I thought Australians had a queer accent, like the English.'

'They've all kind of accents, but you can never mistake their voice. It's got the sun in it. Canadians have got grinding ice in theirs, and Virginians have got butter. So have the Irish. In Britain there are no voices, only speaking-tubes. It isn't safe to judge men by their accent only. You yourself I take to be Scotch, but for all I know you may be a senator from Chicago or a Boer General.'

'I'm from Glasgow. My name's Dickson McCunn.' He had a
faint hope that the announcement might affect the other as it
had affected the bagman at Kilchrist.

'Golly, what a name!' exclaimed the young man rudely.

Dickson was nettled. 'It's very old Highland,' he said. 'It
means the son of a dog.'

'Which – Christian name or surname?' Then the young man
appeared to think he had gone too far, for he smiled pleasantly.
'And a very good name too. Mine is prosaic by comparison.
They call me John Heritage.'

'That,' said Dickson, mollified, 'is like a name out of a book.
With that name by rights you should be a poet.'

Gloom settled on the young man's countenance. 'It's a dashed
sight too poetic. It's like Edwin Arnold and Alfred Austin and
Dante Gabriel Rossetti. Great poets have vulgar monosyllables for
names, like Keats. The new Shakespeare when he comes along
will probably be called Grubb or Jubber, if he isn't Jones. With a
name like yours I might have a chance. *You* should be the poet.'

'I'm very fond of reading,' said Dickson modestly.

A slow smile crumpled Mr Heritage's face. 'There's a fire in
the smoking-room,' he observed as he rose. 'We'd better bag the
arm-chairs before these fishing louts take them.' Dickson
followed obediently. This was the kind of chance acquaintance
for whom he had hoped, and he was prepared to make the most
of him.

The fire burned bright in the little dusky smoking-room,
lighted by one oil-lamp. Mr Heritage flung himself into a chair,
stretched his long legs, and lit a pipe.

'You like reading?' he asked. 'What sort? Any use for poetry?'

'Plenty,' said Dickson. 'I've aye been fond of learning it up
and repeating it to myself when I had nothing to do. In church
and waiting on trains, like. It used to be Tennyson, but now it's
more Browning. I can say a lot of Browning.'

The other screwed his face into an expression of disgust. 'I
know the stuff. "Damask cheeks and dewy sister eyelids." Or
else the Ercles vein – "God's in His Heaven, all's right with the

world." No good, Mr McCunn. All back numbers. Poetry's not a thing of pretty round phrases or noisy invocations. It's life itself, with the tang of the raw world in it – not a sweet-meat for middle-class women in parlours.'

'Are you a poet, Mr Heritage?'

'No, Dogson, I'm a paper-maker.'

This was a new view to Mr McCunn. 'I just once knew a paper-maker,' he observed reflectively. 'They called him Tosh. He drank a bit.'

'Well, I don't drink,' said the other. 'I'm a paper-maker, but that's for my bread and butter. Some day for my own sake I may be a poet.'

'Have you published anything?'

The eager admiration in Dickson's tone gratified Mr Heritage. He drew from his pocket a slim book. 'My first fruits,' he said, rather shyly.

Dickson received it with reverence. It was a small volume in grey paper boards with a white label on the back, and it was lettered: *Whorls – John Heritage's Book.* He turned the pages and read a little. 'It's a nice wee book,' he observed at length.

'Good God, if you call it nice, I must have failed pretty badly,' was the irritated answer.

Dickson read more deeply and was puzzled. It seemed worse than the worst of Browning to understand. He found one poem about a garden entitled 'Revue'. 'Crimson and resonant clangs the dawn,' said the poet. Then he went on to describe noonday:

Sunflowers, tall Grenadiers, ogle the roses' short-skirted ballet.
The fumes of dark sweet wine hidden in frail petals
Madden the drunkard bees.

This seemed to him an odd way to look at things, and he boggled over a phrase about an 'epicene lily'. Then came evening: 'The painted gauze of the stars flutters in a fold of twilight crape,' sang Mr Heritage; and again, 'The moon's pale leprosy sloughs the fields.'

Dickson turned to other verses which apparently enshrined the writer's memory of the trenches. They were largely compounded of oaths, and rather horrible, lingering lovingly over sights and smells which every one is aware of, but most people contrive to forget. He did not like them. Finally he skimmed a poem about a lady who turned into a bird. The evolution was described with intimate anatomical details which scared the honest reader.

He kept his eyes on the book, for he did not know what to say. The trick seemed to be to describe nature in metaphors mostly drawn from music-halls and haberdashers' shops, and, when at a loss, to fall to cursing. He thought it frankly very bad, and he laboured to find words which would combine politeness and honesty.

'Well?' said the poet.

'There's a lot of fine things here, but – but the lines don't just seem to scan very well.'

Mr Heritage laughed. 'Now I can place you exactly. You like the meek rhyme and the conventional epithet. Well, I don't. The world has passed beyond that prettiness. You want the moon described as a Huntress or a gold disc or a flower – I say it's oftener like a beer barrel or a cheese. You want a wealth of jolly words and real things ruled out as unfit for poetry. I say there's nothing unfit for poetry. Nothing, Dogson! Poetry's everywhere, and the real thing is commoner among drabs and pot-houses and rubbish-heaps than in your Sunday parlours. The poet's business is to distil it out of rottenness, and show that it is all one spirit, the thing that keeps the stars in their place. . . . I wanted to call my book *Drains*, for drains are sheer poetry carrying off the excess and discards of human life to make the fields green and the corn ripen. But the publishers kicked. So I called it *Whorls*, to express my view of the exquisite involution of all things. Poetry is the fourth dimension of the soul. . . . Well, let's hear about your taste in prose.'

Mr McCunn was much bewildered, and a little inclined to be cross. He disliked being called Dogson, which seemed to him an abuse of his etymological confidences. But his habit of politeness held.

He explained rather haltingly his preferences in prose.

Mr Heritage listened with wrinkled brows.

'You're even deeper in the mud than I thought,' he remarked. 'You live in a world of painted laths and shadows. All this passion for the picturesque! Trash, my dear man, like a schoolgirl's novelette heroes. You make up romances about gipsies and sailors, and the blackguards they call pioneers, but you know nothing about them. If you did, you would find they had none of the gilt and gloss you imagine. But the great things they have got in common with all humanity you ignore. It's like – it's like sentimentalizing about a pancake because it looked like a buttercup, and all the while not knowing that it was good to eat.'

At that moment the Australian entered the room to get a light for his pipe. He wore a motor-cyclist's overalls and appeared to be about to take the road. He bade them good night, and it seemed to Dickson that his face, seen in the glow of the fire, was drawn and anxious, unlike that of the agreeable companion at dinner.

'There,' said Mr Heritage, nodding after the departing figure. 'I dare say you have been telling yourself stories about that chap – life in the bush, stock-riding, and the rest of it. But probably he's a bank-clerk from Melbourne. . . . Your romanticism is one vast self-delusion, and it blinds your eye to the real thing. We have got to clear it out, and with it all the damnable humbug of the Kelt.'

Mr McCunn, who spelt the word with a soft 'C', was puzzled. 'I thought a kelt was a kind of a no-weel fish,' he interposed.

But the other, in the flood-tide of his argument, ignored the interruption. 'That's the value of the war,' he went on. 'It has bust up all the old conventions, and we've got to finish the destruction before we can build. It is the same with literature and religion, and society and politics. At them with the axe, say I. I have no use for priests and pedants. I've no use for upper classes and middle classes. There's only one class that matters, the plain man, the workers, who live close to life.'

'The place for you,' said Dickson dryly, 'is in Russia among the Bolsheviks.'

Mr Heritage approved. 'They are doing a great work in their own fashion. We needn't imitate all their methods – they're a trifle crude and have too many Jews among them – but they've got hold of the right end of the stick. They seek truth and reality.'

Mr McCunn was slowly being roused.

'What brings you wandering hereaways?' he asked.

'Exercise,' was the answer. 'I've been kept pretty closely tied up all winter. And I want leisure and quiet to think over things.'

'Well, there's one subject you might turn your attention to. You'll have been educated like a gentleman?'

'Nine wasted years – five at Harrow, four at Cambridge.'

'See here, then. You're daft about the working-class and have no use for any other. But what in the name of goodness do you know about working-men? . . . I come out of them myself, and have lived next door to them all my days. Take them one way and another, they're a decent sort, good and bad like the rest of us. But there's a wheen daft folk that would set them up as models – close to truth and reality, says you. It's sheer ignorance, for you're about as well acquainted with the working-man as with King Solomon. You say I make up fine stories about tinklers and sailor-men because I know nothing about them. That's maybe true. But you're at the same job yourself. You idealize the working-man, you and your kind, because you're ignorant. You say that he's seeking for truth, when he's only looking for a drink and a rise in wages. You tell me he's near reality, but I tell you that his notion of reality is often just a short working day and looking on at a footba'-match on Saturday. . . . And when you run down what you call the middle-classes that do three-quarters of the world's work and keep the machine going and the working-man in a job; then I tell you you're talking havers. Havers!'

Mr McCunn, having delivered his defence of the bourgeoisie, rose abruptly and went to bed. He felt jarred and irritated. His innocent little private domain had been badly trampled by this stray bull of a poet. But as he lay in bed, before blowing out his candle, he had recourse to Walton, and found a passage on which, as on a pillow, he went peacefully to sleep:

'As I left this place, and entered into the next field, a second pleasure entertained me; 'twas a handsome milkmaid, that had not yet attained so much age and wisdom as to load her mind with any fears of many things that will never be, as too many men too often do; but she cast away all care, and sang like a nightingale; her voice was good, and the ditty fitted for it; it was the smooth song that was made by *Kit Marlow* now at least fifty years ago. And the milkmaid's mother sung an answer to it, which was made by *Sir Walter Raleigh* in his younger days. They were old-fashioned poetry, but choicely good; I think much better than the strong lines that are now in fashion in this critical age.'

THREE

How Childe Roland and Another Came to the Dark Tower

DICKSON woke with a vague sense of irritation. As his recollections took form they produced a very unpleasant picture of Mr John Heritage. The poet had loosened all his placid idols, so that they shook and rattled in the niches where they had been erstwhile so secure. Mr McCunn had a mind of a singular candour, and was prepared most honestly at all times to revise his views. But by this iconoclast he had been only irritated and in no way convinced. '*Sich* poetry!' he muttered to himself as he shivered in his bath (a daily cold tub instead of his customary hot one on Saturday night being part of the discipline of his holiday). 'And yon blethers about the working-man!' he ingeminated as he shaved. He breakfasted alone, having outstripped even the fishermen, and as he ate he arrived at conclusions. He had a great respect for youth, but a line must be drawn somewhere. 'The man's a child,' he decided, 'and not like to grow up. The way he's besotted on everything daftlike, if it's only *new*. And he's no rightly young either – speaks like an auld dominie, whiles. And he's rather impident,' he concluded, with memories of 'Dogson' . . . He was very clear that he never wanted to see him again; that was the reason of his early breakfast. Having clarified his mind by definitions, Dickson felt comforted. He paid his bill, took an affectionate farewell of the landlord, and at 7.30 precisely stepped out into the gleaming morning.

It was such a day as only a Scots April can show. The cobbled streets of Kirkmichael still shone with the night's rain, but the storm clouds had fled before a mild south wind, and the whole circumference of the sky was a delicate translucent blue.

Homely breakfast smells came from the houses and delighted Mr McCunn's nostrils; a squalling child was a pleasant reminder of an awakening world, the urban counterpart to the morning song of birds; even the sanitary cart seemed a picturesque vehicle. He bought his ration of buns and ginger biscuits at a baker's shop whence various ragamuffin boys were preparing to distribute the householders' bread, and took his way up the Gallows Hill to the Burgh Muir almost with regret at leaving so pleasant a habitation.

A chronicle of ripe vintages must pass lightly over small beer. I will not dwell on his leisurely progress in the bright weather, or on his luncheon in a coppice of young firs, or on his thoughts which had returned to the idyllic. I take up the narrative at about three o'clock in the afternoon, when he is revealed seated on a milestone examining his map. For he had come, all unwitting, to a turning of the ways, and his choice is the cause of this veracious history.

The place was high up on a bare moor, which showed a white lodge among pines, a white cottage in a green nook by a burnside, and no other marks of human dwelling. To his left, which was the east, the heather rose to a low ridge of hill, much scarred with peat-bogs, behind which appeared the blue shoulder of a considerable mountain. Before him the road was lost momentarily in the woods of a shooting-box, but reappeared at a great distance climbing a swell of upland which seemed to be the glacis of a jumble of bold summits. There was a pass there, the map told him, which led into Galloway. It was the road he had meant to follow, but as he sat on the milestone his purpose wavered. For there seemed greater attractions in the country which lay to the westward. Mr McCunn, be it remembered, was not in search of brown heath and shaggy wood; he wanted greenery and the spring.

Westward there ran out a peninsula in the shape of an isosceles triangle, of which his present high-road was the base. At a distance of a mile or so a railway ran parallel to the road, and he could see the smoke of a goods train waiting at a tiny station islanded in acres of bog. Thence the moor swept down to meadows and scattered copses, above which hung a thin haze of smoke which betokened a village. Beyond it were further woodlands, not firs but old shady trees, and as they narrowed to a point the gleam of two tiny estuaries appeared on either side. He could not see the final cape, but he saw the sea beyond it, flawed with catspaws, gold in the afternoon sun, and on it a small herring smack flapping listless sails.

Something in the view caught and held his fancy. He conned his map, and made out the names. The peninsula was called the Cruives – an old name apparently, for it was in antique lettering. He vaguely remembered that 'cruives' had something to do with fishing, doubtless in the two streams which flanked it. One he had already crossed, the Laver, a clear tumbling water springing from green hills; the other, the Garple, descended from the rougher mountains to the south. The hidden village bore the name of Dalquharter, and the uncouth syllables awoke some vague recollection in his mind. The great house in the trees beyond – it must be a great house, for the map showed large policies – was Huntingtower.

The last name fascinated and almost decided him. He pictured an ancient keep by the sea, defended by converging rivers, which some old Comyn lord of Galloway had built to command the shore road, and from which he had sallied to hunt in his wild hills . . . He liked the way the moor dropped down to green meadows, and the mystery of the dark woods beyond. He wanted to explore the twin waters, and see how they entered that strange shimmering sea. The odd names, the odd cul-de-sac of a peninsula, powerfully attracted him. Why should he not spend a night there, for the map showed clearly that Dalquharter had an inn? He must decide promptly, for before him a side-road left the highway, and the signpost bore the legend, 'Dalquharter and Huntingtower'.

Mr McCunn, being a cautious and pious man, took the omens. He tossed a penny – heads go on, tails turn aside. It fell tails.

He knew as soon as he had taken three steps down the side-road that he was doing something momentous, and the exhilaration of enterprise stole into his soul. It occurred to him that this was the kind of landscape that he had always especially hankered after, and had made pictures of when he had a longing for the country on him – a wooded cape between streams, with meadows inland and then a long lift of heather. He had the same feeling of expectancy, of something most interesting and curious on the eve of happening, that he had had long ago when he waited on the curtain rising at his first play. His spirits soared like the lark, and he took to singing. If only the inn at Dalquharter were snug and empty, this was going to be a day in ten thousand. Thus mirthfully he swung down the rough grass-grown road, past the railway, till he came to a point where heath began to merge in pasture, and dry-stone walls split the moor into fields. Suddenly his pace slackened and song died on his lips. For approaching from the right by a tributary path was the Poet.

Mr Heritage saw him afar off and waved a friendly hand. In spite of his chagrin Dickson could not but confess that he had misjudged his critic. Striding with long steps over the heather, his jacket open to the wind, his face aglow, and his capless head like a whin-bush for disorder, he cut a more wholesome and picturesque figure than in the smoking-room the night before. He seemed to be in a companionable mood, for he brandished his stick and shouted greetings.

'Well met!' he cried; 'I was hoping to fall in with you again. You must have thought me a pretty fair cub last night.'

'I did that,' was the dry answer.

'Well, I want to apologize. God knows what made me treat you to a university-extension lecture. I may not agree with you, but every man's entitled to his own views, and it was dashed poor form for me to start jawing you.'

Mr McCunn had no gift of nursing anger, and was very susceptible to apologies.

'That's all right,' he murmured. 'Don't mention it. I'm wondering what brought you down here, for it's off the road.'

'Caprice. Pure caprice. I liked the look of this butt-end of nowhere.'

'Same here. I've aye thought there was something terrible nice about a wee cape with a village at the neck of it and a burn each side.'

'Now that's interesting,' said Mr Heritage. 'You're obsessed by a particular type of landscape. Ever read Freud?'

Dickson shook his head.

'Well, you've got an odd complex somewhere. I wonder where the key lies. Cape – woods – two rivers – moor behind. Ever been in love, Dogson?'

Mr McCunn was startled. 'Love' was a word rarely mentioned in his circle except on death-beds. 'I've been a married man for thirty years,' he said hurriedly.

'That won't do. It should have been a hopeless affair – the last sight of the lady on a spur of coast with water on three sides – that kind of thing, you know. Or it might have happened to an ancestor . . . But you don't look the kind of breed for hopeless attachments. More likely some scoundrelly old Dogson long ago found sanctuary in this sort of place. Do you dream about it?'

'Not exactly.'

'Well, I do. The queer thing is that I've got the same prepossession as you. As soon as I spotted this Cruives place on the map this morning, I saw it was what I was after. When I came in sight of it I almost shouted. I don't very often dream, but when I do that's the place I frequent. Odd, isn't it?'

Mr McCunn was deeply interested at this unexpected revelation of romance. 'Maybe it's being in love,' he daringly observed.

The Poet demurred. 'No. I'm not a connoisseur of obvious sentiment. That explanation might fit your case, but not mine. I'm pretty certain there's something hideous at the back of *my* complex – some grim old business tucked away back in the ages. For though I'm attracted by the place, I'm frightened too!'

There seemed no room for fear in the delicate landscape now opening before them. In front in groves of birch and rowan

smoked the first houses of a tiny village. The road had become
a green 'loaning', on the ample margin of which cattle grazed.
The moorland still showed itself in spits of heather, and some
distance off, where a rivulet ran in a hollow, there were signs of
a fire and figures near it. These last Mr Heritage regarded with
disapproval.

'Some infernal trippers!' he murmured. 'Or Boy Scouts. They
desecrate everything. Why can't the *tunicatus popellus* keep away
from a paradise like this!' Dickson, a democrat who felt nothing
incongruous in the presence of other holiday-makers, was
meditating a sharp rejoinder, when Mr Heritage's tone changed.

'Ye gods! What a village!' he cried, as they turned a corner.
There were not more than a dozen whitewashed houses, all set
in little gardens of wallflower and daffodil and early fruit
blossom. A triangle of green filled the intervening space, and in
it stood an ancient wooden pump. There was no schoolhouse or
kirk; not even a post-office – only a red box in a cottage side.
Beyond rose the high wall and the dark trees of the demesne,
and to the right up a by-road which clung to the park edge stood
a two-storeyed building which bore the legend 'The Cruives
Inn'.

The Poet became lyrical. 'At last!' he cried. 'The village of my
dreams! Not a sign of commerce! No church or school or beastly
recreation hall! Nothing but these divine little cottages and an
ancient pub! Dogson, I warn you, I'm going to have the devil of
a tea.' And he declaimed:

> *Thou shalt hear a song*
> *After a while which Gods may listen to;*
> *But place the flask upon the board and wait*
> *Until the stranger hath allayed his thirst,*
> *For poets, grasshoppers, and nightingales*
> *Sing cheerily but when the throat is moist.*

Dickson, too, longed with sensual gusto for tea. But, as they
drew nearer, the inn lost its hospitable look. The cobbles of the

yard were weedy, as if rarely visited by traffic, a pane in a window was broken, and the blinds hung tattered. The garden was a wilderness, and the doorstep had not been scoured for weeks. But the place had a landlord, for he had seen them approach and was waiting at the door to meet them.

He was a big man in his shirt sleeves, wearing old riding breeches unbuttoned at the knees, and thick ploughman's boots. He had no leggings, and his fleshy calves were imperfectly covered with woollen socks. His face was large and pale, his neck bulged, and he had a gross unshaven jowl. He was a type familiar to students of society; not the innkeeper, which is a thing consistent with good breeding and all the refinements; a type not unknown in the House of Lords, especially among recent creations, common enough in the House of Commons and the City of London, and by no means infrequent in the governing circles of Labour; the type known to the discerning as the Licensed Victualler.

His face was wrinkled in official smiles, and he gave the travellers a hearty good afternoon.

'Can we stop here for the night?' Dickson asked.

The landlord looked sharply at him, and then replied to Mr Heritage. His expression passed from official bonhomie to official contrition.

'Impossible, gentlemen. Quite impossible. . . . Ye couldn't have come at a worse time. I've only been here a fortnight myself, and we haven't got right shaken down yet. Even then I might have made shift to do with ye, but the fact is we've illness in the house, and I'm fair at my wits' end. It breaks my heart to turn gentlemen away and me that keen to get the business started. But there it is!' He spat vigorously as if to emphasize the desperation of his quandary.

The man was clearly Scots, but his native speech was overlaid with something alien, something which might have been acquired in America or in going down to the sea in ships. He hitched his breeches, too, with a nautical air.

'Is there nowhere else we can put up?' Dickson asked.

'Not in this one-horse place. Just a wheen auld wives that
packed thegether they haven't room for an extra hen. But it's
grand weather, and it's not above seven miles to Auchenlochan.
Say the word and I'll yoke the horse and drive ye there.'

'Thank you. We prefer to walk,' said Mr Heritage. Dickson
would have tarried to inquire after the illness in the house, but
his companion hurried him off. Once he looked back, and saw
the landlord still on the doorstep gazing after them.

'That fellow's a swine,' said Mr Heritage sourly. 'I wouldn't
trust my neck in his pot-house. Now, Dogson, I'm hanged if I'm
going to leave this place. We'll find a corner in the village
somehow. Besides, I'm determined on tea.'

The little street slept in the clear pure light of an early April
evening. Blue shadows lay on the white road, and a delicate
aroma of cooking tantalized hungry nostrils. The near meadows
shone like pale gold against the dark lift of the moor. A light
wind had begun to blow from the west and carried the faintest
tang of salt. The village at that hour was pure Paradise, and
Dickson was of the Poet's opinion. At all costs they must spend
the night there.

They selected a cottage whiter and neater than the others,
which stood at a corner, where a narrow lane turned southward.
Its thatched roof had been lately repaired, and starched curtains
of a dazzling whiteness decorated the small, closely-shut
windows. Likewise it had a green door and a polished brass
knocker.

Tacitly the duty of envoy was entrusted to Mr McCunn.
Leaving the other at the gate, he advanced up the little path
lined with quartz stones, and politely but firmly dropped the
brass knocker. He must have been observed; for ere the noise
had ceased the door opened, and an elderly woman stood before
him. She had a sharply-cut face, the rudiments of a beard, big
spectacles on her nose, and an old-fashioned lace cap on her
smooth white hair. A little grim she looked at first sight, because
of her thin lips and Roman nose, but her mild curious eyes
corrected the impression and gave the envoy confidence.

'Good afternoon, mistress,' he said, broadening his voice to something more rustical than his normal Glasgow speech. 'Me and my friend are paying our first visit here, and we're terrible taken up with the place. We would like to bide the night, but the inn is no' taking folk. Is there any chance, think you, of a bed here?'

'I'll no tell ye a lee,' said the woman. 'There's twae guid beds in the loft. But I dinna tak' lodgers and I dinna want to be bothered wi' ye. I'm an auld wumman and no' as stoot as I was. Ye'd better try doun the street. Eppie Home micht tak' ye.'

Dickson wore his most ingratiating smile. 'But, mistress, Eppie Home's house is no' yours. We've taken a tremendous fancy to this bit. Can you no' manage to put up with us for the one night? We're quiet auld-fashioned folk and we'll no' trouble you much. Just our tea and maybe an egg to it, and a bowl of porridge in the morning.'

The woman seemed to relent. 'Whaur's your freend?' she asked, peering over her spectacles towards the garden gate. The waiting Mr Heritage, seeing her eyes moving in his direction, took off his cap with a brave gesture and advanced. 'Glorious weather, madam,' he declared.

'English,' whispered Dickson to the woman, in explanation.

She examined the Poet's neat clothes and Mr McCunn's homely garments, and apparently found them reassuring. 'Come in,' she said shortly. 'I see ye're wilfu' folk and I'll hae to dae my best for ye.'

A quarter of an hour later the two travellers, having been introduced to two spotless beds in the loft, and having washed luxuriously at the pump in the back yard, were seated in Mrs Morran's kitchen before a meal which fulfilled their wildest dreams. She had been baking that morning, so there were white scones and barley scones, and oaten farles, and russet pancakes. There were three boiled eggs for each of them; there was a segment of an immense currant cake ('a present from my guid brither last Hogmanay'); there was skim-milk cheese; there were several kinds of jam, and there was a pot of dark-gold heather honey. 'Try hinny and aitcake,' said their hostess. 'My man used to say he never fund onything as guid in a' his days.'

Presently they heard her story. Her name was Morran, and she had been a widow these ten years. Of her family her son was in South Africa, one daughter a lady's-maid in London, and the other married to a schoolmaster in Kyle. The son had been in France fighting, and had come safely through. He had spent a month or two with her before his return, and, she feared, had found it dull. 'There's no' a man body in the place. Naething but auld wives.'

That was what the innkeeper had told them. Mr McCunn inquired concerning the inn.

'There's new folk just come. What's this they ca' them? – Robson – Dobson – aye, Dobson. What for wad they no' tak' ye in? Does the man think he's a laird to refuse folk that gait?'

'He said he had illness in the house.'

Mrs Morran meditated. 'Whae in the world can be lyin' there? The man bides his lane. He got a lassie frae Auchenlochan to cook, but she and her box gaed off in the post-cairt yestreen. I doot he tell't ye a lee, though it's no for me to juidge him. I've never spoken a word to ane o' thae new folk.'

Dickson inquired about the 'new folk'.

'They're a' new come in the last three weeks, and there's no' a man o' the auld stock left. John Blackstocks at the Wast Lodge dee'd o' pneumony last back-end, and auld Simon Tappie at the Gairdens flitted to Maybole a year come Mairtinmas. There's naebody at the Gairdens noo, but there's a man come to the Wast Lodge, a blackavised body wi' a face like bend-leather. Tam Robison used to bide at the South Lodge, but Tam got killed about Mesopotamy, and his wife took the bairns to her guidsire up at the Garpleheid. I seen the man that's in the South Lodge gaun up the street when I was finishin' my denner – a shilpit body and a lameter, but he hirples as fast as ither folk run. He's no' bonny to look at. I canna think what the factor's ettlin' at to let sic ill-faured chiels come about the toun.'

Their hostess was rapidly rising in Dickson's esteem. She sat very straight in her chair, eating with the careful gentility of a bird, and primming her thin lips after every mouthful of tea.

'Who bides in the Big House?' he asked. 'Huntingtower is the name, isn't it?'

'When I was a lassie they ca'ed it Dalquharter Hoose, and Huntingtower was the auld rickle o' stanes at the sea-end. But naething wad serve the last laird's faither but he maun change the name, for he was clean daft about what they ca' antickities. Ye speir whae bides in the Hoose? Naebody, since the young laird dee'd. It's standin' cauld and lanely and steikit, and it aince the cheeriest dwallin' in a' Carrick.'

Mrs Morran's tone grew tragic. 'It's a queer warld wi'out the auld gentry. My faither and my guidsire and his faither afore him served the Kennedys, and my man Dauvit Morran was gemkeeper to them, and afore I mairried I was ane o' the table-maids. They were kind folk, the Kennedys, and, like a' the rale gentry, maist mindfu' o' them that served them. Sic merry nichts I've seen in the auld Hoose, at Hallowe'en and Hogmanay, and at the servants' balls and the waddin's o' the young leddies! But the laird bode to waste his siller in stane and lime, and hadna that much to leave to his bairns. And now they're a' scattered or deid.'

Her grave face wore the tenderness which comes from affectionate reminiscence.

'There was never sic a laddie as young Maister Quentin. No' a week gaed by but he was in here, cryin', "Phemie Morran, I've come till my tea!" Fine he likit my treacle scones, puir man. There wasna ane in the countryside sae bauld a rider at the hunt, or sic a skeely fisher. And he was clever at his books tae, a graund scholar, they said, and ettlin' at bein' what they ca' a dipplemat. But that's a' bye wi'.'

'Quentin Kennedy – the fellow in the Tins?' Heritage asked. 'I saw him in Rome when he was with the Mission.'

'I dinna ken. He was a brave sodger, but he wasna long fechtin' in France till he got a bullet in his breist. Syne we heard

tell o' him in far awa' bits like Russia; and syne cam' the end o'
the war and we lookit to see him back, fishin' the waters and
ridin' like Jehu as in the auld days. But wae's me! It wasna
permitted. The next news we got, the puir laddie was deid o'
influenzy and buried somewhere about France. The wanchancy
bullet maun have weakened his chest, nae doot. So that's the
end o' the guid stock o' Kennedy o' Huntingtower, whae hae
been great folk sin' the time o' Robert Bruce. And noo the Hoose
is shut up till the lawyers can get somebody sae far left to himsel'
as to tak' it on lease, and in thae dear days it's no' just onybody
that wants a muckle castle.'

'Who are the lawyers?' Dickson asked.

'Glendonan and Speirs in Embro. But they never look near
the place, and Maister Loudon in Auchenlochan does the
factorin'. He's let the public an' filled the twae lodges, and he'll
be thinkin' nae doot that he's done eneuch.'

Mrs Morran had poured some hot water into the big slop-
bowl, and had begun the operation known as 'synding out' the
cups. It was a hint that the meal was over, and Dickson and
Heritage rose from the table. Followed by an injunction to be
back for supper 'on the chap o' nine', they strolled out into the
evening. Two hours of some sort of daylight remained, and the
travellers had that impulse to activity which comes to all men
who, after a day of exercise and emptiness, are stayed with a
satisfying tea.

'You should be happy, Dogson,' said the Poet. 'Here we have
all the materials for your blessed romance – old mansion,
extinct family, village deserted of men, and an innkeeper whom
I suspect of being a villain. I feel almost a convert to your
nonsense myself. We'll have a look at the House.'

They turned down the road which ran north by the park wall,
past the inn, which looked more abandoned than ever, till they
came to an entrance which was clearly the West Lodge. It had
once been a pretty, modish cottage, with a thatched roof and
dormer windows, but now it was badly in need of repair. A
window-pane was broken and stuffed with a sack, the posts of

the porch were giving inwards, and the thatch was crumbling under the attentions of a colony of starlings. The great iron gates were rusty, and on the coat of arms above them the gilding was patchy and tarnished.

Apparently the gates were locked, and even the side wicket failed to open to Heritage's vigorous shaking. Inside a weedy drive disappeared among ragged rhododendrons.

The noise brought a man to the lodge door. He was a sturdy fellow in a suit of black clothes which had not been made for him. He might have been a butler *en déshabillé*, but for the presence of a pair of field boots into which he had tucked the ends of his trousers. The curious thing about him was his face, which was decorated with features so tiny as to give the impression of a monstrous child. Each in itself was well enough formed, but eyes, nose, mouth, chin were of a smallness curiously out of proportion to the head and body. Such an anomaly might have been redeemed by the expression; good-humour would have invested it with an air of agreeable farce. But there was no friendliness in the man's face. It was set like a judge's in a stony impassiveness.

'May we walk up to the House?' Heritage asked. 'We are here for a night and should like to have a look at it.'

The man advanced a step. He had either a bad cold, or a voice comparable in size to his features.

'There's no entrance here,' he said huskily. 'I have strict orders.'

'Oh, come now,' said Heritage. 'It can do nobody any harm if you let us in for half an hour.'

The man advanced another step.

'You shall not come in. Go away from here. Go away, I tell you. It is private.' The words spoken by the small mouth in the small voice had a kind of childish ferocity.

The travellers turned their back on him and continued their way.

'Sich a curmudgeon!' Dickson commented. His face had flushed, for he was susceptible to rudeness. 'Did you notice? That man's a foreigner.'

'He's a brute,' said Heritage. 'But I'm not going to be done in by that class of lad. There can be no gates on the sea side, so we'll work round that way, for I won't sleep till I've seen the place.'

Presently the trees grew thinner, and the road plunged through thickets of hazel till it came to a sudden stop in a field. There the cover ceased wholly, and below them lay the glen of the Laver. Steep green banks descended to a stream which swept in coils of gold into the eye of the sunset. A little farther down the channel broadened, the slopes fell back a little, and a tongue of glittering sea ran up to meet the hill waters. The Laver is a gentle stream after it leaves its cradle heights, a stream of clear pools and long bright shallows, winding by moorland steadings and upland meadows; but in its last half-mile it goes mad, and imitates its childhood when it tumbled over granite shelves. Down in that green place the crystal water gushed and frolicked as if determined on one hour of rapturous life before joining the sedater sea.

Heritage flung himself on the turf.

'This is a good place! Ye gods, what a good place! Dogson, aren't you glad you came? I think everything's bewitched tonight. That village is bewitched, and that old woman's tea. Good white magic! And that foul innkeeper and that brigand at the gate. Black magic! And now here is the home of all enchantment – "island valley of Avilion" – "waters that listen for lovers" – all the rest of it!'

Dickson observed and marvelled.

'I can't make you out, Mr Heritage. You were saying last night you were a great democrat, and yet you were objecting to yon laddies camping on the moor. And you very near bit the neb off me when I said I liked Tennyson. And now . . .' Mr McCunn's command of language was inadequate to describe the transformation.

'You're a precise, pragmatical Scot,' was the answer. 'Hang it, man, don't remind me that I'm inconsistent. I've a poet's licence to play the fool, and if you don't understand me, I don't in the least understand myself. All I know is that I'm feeling young and jolly, and that it's the spring.'

Mr Heritage was assuredly in a strange mood. He began to whistle with a far-away look in his eye.

'Do you know what that is?' he asked suddenly.

Dickson, who could not detect any tune, said no.

'It's an aria from a Russian opera that came out just before the war. I've forgotten the name of the fellow who wrote it. Jolly thing, isn't it? I always remind myself of it when I'm in this mood, for it is linked with the greatest experience of my life. You said, I think, that you had never been in love?'

Dickson replied in the native fashion. 'Have you?' he asked.

'I have, and I am – been for two years. I was down with my battalion on the Italian front early in 1918, and because I could speak the language they hoicked me out and sent me to Rome on a liaison job. It was Easter time and fine weather, and, being glad to get out of the trenches, I was pretty well pleased with myself and enjoying life . . . In the place where I stayed there was a girl. She was a Russian, a princess of a great family, but a refugee, and of course as poor as sin . . . I remember how badly dressed she was among all the well-to-do Romans. But, my God, what a beauty! There was never anything in the world like her . . . She was little more than a child, and she used to sing that air in the morning as she went down the stairs . . . They sent me back to the front before I had a chance of getting to know her, but she used to give me little timid good mornings, and her voice and eyes were like an angel's . . . I'm over my head in love, but it's hopeless, quite hopeless. I shall never see her again.'

'I'm sure I'm honoured by your confidence,' said Dickson reverently.

The Poet, who seemed to draw exhilaration from the memory of his sorrows, arose and fetched him a clout on the back. 'Don't talk of confidence, as if you were a reporter,' he said. 'What about that House? If we're to see it before the dark comes we'd better hustle.'

The green slopes on their left, as they ran seaward, were clothed towards their summit with a tangle of broom and light scrub. The two forced their way through it, and found to their surprise that on this side there were no defences of the Huntingtower demesne. Along the crest ran a path which had once been gravelled and trimmed. Beyond, through a thicket of laurels and rhododendrons, they came on a long unkempt aisle of grass, which seemed to be one of those side avenues often found in connexion with old Scots dwellings. Keeping along this they reached a grove of beech and holly through which showed a dim shape of masonry. By a common impulse they moved stealthily, crouching in cover, till at the far side of the wood they found a sunk fence and looked over an acre or two of what had once been lawn and flower-beds to the front of the mansion.

The outline of the building was clearly silhouetted against the glowing west, but since they were looking at the east face the detail was all in shadow. But, dim as it was, the sight was enough to give Dickson the surprise of his life. He had expected something old and baronial. But this was new, raw and new, not twenty years built. Some madness had prompted its creator to set up a replica of a Tudor house in a countryside where the thing was unheard of. All the tricks were there – oriel windows, lozenged panes, high twisted chimney stacks; the very stone was red, as if to imitate the mellow brick of some ancient Kentish manor. It was new, but it was also decaying. The creepers had fallen from the walls, the pilasters on the terrace were tumbling down, lichen and moss were on the doorsteps. Shuttered, silent, abandoned, it stood like a harsh *memento mori* of human hopes.

Dickson had never before been affected by an inanimate thing with so strong a sense of disquiet. He had pictured an old stone tower on a bright headland; he found instead this raw thing among trees. The decadence of the brand-new repels as something against nature, and this new thing was decadent. But there was a mysterious life in it, for though not a chimney

smoked, it seemed to enshrine a personality and to wear a sinis-
ter aura. He felt a lively distaste, which was almost fear. He
wanted to get far away from it as fast as possible. The sun, now
sinking very low, sent up rays which kindled the crests of a
group of firs to the left of the front door. He had the absurd
fancy that they were torches flaming before a bier.

It was well that the two had moved quietly and kept in shadow.
Footsteps fell on their ears, on the path which threaded the lawn
just beyond the sunk fence. It was the keeper of the West Lodge
and he carried something on his back, but both that and his face
were indistinct in the half-light.

Other footsteps were heard, coming from the other side of
the lawn. A man's shod feet rang on the stone of a flagged path,
and from their irregular fall it was plain that he was lame. The
two men met near the door, and spoke together. Then they separated, and moved one down each side of the house. To the two
watchers they had the air of a patrol, or of warders pacing the
corridors of a prison.

'Let's get out of this,' said Dickson, and turned to go.

The air had the curious stillness which precedes the moment
of sunset, when the birds of day have stopped their noises and
the sounds of night have not begun. But suddenly in the silence
fell notes of music. They seemed to come from the house, a
voice singing softly but with great beauty and clearness.

Dickson halted in his steps. The tune, whatever it was, was
like a fresh wind to blow aside his depression. The house no
longer looked sepulchral. He saw that the two men had hurried
back from their patrol, had met and exchanged some message,
and made off again as if alarmed by the music. Then he noticed
his companion . . .

Heritage was on one knee with his face rapt and listening. He
got to his feet and appeared to be about to make for the House.
Dickson caught him by the arm and dragged him into the
bushes, and he followed unresistingly, like a man in a dream.
They ploughed through the thicket, recrossed the grass avenue,
and scrambled down the hillside to the banks of the stream.

Then for the first time Dickson observed that his companion's face was very white, and that sweat stood on his temples. Heritage lay down and lapped up water like a dog. Then he turned a wild eye on the other.

'I am going back,' he said. 'That is the voice of the girl I saw in Rome, and it is singing her song!'

FOUR

Dougal

'You'll do nothing of the kind,' said Dickson. 'You're coming home to your supper. It was to be on the chap of nine.'

'I'm going back to that place.'

The man was clearly demented and must be humoured. 'Well, you must wait till the morn's morning. It's very near dark now, and those are two ugly customers wandering about yonder. You'd better sleep the night on it.'

Mr Heritage seemed to be persuaded. He suffered himself to be led up the now dusky slopes to the gate where the road from the village ended. He walked listlessly like a man engaged in painful reflexion. Once only he broke the silence.

'You heard the singing?' he asked.

Dickson was a very poor hand at a lie. 'I heard something,' he admitted.

'You heard a girl's voice singing?'

'It sounded like that,' was the admission. 'But I'm thinking it might have been a seagull.'

'You're a fool,' said the Poet rudely.

The return was a melancholy business, compared to the bright speed of the outward journey. Dickson's mind was a chaos of feelings, all of them unpleasant. He had run up against something which he violently, blindly detested, and the trouble was that he could not tell why. It was all perfectly absurd, for why on earth should an ugly house, some over-grown trees, and a couple of ill-favoured servants so malignly affect him? Yet this was the fact; he had strayed out of Arcady into a sphere that filled him with revolt and a nameless fear. Never in his experience had he felt like this, this foolish childish panic which took all the colour and zest out of life. He tried to laugh at himself but failed. Heritage, stumbling along by his side, effectually crushed his effort to discover humour in the situation. Some exhalation from that infernal place had driven the Poet mad. And then that voice singing! A seagull, he had said. More like a nightingale, he reflected – a bird which in the flesh he had never met.

Mrs Morran had the lamp lit and a fire burning in her cheerful kitchen. The sight of it somewhat restored Dickson's equanimity, and to his surprise he found that he had an appetite for supper. There was new milk, thick with cream, and most of the dainties which had appeared at tea, supplemented by a noble dish of shimmering 'potted-head'. The hostess did not share their meal, being engaged in some duties in the little cubbyhole known as the back kitchen.

Heritage drank a glass of milk but would not touch food.

'I called this place Paradise four hours ago,' he said. 'So it is, but I fancy it is next door to Hell. There is something devilish going on inside that park wall, and I mean to get to the bottom of it.'

'Hoots! Nonsense!' Dickson replied with affected cheerfulness. 'Tomorrow you and me will take the road for Auchenlochan. We needn't trouble ourselves about an ugly old house and a wheen impident lodge-keepers.'

'Tomorrow I'm going to get inside the place. Don't come unless you like, but it's no use arguing with me. My mind is made up.'

Heritage cleared a space on the table and spread out a section of a large-scale ordnance map.

'I must clear my head about the topography, the same as if this were a battle-ground. Look here, Dogson . . . The road past the inn that we went by tonight runs north and south.' He tore a page from a note-book and proceeded to make a rough sketch . . . 'One end we know abuts on the Laver glen, and the other stops at the South Lodge. Inside the wall which follows the road is a long belt of plantation – mostly beeches and ash – then to the west a kind of park, and beyond that the lawns of the House. Strips of plantation with avenues between follow the north and south sides of the park. On the sea side of the House are the stables and what looks like a walled garden, and beyond them what seems to be open ground with an old dovecot marked, and the ruins of Huntingtower keep. Beyond that there is more open ground, till you come to the cliffs of the cape. Have you got that? ... It looks possible from the contouring to get on to the sea cliffs by following the Laver, for all that side is broken up into ravines ... But look at the other side – the Garple glen. It's evidently a deep-cut gully, and at the bottom it opens out into a little harbour. There's deep water there, you observe. Now the House on the south side – the Garple side – is built fairly close to the edge of the cliffs. Is that all clear in your head? We can't reconnoitre unless we've got a working notion of the lie of the land.'

Dickson was about to protest that he had no intention of reconnoitring, when a hubbub arose in the back kitchen. Mrs Morran's voice was heard in shrill protest.

'Ye ill laddie! Eh – ye – ill – laddie! [*crescendo*] Makin' a hash o' my back door wi' your dirty feet! What are ye slinkin' roond here for, when I tell't ye this mornin' that I wad sell ye nae mair scones till ye paid for the last lot? Ye're a wheen thievin' hungry callants, and if there were a polisman in the place I'd gie ye in chairge ... What's that ye say? Ye're no' wantin' meat? Ye want to speak to the gentlemen that's bidin' here? Ye ken the auld ane, says you? I believe it's a muckle lee, but there's the gentlemen to answer ye theirsels.'

Mrs Morran, brandishing a dishclout dramatically, flung open the door, and with a vigorous push propelled into the kitchen a singular figure.

It was a stunted boy, who from his face might have been fifteen years old, but had the stature of a child of twelve. He had a thatch of fiery red hair above a pale freckled countenance. His nose was snub, his eyes a sulky grey-green, and his wide mouth disclosed large and damaged teeth. But remarkable as was his

visage, his clothing was still stranger. On his head was the regu-
lation Boy Scout hat, but it was several sizes too big, and was
squashed down upon his immense red ears. He wore a very
ancient khaki shirt, which had once belonged to a full-grown
soldier, and the spacious sleeves were rolled up at the shoulders
and tied with string, revealing a pair of skinny arms. Round his
middle hung what was meant to be a kilt – a kilt of home manu-
facture, which may once have been a tablecloth, for its bold
pattern suggested no known clan tartan. He had a massive belt,
in which was stuck a broken gully-knife, and round his neck
was knotted the remnant of what had once been a silk bandanna.
His legs and feet were bare, blue, scratched, and very dirty, and
his toes had the prehensile look common to monkeys and small
boys who summer and winter go bootless. In his hand was a
long ash-pole, new cut from some coppice.

The apparition stood glum and lowering on the kitchen floor.
As Dickson stared at it he recalled Mearns Street and the band
of irregular Boy Scouts who paraded to the roll of tin cans.
Before him stood Dougal, Chieftain of the Gorbals Die-Hards.
Suddenly he remembered the philanthropic Mackintosh, and
his own subscription of ten pounds to the camp fund. It pleased
him to find the rascals here, for in the unpleasant affairs on the
verge of which he felt himself they were a comforting reminder
of the peace of home.

'I'm glad to see you, Dougal,' he said pleasantly. 'How are you
all getting on?' And then, with a vague reminiscence of the
Scouts' code – 'Have you been minding to perform a good deed
every day?'

The Chieftain's brow darkened.

' "*Good deeds!*" ' he repeated bitterly. 'I tell ye I'm fair wore out
wi' good deeds. Yon man Mackintosh tell't me this was going to
be a grand holiday. Holiday! Govey Dick! It's been like a
Setterday night in Main Street – a' fechtin', fechtin'.'

No collocation of letters could reproduce Dougal's accent,
and I will not attempt it. There was a touch of Irish in it, a spice
of music-hall patter, as well as the odd lilt of the Glasgow

vernacular. He was strong in vowels, but the consonants, especially the letter 't', were only aspirations.

'Sit down and let's hear about things,' said Dickson.

The boy turned his head to the still open back door, where Mrs Morran could be heard at her labours. He stepped across and shut it. 'I'm no' wantin' that auld wife to hear,' he said. Then he squatted down on the patchwork rug by the hearth, and warmed his blue-black shins. Looking into the glow of the fire, he observed, 'I seen you two up by the Big Hoose the night.'

'The devil you did,' said Heritage, roused to a sudden attention. 'And where were you?'

'Seven feet from your head, up a tree. It's my chief hidy-hole, an Gosh! I need one, for Lean's after me wi' a gun. He had a shot at me two days syne.'

Dickson exclaimed, and Dougal with morose pride showed a rent in his kilt. 'If I had had on breeks, he'd ha' got me.'

'Who's Lean?' Heritage asked.

'The man wi' the black coat. The other – the lame one – they ca' Spittal.'

'How d'you know?'

'I've listened to them crackin' thegither.'

'But what for did the man want to shoot at you?' asked the scandalized Dickson.

'What for? Because they're frightened to death o' onybody going near their auld Hoose. They're a pair of deevils, worse nor any Red Indian, but for a' that they're sweatin' wi' fright. What for? says you. Because they're hidin' a Secret. I knew it as soon as I seen the man Lean's face. I once seen the same kind o' scoondrel at the picters. When he opened his mouth to swear, I kenned he was a foreigner, like the lads down at the Broomielaw. That looked black, but I hadn't got at the worst of it. Then he loosed off at me wi' his gun.'

'Were you not feared?' said Dickson.

'Ay, I was feared. But ye'll no' choke off the Gorbals Die-Hards wi' a gun. We held a meetin' round the camp fire, and we resolved to get to the bottom o' the business. Me bein' their

Chief, it was my duty to make what they ca' a reckonissince, for that was the dangerous job. So a' this day I've been going on my belly about thae policies. I've found out some queer things.'

Heritage had risen and was staring down at the small squatting figure.

'What have you found out? Quick. Tell me at once.' His voice was sharp and excited.

'Bide a wee,' said the unwinking Dougal. 'I'm no' going to let ye into this business till I ken that ye'll help. It's a far bigger job than I thought. There's more in it than Lean and Spittal. There's the big man that keeps the public – Dobson, they ca' him. He's a Namerican, which looks bad. And there's two-three tinklers campin' down in the Garple Dean. They're in it, for Dobson was colloguin' wi' them a' mornin'. When I seen ye, I thought ye were more o' the gang, till I mindit that one o' ye was auld McCunn that has the shop in Mearns Street. I seen that ye didn't like the look o' Lean, and I followed ye here, for I was thinkin' I needit help.'

Heritage plucked Dougal by the shoulder and lifted him to his feet.

'For God's sake, boy,' he cried, 'tell us what you know!'

'Will ye help?'

'Of course, you little fool.'

'Then swear,' said the ritualist. From a grimy wallet he extracted a limp little volume which proved to be a damaged copy of a work entitled *Sacred Songs and Solos*. 'Here! Take that in your right hand and put your left hand on my pole, and say after me, "I swear no' to blab what is telled me in secret, and to be swift and sure in obeyin' orders, s'help me God!" Syne kiss the bookie.'

Dickson at first refused, declaring it was all havers, but Heritage's docility persuaded him to follow suit. The two were sworn.

'Now,' said Heritage.

Dougal squatted again on the hearth-rug, and gathered the eyes of his audience. He was enjoying himself.

'This day,' he said slowly, 'I got inside the Hoose.'

'Stout fellow,' said Heritage; 'and what did you find there?'

'I got inside that Hoose, but it wasn't once or twice I tried. I found a corner where I was out o' sight o' anybody unless they had come there seekin' me, and I sklimmed up a rone pipe, but a' the windies were lockit and I verra near broke my neck. Syne I tried the roof, and a sore sklim I had, but when I got there there were no skylights. At the end I got in by the coal-hole. That's why ye're maybe thinkin' I'm no' very clean.'

Heritage's patience was nearly exhausted.

'I don't want to hear how you got in. What did you find, you little devil?'

'Inside the Hoose,' said Dougal slowly (and there was a melancholy sense of anti-climax in his voice, as of one who had hoped to speak of gold and jewels and armed men) – 'inside that Hoose there's nothing but two women.'

Heritage sat down before him with a stern face.

'Describe them,' he commanded.

'One o' them is dead auld, as auld as the wife here. She didn't look to me very right in the head.'

'And the other?'

'Oh, just a lassie.'

'What was she like?'

Dougal seemed to be searching for adequate words. 'She is . . .' he began. Then a popular song gave him inspiration. 'She's pure as the lully in the dell!'

In no way discomposed by Heritage's fierce interrogatory air, he continued: 'She's either foreign or English, for she couldn't understand what I said, and I could make nothing o' her clippit tongue. But I could see she had been greetin'. She looked feared, yet kind o' determined. I speired if I could do anything for her, and when she got my meaning she was terrible anxious to ken if I had seen a man – a big man, she said, wi' a yellow beard. She didn't seem to ken his name, or else she wouldn't tell me. The auld wife was mortal feared, and was aye speakin' in a foreign langwidge. I seen at once that what frightened them was Lean and his friends, and I was just starting to speir about them when there came a sound like a man walkin' along the passage. She was for hidin' me in behind a sofy, but I wasn't going to be trapped like that, so I got out by the other door and down the kitchen stairs and into the coal-hole. Gosh, it was a near thing!'

The boy was on his feet. 'I must be off to the camp to give out the orders for the morn. I'm going back to that Hoose, for it's a fight atween the Gorbals Die-Hards and the scoondrels that are frightenin' thae women. The question is, Are ye comin' with me? Mind, ye've sworn. But if ye're no', I'm going mysel', though I'll no' deny I'd be glad o' company. *You* anyway –' he added, nodding at Heritage. 'Maybe auld McCunn wouldn't get through the coal-hole.'

'You're an impident laddie,' said the outraged Dickson. 'It's no' likely we're coming with you. Breaking into other folks' houses! It's a job for the police!'

'Please yersel',' said the Chieftain, and looked at Heritage.

'I'm on,' said that gentleman.

'Well, just you set out the morn as if ye were for a walk up the Garple glen. I'll be on the road and I'll have orders for ye.'

Without more ado Dougal left by way of the back kitchen. There was a brief denunciation from Mrs Morran, then the outer door banged and he was gone.

The Poet sat still with his head in his hands, while Dickson, acutely uneasy, prowled about the floor. He had forgotten even to light his pipe.

'You'll not be thinking of heeding that ragamuffin boy,' he ventured.

'I'm certainly going to get into the House tomorrow,' Heritage answered, 'and if he can show me a way so much the better. He's a spirited youth. Do you breed many like him in Glasgow?'

'Plenty,' said Dickson sourly. 'See here, Mr Heritage. You can't expect me to be going about burgling houses on the word of a blagyird laddie. I'm a respectable man – aye been. Besides, I'm here for a holiday, and I've no call to be mixing myself up in strangers' affairs.'

'You haven't. Only, you see, I think there's a friend of mine in that place, and anyhow there are women in trouble. If you like, we'll say goodbye after breakfast, and you can continue as if you had never turned aside to this damned peninsula. But I've got to stay.'

Dickson groaned. What had become of his dream of idylls, his gentle bookish romance? Vanished before a reality which smacked horribly of crude melodrama and possibly of sordid crime. His gorge rose at the picture, but a thought troubled him. Perhaps all romance in its hour of happening was rough and ugly like this, and only shone rosy in the retrospect. Was he being false to his deepest faith?

'Let's have Mrs Morran in,' he ventured. 'She's a wise old body and I'd like to hear her opinion of this business. We'll get common sense from her.'

'I don't object,' said Heritage. 'But no amount of common sense will change my mind.'

Their hostess forestalled them by returning at that moment to the kitchen.

'We want your advice, mistress,' Dickson told her, and accordingly, like a barrister with a client, she seated herself carefully in the big easy chair, found and adjusted her spectacles, and waited with hands folded on her lap to hear the business. Dickson narrated their pre-supper doings, and gave a sketch of Dougal's evidence. His exposition was cautious and colourless, and without conviction. He seemed to expect a robust incredulity in his hearer.

Mrs Morran listened with the gravity of one in church. When Dickson finished she seemed to meditate.

'There's no blagyird trick that would surprise me in thae new folk. What's that ye ca' them – Lean and Spittal? Eppie Home threepit to me they were furriners, and these are no furrin names.'

'What I want to hear from you, Mrs Morran,' said Dickson impressively, 'is whether you think there's anything in that boy's story?'

'I think it's maist likely true. He's a terrible impident callant, but he's no' a leear.'

'Then you think that a gang of ruffians have got two lone women shut up in that house for their own purposes?'

'I wadna wonder.'

'But it's ridiculous! This is a Christian and law-abiding country. What would the police say?'

'They never troubled Dalquharter muckle. There's no' a polis-man nearer than Knockraw – yin Johnnie Trummle, and he's as useless as a frostit tattie.'

'The wiselike thing, as I think,' said Dickson, 'would be to turn the Procurator-Fiscal on to the job. It's his business, no' ours.'

'Well, I wadna say but ye're richt,' said the lady.

'What would you do if you were us?' Dickson's tone was subtly confidential. 'My friend here wants to get into the House the morn with that red-haired laddie to satisfy himself about the facts. I say no. Let sleeping dogs lie, I say, and if you think the beasts are mad, report to the authorities. What would you do yourself?'

'If I were you,' came the emphatic reply, 'I would tak' the first train hame the morn, and when I got hame I wad bide there. Ye're a dacent body, but ye're no' the kind to be traivellin' the roads.'

'And if you were me?' Heritage asked with his queer crooked smile.

'If I was young and yauld like you I wad gang into the Hoose, and I wadna rest till I had riddled oot the truith and jyled every scoondrel about the place. If ye dinna gang, 'faith I'll kilt my coats and gang mysel'. I havena served the Kennedys for forty year no' to hae the honour o' the Hoose at my hert . . . Ye speired my advice, sirs, and ye've gotten it. Now I maun clear awa' your supper.'

Dickson asked for a candle, and, as on the previous night, went abruptly to bed. The oracle of prudence to which he had appealed had betrayed him and counselled folly. But was it folly? For him, assuredly, for Dickson McCunn, late of Mearns Street, Glasgow, wholesale and retail provision merchant, elder in the Guthrie Memorial Kirk, and fifty-five years of age. Ay, that was the rub. He was getting old. The woman had seen it and had advised him to go home. Yet the plea was curiously irksome, though it gave him the excuse he needed. If you played at being young, you had to take up the obligations of youth, and he thought derisively of his boyish exhilaration of the past days. Derisively, but also sadly. What had become of that innocent joviality he had dreamed of, that happy morning pilgrimage of spring enlivened by tags from the poets? His goddess had played him false. Romance had put upon him too hard a trial.

He lay long awake, torn between common sense and a desire to be loyal to some vague whimsical standard. Heritage a yard distant appeared also to be sleepless, for the bed creaked with his turning. Dickson found himself envying one whose troubles, whatever they might be, were not those of a divided mind.

FIVE

Of the Princess in the Tower

VERY early next morning, while Mrs Morran was still cooking breakfast, Dickson and Heritage might have been observed taking the air in the village street. It was the Poet who had insisted upon this walk, and he had his own purpose. They looked at the spires of smoke piercing the windless air, and studied the daffodils in the cottage gardens. Dickson was glum, but Heritage seemed in high spirits. He varied his garrulity with spells of cheerful whistling.

They strode along the road by the park wall till they reached the inn. There Heritage's music waxed peculiarly loud. Presently from the yard, unshaven and looking as if he had slept in his clothes, came Dobson the innkeeper.

'Good morning,' said the Poet. 'I hope the sickness in your house is on the mend?'

'Thank ye, it's no worse,' was the reply, but in the man's heavy face there was little civility. His small grey eyes searched their faces.

'We're just waiting for breakfast to get on the road again. I'm jolly glad we spent the night here. We found quarters after all, you know.'

'So I see. Whereabouts, may I ask?'

'Mrs Morran's. We could always have got in there, but we didn't want to fuss an old lady, so we thought we'd try the inn first. She's my friend's aunt.'

At this amazing falsehood Dickson started, and the man observed his surprise. The eyes were turned on him like a searchlight. They roused antagonism in his peaceful soul, and with that antagonism came an impulse to back up the Poet. 'Ay,' he said, 'she's my Auntie Phemie, my mother's half-sister.'

The man turned on Heritage.

'Where are ye for the day?'

'Auchenlochan,' said Dickson hastily. He was still determined to shake the dust of Dalquharter from his feet.

The innkeeper sensibly brightened. 'Well, ye'll have a fine walk. I must go in and see about my own breakfast. Good day to ye, gentlemen.'

'That,' said Heritage as they entered the village street again, 'is the first step in camouflage, to put the enemy off his guard.'

'It was an abominable lie,' said Dickson crossly.

'Not at all. It was a necessary and proper *ruse de guerre*. It explained why we spent the night here, and now Dobson and his friends can get about their day's work with an easy mind. Their suspicions are temporarily allayed, and that will make our job easier.'

'I'm not coming with you.'

'I never said you were. By "we" I refer to myself and the red-headed boy.'

'Mistress, you're my auntie,' Dickson informed Mrs Morran as she set the porridge on the table. 'This gentleman has just been telling the man at the inn that you're my Auntie Phemie.'

For a second their hostess looked bewildered. Then the corners of her prim mouth moved upwards in a slow smile.

'I see,' she said. 'Weel, maybe it was weel done. But if ye're my nevoy ye'll hae to keep up my credit, for we're a bauld and siccar lot.'

Half an hour later there was a furious dissension when Dickson attempted to pay for the night's entertainment. Mrs Morran would have none of it. 'Ye're no' awa' yet,' she said tartly, and the matter was complicated by Heritage's refusal to take part in the debate. He stood aside and grinned, till Dickson in despair returned his notecase to his pocket, murmuring darkly that 'he would send it from Glasgow'.

The road to Auchenlochan left the main village street at right angles by the side of Mrs Morran's cottage. It was a better road than that by which they had come yesterday, for by it

twice daily the post-cart travelled to the post-town. It ran on
the edge of the moor and on the lip of the Garple glen, till it
crossed that stream and, keeping near the coast, emerged after
five miles into the cultivated flats of the Lochan valley. The
morning was fine, the keen air invited to high spirits, plovers
piped entrancingly over the bent and linnets sang in the
whins, there was a solid breakfast behind him, and the
promise of a cheerful road till luncheon. The stage was set for
good humour, but Dickson's heart, which should have been
ascending with the larks, stuck leadenly in his boots. He was
not even relieved at putting Dalquharter behind him. The
atmosphere of that unhallowed place lay still on his soul. He
hated it, but he hated himself more. Here was one who had
hugged himself all his days as an adventurer waiting his
chance, running away at the first challenge of adventure; a
lover of Romance who fled from the earliest overture of his
goddess. He was ashamed and angry, but what else was there
to do? Burglary in the company of a queer poet and a queerer
urchin? It was unthinkable.

Presently, as they tramped silently on, they came to the bridge
beneath which the peaty waters of the Garple ran in porter-
coloured pools and tawny cascades. From a clump of elders on
the other side Dougal emerged. A barefoot boy, dressed in
much the same parody of a Boy Scout's uniform, but with
corduroy shorts instead of a kilt, stood before him at rigid attention. Some command was issued, the child saluted, and trotted
back past the travellers with never a look at them. Discipline
was strong among the Gorbals Die-Hards; no Chief of Staff ever
conversed with his General under a stricter etiquette.

Dougal received the travellers with the condescension of a
regular towards civilians.

'They're off their gawrd,' he announced. 'Thomas Yownie has
been shadowin' them since skreigh o' day, and he reports that
Dobson and Lean followed ye till ye were out o' sight o' the
houses, and syne Lean got a spy-glass and watched ye till the
road turned in among the trees. That satisfied them, and they're

both away back to their jobs. Thomas Yownie's the fell yin. Ye'll no fickle Thomas Yownie.'

Dougal extricated from his pouch the fag of a cigarette, lit it, and puffed meditatively. 'I did a reckonissince mysel' this morning. I was up at the Hoose afore it was light, and tried the door o' the coal-hole. I doot they've gotten on our tracks, for it was lockit – aye, and wedged from the inside.'

Dickson brightened. Was the insane venture off?

'For a wee bit I was fair beat. But I mindit that the lassie was allowed to walk in a kind o' a glass hoose on the side farthest away from the Garple. That was where she was singin' yest'reen. So I reckonissinced in that direction, and I fund a queer place.' *Sacred Songs and Solos* was requisitioned, and on a page of it Dougal proceeded to make marks with the stump of a carpenter's pencil. 'See here,' he commanded. 'There's the glass place wi' a door into the Hoose. That door maun be open or the lassie maun hae the key, for she comes there whenever she likes. Now, at each end o' the place the doors are lockit, but the front that looks on the garden is open, wi' muckle posts and flowerpots. The trouble is that that side there's maybe twenty feet o' a wall between the pawrapet and the ground. It's an auld wall wi' cracks and holes in it, and it wouldn't be ill to sklim. That's why they let her gang there when she wants, for a lassie couldn't get away without breakin' her neck.'

'Could we climb it?' Heritage asked.

The boy wrinkled his brows. 'I could manage it mysel' – I think – and maybe you. I doubt if auld McCunn could get up. Ye'd have to be mighty carefu' that nobody saw ye, for your hinder end, as ye were sklimmin', wad be a grand mark for a gun.'

'Lead on,' said Heritage. 'We'll try the veranda.'

They both looked at Dickson, and Dickson, scarlet in the face, looked back at them. He had suddenly found the thought of a solitary march to Auchenlochan intolerable. Once again he was at the parting of the ways, and once more caprice determined his decision. That the coal-hole was out of the question had worked a change in his views. Somehow it seemed to him less burglarious to enter by a veranda. He felt very frightened but – for the moment – quite resolute.

'I'm coming with you,' he said.

'Sportsman,' said Heritage, and held out his hand. 'Well done, the auld yin,' said the Chieftain of the Gorbals Die-Hards. Dickson's quaking heart experienced a momentary bound as he followed Heritage down the track into the Garple Dean.

The track wound through a thick covert of hazels, now close to the rushing water, now high upon the bank so that clear sky showed through the fringes of the wood. When they had gone a little way Dougal halted them.

'It's a ticklish job,' he whispered. 'There's the tinklers, mind, that's campin' in the Dean. If they're still in their camp we can get by easy enough, but they're maybe wanderin' about the wud after rabbits . . . Then we maun ford the water, for ye'll no' cross it lower down where it's deep . . . Our road is on the Hoose side o' the Dean, and it's awfu' public if there's onybody on the other side, though it's hid well enough from folk up in the policies . . . Ye maun do exactly what I tell ye. When we get near danger I'll scout on ahead, and I daur ye to move a hair o' your heid till I give the word.'

Presently, when they were at the edge of the water, Dougal announced his intention of crossing. Three boulders in the stream made a bridge for an active man, and Heritage hopped lightly over. Not so Dickson, who stuck fast on the second stone, and would certainly have fallen in had not Dougal plunged into the current and steadied him with a grimy hand. The leap was at last successfully taken, and the three scrambled up a rough scaur, all reddened with iron springs, till they struck a slender track running down the Dean on its northern side. Here the undergrowth was very thick, and they had gone the better part of half a mile before the covert thinned sufficiently to show them the stream beneath. Then Dougal halted them with a finger on his lips, and crept forward alone.

He returned in three minutes. 'Coast's clear,' he whispered. 'The tinklers are eatin' their breakfast. They're late at their meat though they're up early seekin' it.'

Progress was now very slow and secret, and mainly on all fours. At one point Dougal nodded downward, and the other two saw on a patch of turf, where the Garple began to widen into its estuary, a group of figures round a small fire. There were four of them, all men, and Dickson thought he had never seen such ruffianly-looking customers. After that they moved high up the slope, in a shallow glade of a tributary burn, till they came out of the trees and found themselves looking seaward.

On one side was the House, a hundred yards or so back from the edge, the roof showing above the precipitous scarp. Halfway down the slope became easier, a jumble of boulders and boiler-plates, till it reached the waters of the small haven, which lay calm as a mill-pond in the windless forenoon. The haven broadened out at its foot and revealed a segment of blue sea. The opposite shore was flatter, and showed what looked like an old wharf and the ruins of buildings, behind which rose a bank clad with scrub and surmounted by some gnarled and wind-crooked firs.

'There's dashed little cover here,' said Heritage.

'There's no muckle,' Dougal assented. 'But they canna see us from the policies, and it's no' like there's anybody watchin' from the Hoose. The danger is somebody on the other side, but we'll have to risk it. Once among thae big stones we're safe. Are ye ready?'

Five minutes later Dickson found himself gasping in the lee of a boulder, while Dougal was making a cast forward. The scout returned with a hopeful report. 'I think we're safe till we get into the policies. There's a road that the auld folk made when ships used to come here. Down there it's deeper than Clyde at the Broomielaw. Has the auld yin got his wind yet? There's no time to waste.'

Up that broken hillside they crawled, well in the cover of the tumbled stones, till they reached a low wall which was the boundary of the garden. The House was now behind them on their right rear, and as they topped the crest they had a glimpse of an ancient dovecot and the ruins of the old Huntingtower on the short thymy turf which ran seaward to the cliffs. Dougal led them along a sunk fence which divided the downs from the lawns behind the House, and, avoiding the stables, brought them by devious ways to a thicket of rhododendrons and broom. On all fours they travelled the length of the place, and came to the edge where some forgotten gardeners had once tended a herbaceous border. The border was now rank and wild, and, lying flat under the shade of an azalea and peering through the young spears of iris, Dickson and Heritage regarded the north-western façade of the House.

The ground before them had been a sunken garden, from which a steep wall, once covered with creepers and rock plants, rose to a long veranda, which was pillared and open on that side; but at each end built up half-way and glazed for the rest. There was a glass roof, and inside untended shrubs sprawled in broken plaster vases.

'Ye maun bide here,' said Dougal, 'and no cheep above your breath. Afore we dare to try that wall, I maun ken where Lean and Spittal and Dobson are. I'm off to spy the policies.' He glided out of sight behind a clump of pampas grass.

For hours, so it seemed, Dickson was left to his own unpleasant reflexions. His body, prone on the moist earth, was fairly comfortable, but his mind was ill at ease. The scramble up the hillside had convinced him that he was growing old, and there was no rebound in his soul to counter the conviction. He felt listless, spiritless – an apathy with fright trembling somewhere at the back of it. He regarded the veranda wall with foreboding. How on earth could he climb that? And if he did there would be his exposed hinder-parts inviting a shot from some malevolent gentleman among the trees. He reflected that he would give a large sum of money to be out of this preposterous adventure.

Heritage's hand was stretched towards him, containing two of Mrs Morran's jellied scones, of which the Poet had been wise enough to bring a supply in his pocket. The food cheered him, for he was growing very hungry, and he began to take an interest in the scene before him instead of his own thoughts. He

observed every detail of the veranda. There was a door at one
end, he noted, giving on a path which wound down to the sunk
garden. As he looked he heard a sound of steps and saw a man
ascending this path.

It was the lame man whom Dougal had called Spittal, the
dweller in the South Lodge. Seen at closer quarters he was an
odd-looking being, lean as a heron, wry-necked, but amazingly
quick on his feet. Had not Mrs Morran said that he hobbled as
fast as other folk ran? He kept his eyes on the ground and
seemed to be talking to himself as he went, but he was alert
enough, for the dropping of a twig from a dying magnolia
transferred him in an instant into a figure of active vigilance.
No risks could be run with that watcher. He took a key from
his pocket, opened the garden door, and entered the veranda.
For a moment his shuffle sounded on its tiled floor, and then
he entered the door admitting from the veranda to the House.
It was clearly unlocked, for there came no sound of a turning
key.

Dickson had finished the last crumbs of his scones before the
man emerged again. He seemed to be in a greater hurry than
ever as he locked the garden door behind him and hobbled
along the west front of the House till he was lost to sight. After
that the time passed slowly. A pair of yellow wagtails arrived and
played at hide-and-seek among the stuccoed pillars. The little
dry scratch of their claws was heard clearly in the still air.
Dickson had almost fallen asleep when a smothered exclamation from Heritage woke him to attention. A girl had appeared
in the veranda.

Above the parapet he saw only her body from the waist up.
She seemed to be clad in bright colours, for something red was
round her shoulders and her hair was bound with an orange
scarf. She was tall – that he could tell, tall and slim and very
young. Her face was turned seaward, and she stood for a little
scanning the broad channel, shading her eyes as if to search for
something on the extreme horizon. The air was very quiet and
he thought that he could hear her sigh. Then she turned and

re-entered the House, while Heritage by his side began to curse under his breath with a shocking fervour.

One of Dickson's troubles had been that he did not really believe Dougal's story, and the sight of the girl removed one doubt. That bright exotic thing did not belong to the Cruives or to Scotland at all, and that she should be in the House removed the place from the conventional dwelling to which the laws against burglary applied.

There was a rustle among the rhododendrons and the fiery face of Dougal appeared. He lay between the other two, his chin on his hands, and grunted out his report.

'After they had their dinner Dobson and Lean yokit a horse and went off to Auchenlochan. I seen them pass the Garple brig, so that's two accounted for. Has Spittal been round here?'

'Half an hour ago,' said Heritage, consulting a wrist watch.

'It was him that keepit me waitin' so long. But he's safe enough now, for five minutes syne he was splittin' firewood at the back door o' his hoose . . . I've found a ladder, an auld yin in ahint yon lot o' bushes. It'll help wi' the wall. There! I've gotten my breath again and we can start.'

The ladder was fetched by Heritage and proved to be ancient and wanting many rungs, but sufficient in length. The three stood silent for a moment, listening like stags, and then ran across the intervening lawn to the foot of the veranda wall. Dougal went up first, then Heritage, and lastly Dickson, stiff and giddy from his long lie under the bushes. Below the parapet the veranda floor was heaped with old garden litter, rotten matting, dead or derelict bulbs, fibre, withies, and strawberry nets. It was Dougal's intention to pull up the ladder and hide it among the rubbish against the hour of departure. But Dickson had barely put his foot on the parapet when there was a sound of steps within the House approaching the veranda door.

The ladder was left alone. Dougal's hand brought Dickson summarily to the floor, where he was fairly well concealed by a mess of matting. Unfortunately his head was in the vicinity of some upturned pot-plants, so that a cactus tickled his brow and a spike of aloe supported painfully the back of his neck. Heritage was prone behind two old water-butts, and Dougal was in a hamper which had once contained seed potatoes. The house door had panels of opaque glass, so the newcomer could not see the doings of the three till it was opened, and by that time all were in cover.

The man – it was Spittal – walked rapidly along the veranda and out of the garden door. He was talking to himself again, and Dickson, who had a glimpse of his face, thought he looked both evil and furious. Then came some anxious moments, for had the man glanced back when he was once outside, he must have seen the tell-tale ladder. But he seemed immersed in his own reflexions, for he hobbled steadily along the house front till he was lost to sight.

'That'll be the end o' them the day,' said Dougal, as he helped Heritage to pull up the ladder and stow it away. 'We've got the place to oursels, now. Forward, men, forward.' He tried the handle of the House door and led the way in.

A narrow paved passage took them into what had once been the garden room, where the lady of the house had arranged her flowers, and the tennis racquets and croquet mallets had been kept. It was very dusty, and on the cobwebbed walls still hung a few soiled garden overalls. A door beyond opened into a huge murky hall, murky, for the windows were shuttered, and the only light came through things like port-holes far up in the wall. Dougal, who seemed to know his way about, halted them. 'Stop here till I scout a bit. The women bide in a wee room through that muckle door.' Bare feet stole across the oak flooring, there was the sound of a door swinging on its hinges, and then silence and darkness. Dickson put out a hand for companionship and clutched Heritage's; to his surprise it was cold and all a-tremble. They listened for voices, and thought they could detect a faraway sob.

It was some minutes before Dougal returned. 'A bonny kettle o' fish,' he whispered. 'They're both greetin'. We're just in time. Come on, the pair o' ye.'

Through a green baize door they entered a passage which led to the kitchen regions, and turned in at the first door on their right. From its situation Dickson calculated that the room lay on the seaward side of the House next to the veranda. The light was bad, for the two windows were partially shuttered, but it had plainly been a smoking-room, for there were pipe-racks by the hearth, and on the walls a number of old school and college photographs, a couple of oars with emblazoned names, and a variety of stags' and roebucks' heads. There was no fire in the grate, but a small oil-stove burned inside the fender. In a stiff-backed chair sat an elderly woman, who seemed to feel the cold, for she was muffled to the neck in a fur coat. Beside her, so that the late afternoon light caught her face and head, stood a girl.

Dickson's first impression was of a tall child. The pose, startled and wild and yet curiously stiff and self-conscious, was that of a child striving to remember a forgotten lesson. One hand clutched a handkerchief, the other was closing and unclosing on a knob of the chair back. She was staring at Dougal, who stood like a gnome in the centre of the floor. 'Here's the gentlemen I was tellin' ye about,' was his introduction, but her eyes did not move.

Then Heritage stepped forward. 'We have met before, Mademoiselle,' he said. 'Do you remember Easter in 1918 – in the house in the Trinità dei Monti?'

The girl looked at him.

'I do not remember,' she said slowly.

'But I was the English officer who had the apartments on the floor below you. I saw you every morning. You spoke to me sometimes.'

'You are a soldier?' she asked, with a new note in her voice.

'I was then – till the war finished.'

'And now? Why have you come here?'

'To offer you help if you need it. If not, to ask your pardon and go away.'

The shrouded figure in the chair burst suddenly into rapid hysterical talk in some foreign tongue which Dickson suspected of being French. Heritage replied in the same language, and the girl joined in with sharp questions. Then the Poet turned to Dickson.

'This is my friend. If you will trust us we will do our best to help you.'

The eyes rested on Dickson's face, and he realized that he was in the presence of something the like of which he had never met in his life before. It was a loveliness greater than he had imagined was permitted by the Almighty to His creatures. The little face was more square than oval, with a low broad brow and proud exquisite eyebrows. The eyes were of a colour which he could never decide on; afterwards he used to allege obscurely that they were the colour of everything in spring. There was a delicate pallor in the cheeks, and the face bore signs of suffering and care, possibly even of hunger; but for all that there was youth there, eternal and triumphant! Not youth such as he had known it, but youth with all history behind it, youth with centuries of command in its blood and the world's treasures of beauty and pride in its ancestry. Strange, he thought, that a thing so fine should be so masterful. He felt abashed in every inch of him.

As the eyes rested on him their sorrowfulness seemed to be shot with humour. A ghost of a smile lurked there, to which Dickson promptly responded. He grinned and bowed.

'Very pleased to meet you, Mem. I'm Mr McCunn from Glasgow.'

'You don't even know my name,' she said.

'We don't,' said Heritage.

'They call me Saskia. This,' nodding to the chair, 'is my cousin Eugénie . . . We are in very great trouble. But why should I tell you? I do not know you. You cannot help me.'

'We can try,' said Heritage. 'Part of your trouble we know already through that boy. You are imprisoned in this place by scoundrels. We are here to help you to get out. We want to ask no questions – only to do what you bid us.'

'You are not strong enough,' she said sadly. 'A young man – an old man – and a little boy. There are many against us, and any moment there may be more.'

It was Dougal's turn to break in. 'There's Lean and Spittal and Dobson and four tinklers in the Dean – that's seven; but there's us three and five more Gorbals Die-Hards – that's eight.'

There was something in the boy's truculent courage that cheered her.

'I wonder,' she said, and her eyes fell on each in turn.

Dickson felt impelled to intervene.

'I think this is a perfectly simple business. Here's a lady shut up in this house against her will by a wheen blagyirds. This is a free country and the law doesn't permit that. My advice is for one of us to inform the police at Auchenlochan and get Dobson and his friends took up and the lady set free to do what she likes. That is, if these folks are really molesting her, which is not yet quite clear to my mind.'

'Alas! It is not so simple as that,' she said. 'I dare not invoke your English law, for perhaps in the eyes of that law I am a thief.'

'Deary me, that's a bad business,' said the startled Dickson.

The two women talked together in some strange tongue, and the elder appeared to be pleading and the younger objecting. Then Saskia seemed to come to a decision.

'I will tell you all,' and she looked straight at Heritage. 'I do not think you would be cruel or false, for you have honourable faces . . . Listen, then. I am a Russian, and for two years have been an exile. I will not speak of my house, for it is no more, or how I escaped, for it is the common tale of all of us. I have seen things more terrible than any dream and yet lived, but I have paid a price for such experience. First I went to Italy where there were friends, and I wished only to have peace among kindly people. About poverty I do not care, for, to us, who have lost all the great things, the want of bread is a little matter. But peace was forbidden me, for I learned that we Russians had to win back our fatherland again, and that the weakest must work in that cause. So I was set my task, and it was very hard . . . There were jewels which once belonged to my Emperor – they had been stolen by the brigands and must be recovered. There were others still hidden in Russia which must be brought to a safe place. In that work I was ordered to share.'

She spoke in almost perfect English, with a certain foreign precision. Suddenly she changed to French, and talked rapidly to Heritage.

'She has told me about her family,' he said, turning to Dickson. 'It is among the greatest in Russia, the very greatest after the throne.' Dickson could only stare.

'Our enemies soon discovered me,' she went on. 'Oh, but they are very clever, these enemies, and they have all the criminals of the world to aid them. Here you do not understand what they are. You good people in England think they are well-meaning dreamers who are forced into violence by the persecution of Western Europe. But you are wrong. Some honest fools there are among them, but the power – the true power – lies with madmen and degenerates, and they have for allies the special devil that dwells in each country. That is why they cast their nets as wide as mankind.'

She shivered, and for a second her face wore a look which Dickson never forgot, the look of one who has looked over the edge of life into the outer dark.

'There were certain jewels of great price which were about to be turned into guns and armies for our enemies. These our people recovered, and the charge of them was laid on me. Who would suspect, they said, a foolish girl? But our enemies were very clever, and soon the hunt was cried against me. They tried to rob me of them, but they failed, for I too had become clever. Then they asked the help of the law – first in Italy and then in France. Oh, it was subtly done. Respectable bourgeois, who hated the Bolsheviki but had bought long ago the bonds of my country, desired to be repaid their debts out of the property of the Russian Crown which might be found in the West. But behind them were the Jews, and behind the Jews our unsleeping enemies. Once I was enmeshed in the law I would be safe for them, and presently they would find the hiding-place of the treasure, and while the bourgeois were clamouring in the courts it would be safe in their pockets. So I fled. For months I have been fleeing and hiding. They have tried to kidnap me many times, and once they have tried to kill me, but I, too, have become clever – oh, so clever. And I have learned not to fear.'

This simple recital affected Dickson's honest soul with the liveliest indignation. 'Sich doings!' he exclaimed, and he could not forbear from whispering to Heritage an extract from that gentleman's conversation the first night at Kirkmichael. 'We needn't imitate all their methods, but they've got hold of the right end of the stick. They seek truth and reality.' The reply from the Poet was an angry shrug.

'Why and how did you come here?' he asked.

'I always meant to come to England, for I thought it the sanest place in a mad world. Also it is a good country to hide in, for it is apart from Europe, and your police, as I thought, do not permit evil men to be their own law. But especially I had a friend, a Scottish gentleman, whom I knew in the days when we Russians were still a nation. I saw him again in Italy, and since he was kind and brave I told him some part of my troubles. He was called Quentin Kennedy, and now he is dead. He told me that in Scotland he had a lonely château, where I could hide secretly and safely, and against the day when I might be hard-pressed he gave me a letter to his steward, bidding him welcome me as a guest when I made application. At that time I did not think I would need such sanctuary, but a month ago the need became urgent, for the hunt in France was very close on me. So I sent a message to the steward as Captain Kennedy told me.'

'What is his name?' Heritage asked.

She spelt it, 'Monsieur Loudon – L-O-U-D-O-N in the town of Auchenlochan.'

'The factor,' said Dickson. 'And what then?'

'Some spy must have found me out. I had a letter from this Loudon bidding me come to Auchenlochan. There I found no steward to receive me, but another letter saying that that night a carriage would be in waiting to bring me here. It was midnight when we arrived, and we were brought in by strange ways to this House, with no light but a single candle. Here we were welcomed indeed, but by an enemy.'

'Which?' asked Heritage. 'Dobson or Lean or Spittal?'

'Dobson I do not know. Léon was there. He is no Russian, but a Belgian who was a valet in my father's service till he joined the Bolsheviki. Next day the Lett Spidel came, and I knew that I was in very truth entrapped. For of all our enemies he is, save one, the most subtle and unwearied.'

Her voice had trailed off into flat weariness. Again Dickson was reminded of a child, for her arms hung limp by her side; and her slim figure in its odd clothes was curiously like that of a boy in a school blazer. Another resemblance perplexed him. She had a hint of Janet – about the mouth – Janet, that solemn little girl those twenty years in her grave.

Heritage was wrinkling his brows. 'I don't think I quite understand. The jewels? You have them with you?'

She nodded.

'These men wanted to rob you. Why didn't they do it between here and Auchenlochan? You had no chance to hide them on the journey. Why did they let you come here where you were in a better position to baffle them?'

She shook her head. 'I cannot explain – except, perhaps, that Spidel had not arrived that night, and Léon may have been waiting instructions.'

The other still looked dissatisfied. 'They are either clumsier villains than I take them to be, or there is something deeper in the business than we understand. These jewels – are they here?'

His tone was so sharp that she looked startled – almost suspicious. Then she saw that in his face which reassured her. 'I have them hidden here. I have grown very skilful in hiding things.'

'Have they searched for them?'

'The first day they demanded them of me. I denied all knowledge. Then they ransacked this House – I think they ransack it daily, but I am too clever for them. I am not allowed to go beyond the veranda, and when at first I disobeyed there was always one of them in wait to force me back with a pistol behind my head. Every morning Léon brings us food for the day – good food, but not enough, so that Cousin Eugénie is always hungry, and each day he and Spidel question and threaten me. This afternoon Spidel has told me that their patience is at an end. He has given me till tomorrow at noon to produce the jewels. If not, he says I will die.'

'Mercy on us!' Dickson exclaimed.

'There will be no mercy for us,' she said solemnly. 'He and his kind think as little of shedding blood as of spilling water. But I do not think he will kill me. I think I will kill him first, but after that I shall surely die. As for Cousin Eugénie, I do not know.'

Her level matter-of-fact tone seemed to Dickson most shocking, for he could not treat it as mere melodrama. It carried a horrid conviction. 'We must get you out of this at once,' he declared.

'I cannot leave. I will tell you why. When I came to this country I appointed one to meet me here. He is a kinsman who knows England well, for he fought in your army. With him by my side I have no fear. It is altogether needful that I wait for him.'

'Then there is something more which you haven't told us?' Heritage asked.

Was there the faintest shadow of a blush on her cheek? 'There is something more,' she said.

She spoke to Heritage in French, and Dickson caught the name 'Alexis' and a word which sounded like 'prance'. The Poet listened eagerly and nodded. 'I have heard of him,' he said.

'But have you not seen him? A tall man with a yellow beard, who bears himself proudly. Being of my mother's race he has eyes like mine.'

'That's the man she was askin' me about yesterday,' said Dougal, who had squatted on the floor.

Heritage shook his head. 'We only came here last night. When did you expect Prince – your friend?'

'I hoped to find him here before me. Oh, it is his not coming that terrifies me. I must wait and hope. But if he does not come in time another may come before him.'

'The ones already here are not all the enemies that threaten you?'

'Indeed, no. The worst has still to come, and till I know he is here I do not greatly fear Spidel or Léon. They receive orders and do not give them.'

Heritage ran a perplexed hand through his hair. The sunset which had been flaming for some time in the unshuttered panes was now passing into the dark. The girl lit a lamp after first shuttering the rest of the windows. As she turned up the wick the odd dusty room and its strange company were revealed more clearly, and Dickson saw with a shock how haggard was the beautiful face. A great pity seized him and almost conquered his timidity.

'It is very difficult to help you,' Heritage was saying. 'You won't leave this place, and you won't claim the protection of the law. You are very independent, Mademoiselle, but it can't go on for ever. The man you fear may arrive at any moment. At any moment, too, your treasure may be discovered.'

'It is that that weighs on me,' she cried. 'The jewels! They are my solemn trust, but they burden me terribly. If I were only rid of them and knew them to be safe I should face the rest with a braver mind.'

'If you'll take my advice,' said Dickson slowly, 'you'll get them deposited in a bank and take a receipt for them. A Scotch bank is no' in a hurry to surrender a deposit without it gets the proper authority.'

Heritage brought his hands together with a smack. 'That's an idea. Will you trust us to take these things and deposit them safely?'

For a little she was silent and her eyes were fixed on each of the trio in turn. 'I will trust you,' she said at last. 'I think you will not betray me.'

'By God, we won't!' said the Poet fervently. 'Dogson, it's up to you. You march off to Glasgow in double quick time and place the stuff in your own name in your own bank. There's not a moment to lose. D'you hear?'

'I will that.' To his own surprise Dickson spoke without hesitation. Partly it was because of his merchant's sense of property, which made him hate the thought that miscreants should acquire that to which they had no title; but mainly it was the appeal in those haggard childish eyes. 'But I'm not going to be tramping the country in the night carrying a fortune and seeking for trains that aren't there. I'll go the first thing in the morning.'

'Where are they?' Heritage asked.

'That I do not tell. But I will fetch them.'

She left the room, and presently returned with three odd little parcels wrapped in leather and tied with thongs of raw hide. She gave them to Heritage, who held them appraisingly in his hand and then passed them to Dickson.

'I do not ask about their contents. We take them from you as they are, and, please God, when the moment comes they will be returned to you as you gave them. You trust us, Mademoiselle?'

'I trust you, for you are a soldier. Oh, and I thank you from my heart, my friends.' She held out a hand to each, which caused Heritage to grow suddenly very red.

'I will remain in the neighbourhood to await developments,' he said. 'We had better leave you now. Dougal, lead on.'

Before going, he took the girl's hand again, and with a sudden movement bent and kissed it. Dickson shook it heartily. 'Cheer up, Mem,' he observed. 'There's a better time coming.' His last recollection of her eyes was a soft mistiness not far from tears. His pouch and pipe had strange company jostling them in his pocket as he followed the others down the ladder into the night.

Dougal insisted that they must return by the road of the morning. 'We daren't go by the Laver, for that would bring us by the public-house. If the worst comes to the worst, and we fall in wi' any of the deevils, they must think ye've changed your mind and come back from Auchenlochan.'

The night smelt fresh and moist as if a break in the weather were imminent. As they scrambled along the Garple Dean a pinprick of light below showed where the tinklers were busy by their fire. Dickson's spirits suffered a sharp fall and he began to marvel at his temerity. What in Heaven's name had he undertaken? To carry very precious things, to which certainly he had no right, through the enemy to distant Glasgow. How could he escape the notice of the watchers? He was already suspect, and the sight of him back again in Dalquharter would double that suspicion. He must brazen it out, but he distrusted his powers with such tell-tale stuff in his pockets. They might murder him anywhere on the moor road or in an empty railway carriage. An unpleasant memory of various novels he had read in which such things happened haunted his mind . . . There was just one consolation. This job over, he would be quit of the whole business. And honourably quit, too, for he would have played a manly part in a most unpleasant affair. He could retire to the idyllic with the knowledge that he had not been wanting when Romance called. Not a soul should ever hear of it, but he saw himself in the future tramping green roads or sitting by his winter fireside pleasantly retelling himself the tale.

Before they came to the Garple bridge Dougal insisted that they should separate, remarking that 'it would never do if we were seen thegither'. Heritage was despatched by a short cut over fields to the left, which eventually, after one or two plunges into ditches, landed him safely in Mrs Morran's back yard. Dickson and Dougal crossed the bridge and tramped Dalquharter-wards by the highway. There was no sign of human life in that quiet place with owls hooting and rabbits rustling in the undergrowth. Beyond the woods they came in sight of the light in the back kitchen, and both seemed to relax their watchfulness when it was most needed. Dougal sniffed the air and looked seaward.

'It's coming on to rain,' he observed. 'There should be a muckle star there, and when you can't see it it means wet weather wi' this wind.'

'What star?' Dickson asked.

'The one wi' the Irish-lukkin' name. What's that they call it? O'Brien?' And he pointed to where the constellation of the Hunter should have been declining on the western horizon.

There was a bend of the road behind them, and suddenly round it came a dogcart driven rapidly. Dougal slipped like a weasel into a bush, and presently Dickson stood revealed in the glare of a lamp. The horse was pulled up sharply and the driver called out to him. He saw that it was Dobson the innkeeper with Léon beside him.

'Who is it?' cried the voice. 'Oh, you! I thought ye were off the day?'

Dickson rose nobly to the occasion.

'I thought myself I was. But I didn't think much of Auchenlochan, and I took a fancy to come back and spend the last night of my holiday with my Auntie. I'm off to Glasgow first thing the morn's morn.'

'So!' said the voice. 'Queer thing I never saw ye on the Auchenlochan road, where ye can see three mile before ye.'

'I left early and took it easy along the shore.'

'Did ye so? Well, goodnight to ye.'

Five minutes later Dickson walked into Mrs Morran's kitchen, where Heritage was busy making up for a day of short provender.

'I'm for Glasgow tomorrow, Auntie Phemie,' he cried. 'I want you to loan me a wee trunk with a key, and steek the door and windows, for I've a lot to tell you.'

SIX

How Mr McCunn Departed with Relief
and Returned with Resolution

AT seven o'clock on the following morning the post-cart, summoned by an early message from Mrs Morran, appeared outside the cottage. In it sat the ancient postman, whose real home was Auchenlochan, but who slept alternate nights in Dalquharter, and beside him Dobson the innkeeper. Dickson and his hostess stood at the garden-gate, the former with his pack on his back, and at his feet a small stout wooden box, of the kind in which cheeses are transported, garnished with an immense padlock. Heritage for obvious reasons did not appear; at the moment he was crouched on the floor of the loft watching the departure through a gap in the dimity curtains.

The traveller, after making sure that Dobson was looking, furtively slipped the key of the trunk into his knapsack.

'Well, goodbye, Auntie Phemie,' he said. 'I'm sure you've been awful kind to me, and I don't know how to thank you for all you're sending.'

'Tuts, Dickson, my man, they're hungry folk about Glesca that'll be glad o' my scones and jeelie. Tell Mirren I'm rale pleased wi' her man, and haste ye back soon.'

The trunk was deposited on the floor of the cart, and Dickson clambered into the back seat. He was thankful that he had not to sit next to Dobson, for he had tell-tale stuff on his person. The morning was wet, so he wore his waterproof, which concealed his odd tendency to stoutness about the middle.

Mrs Morran played her part well, with all the becoming gravity of an affectionate aunt, but as soon as the post-cart turned the bend of the road her demeanour changed. She was torn with convulsions of silent laughter. She retreated to the kitchen, sank into a chair, wrapped her face in her apron and rocked. Heritage, descending, found her struggling to regain composure. 'D'ye ken his wife's name?' she gasped. 'I ca'ed her Mirren! And maybe the body's no' mairried! Hech sirs! Hech sirs!'

Meantime Dickson was bumping along the moor-road on the back of the post-cart. He had worked out a plan, just as he had been used aforetime to devise a deal in foodstuffs. He had expected one of the watchers to turn up, and was rather relieved that it should be Dobson, whom he regarded as 'the most natural beast' of the three. Somehow he did not think that he would be molested before he reached the station, since his enemies would still be undecided in their minds. Probably they only wanted to make sure that he had really departed to forget all about him. But if not, he had his plan ready.

'Are you travelling today?' he asked the innkeeper.

'Just as far as the station to see about some oil-cake I'm expectin'. What's in your wee kist? Ye came here wi' nothing but the bag on your back.'

'Ay, the kist is no' mine. It's my auntie's. She's a kind body, and nothing would serve but she must pack a box for me to take back. Let me see. There's a baking of scones; three pots of honey and one of rhubarb jam – she was aye famous for her rhubarb jam; a mutton ham, which you can't get for love or money in Glasgow; some home-made black puddings, and a wee skim-milk cheese. I doubt I'll have to take a cab from the station.'

Dobson appeared satisfied, lit a short pipe, and relapsed into meditation. The long uphill road, ever climbing to where far off showed the tiny whitewashed buildings which were the railway station, seemed interminable this morning. The aged postman addressed strange objurgations to his aged horse and muttered reflexions to himself, the innkeeper smoked, and Dickson stared back into the misty hollow where lay Dalquharter. The south-west wind had brought up a screen of rain clouds and washed all the countryside in a soft wet grey. But the eye could

still travel a fair distance, and Dickson thought he had a glimpse
of a figure on a bicycle leaving the village two miles back. He
wondered who it could be. Not Heritage, who had no bicycle.
Perhaps some woman who was conspicuously late for the train.
Women were the chief cyclists nowadays in country places.

Then he forgot about the bicycle and twisted his neck to
watch the station. It was less than a mile off now, and they had
no time to spare, for away to the south among the hummocks of
the bog he saw the smoke of the train coming from
Auchenlochan. The postman also saw it and whipped up his
beast into a clumsy canter. Dickson, always nervous about being
late for trains, forced his eyes away and regarded again the road
behind him. Suddenly the cyclist had become quite plain – a
little more than a mile behind – a man, and pedalling furiously
in spite of the stiff ascent . . . It could only be one person – Léon.
He must have discovered their visit to the House yesterday and
be on the way to warn Dobson. If he reached the station before
the train, there would be no journey to Glasgow that day for one
respectable citizen.

Dickson was in a fever of impatience and fright. He dared not
adjure the postman to hurry, lest Dobson should turn his head
and descry his colleague. But the ancient man had begun to
realize the shortness of time and was urging the cart along at a
fair pace, since they were now on the flatter shelf of land which
carried the railway. Dickson kept his eyes fixed on the bicycle
and his teeth shut tight on his lower lip. Now it was hidden by
the last dip of hill; now it emerged into view not a quarter of a
mile behind, and its rider gave vent to a shrill call. Luckily the
innkeeper did not hear, for at that moment with a jolt the cart
pulled up at the station door, accompanied by the roar of the
incoming train.

Dickson whipped down from the back seat and seized the
solitary porter. 'Label the box for Glasgow and into the van with
it. Quick, man, and there'll be a shilling for you.' He had been
doing some rapid thinking these last minutes and had made up
his mind. If Dobson and he were alone in a carriage he could

not have the box there; that must be elsewhere, so that Dobson could not examine it if he were set on violence, somewhere in which it could still be a focus of suspicion and attract attention from his person. He took his ticket, and rushed on to the platform, to find the porter and the box at the door of the guard's van. Dobson was not there. With the vigour of a fussy traveller he shouted directions to the guard to take good care of his luggage, hurled a shilling at the porter, and ran for a carriage. At that moment he became aware of Dobson hurrying through the entrance. He must have met Léon and heard news from him, for his face was red and his ugly brows darkening.

The train was in motion. 'Here, you!' Dobson's voice shouted. 'Stop! I want a word wi' ye.' Dickson plunged at a third-class carriage, for he saw faces behind the misty panes, and above all things then he feared an empty compartment. He clambered on to the step, but the handle would not turn, and with a sharp pang of fear he felt the innkeeper's grip on his arm. Then some Samaritan from within let down the window, opened the door, and pulled him up. He fell on a seat, and a second later Dobson staggered in beside him.

Thank Heaven, the dirty little carriage was nearly full. There were two herds, each with a dog and a long hazel crook, and an elderly woman who looked like a ploughman's wife out for a day's marketing. And there was one other whom Dickson recognized with peculiar joy – the bagman in the provision line of business whom he had met three days before at Kilchrist.

The recognition was mutual. 'Mr McCunn!' the bagman exclaimed. 'My, but that was running it fine! I hope you've had a pleasant holiday, sir?'

'Very pleasant. I've been spending two nights with friends down hereaways. I've been very fortunate in the weather, for it has broke just when I'm leaving.'

Dickson sank back on the hard cushions. It had been a near thing, but so far he had won. He wished his heart did not beat so fast, and he hoped he did not betray his disorder in his face. Very deliberately he hunted for his pipe and filled it slowly.

Then he turned to Dobson. 'I didn't know you were travelling the day. What about your oil-cake?'

'I've changed my mind,' was the gruff answer.

'Was that you I heard crying on me when we were running for the train?'

'Ay. I thought ye had forgot about your kist.'

'No fear,' said Dickson. 'I'm no' likely to forget my auntie's scones.'

He laughed pleasantly and then turned to the bagman. Thereafter the compartment hummed with the technicalities of the grocery trade. He exerted himself to draw out his companion, to have him refer to the great firm of D. McCunn, so that the innkeeper might be ashamed of his suspicions. What nonsense to imagine that a noted and wealthy Glasgow merchant – the bagman's tone was almost reverential – would concern himself with the affairs of a forgotten village and a tumbledown house!

Presently the train drew up at Kirkmichael station. The woman descended, and Dobson, after making sure that no one else meant to follow her example, also left the carriage. A porter was shouting: 'Fast train to Glasgow – Glasgow next stop.' Dickson watched the innkeeper shoulder his way through the crowd in the direction of the booking office. 'He's off to send a telegram,' he decided. 'There'll be trouble waiting for me at the other end.'

When the train moved on he found himself disinclined for further talk. He had suddenly become meditative, and curled up in a corner with his head hard against the window pane, watching the wet fields and glistening roads as they slipped past. He had his plans made for his conduct at Glasgow, but, Lord! how he loathed the whole business! Last night he had had a kind of gusto in his desire to circumvent villainy; at Dalquharter station he had enjoyed a momentary sense of triumph; now he felt very small, lonely, and forlorn. Only one thought far at the back of his mind cropped up now and then to give him comfort. He was entering on the last lap. Once get this detestable errand

done and he would be a free man, free to go back to the kindly
humdrum life from which he should never have strayed. Never
again, he vowed, never again. Rather would he spend the rest of
his days in hydropathics than come within the pale of such
horrible adventure. Romance, forsooth! This was not the mild
goddess he had sought, but an awful harpy who battened on the
souls of men.

He had some bad minutes as the train passed through the
suburbs and along the grimy embankment by which the southern lines enter the city. But as it rumbled over the river bridge
and slowed down before the terminus his vitality suddenly
revived. He was a business man, and there was now something
for him to do.

After a rapid farewell to the bagman, he found a porter and
hustled his box out of the van in the direction of the left-luggage
office. Spies, summoned by Dobson's telegram, were, he was
convinced, watching his every movement, and he meant to see
that they missed nothing. He received his ticket for the box, and
slowly and ostentatiously stowed it away in his pack. Swinging
the said pack on his arm, he sauntered through the entrance
hall to the row of waiting taxi-cabs, and selected that one which
seemed to him to have the oldest and most doddering driver.
He deposited the pack inside on the seat, and then stood still as
if struck with a sudden thought.

'I breakfasted terrible early,' he told the driver. 'I think I'll
have a bite to eat. Will you wait?'

'Ay,' said the man, who was reading a grubby sheet of newspaper. 'I'll wait as long as ye like, for it's you that pays.'

Dickson left his pack in the cab and, oddly enough for a
careful man, he did not shut the door. He re-entered the station,
strolled to the bookstall, and bought a *Glasgow Herald*. His steps
then tended to the refreshment-room, where he ordered a cup
of coffee and two Bath buns, and seated himself at a small table.
There he was soon immersed in the financial news, and though
he sipped his coffee he left the buns untasted. He took out a
penknife and cut various extracts from the *Herald*, bestowing

them carefully in his pocket. An observer would have seen an elderly gentleman absorbed in market quotations.

After a quarter of an hour had been spent in this performance he happened to glance at the clock and rose with an exclamation. He bustled out to his taxi and found the driver still intent upon his reading. 'Here I am at last,' he said cheerily, and had a foot on the step, when he stopped suddenly with a cry. It was a cry of alarm, but also of satisfaction.

'What's become of my pack? I left it on the seat, and now it's gone! There's been a thief here.'

The driver, roused from his lethargy, protested in the name of his gods that no one had been near it. 'Ye took it into the station wi' ye,' he urged.

'I did nothing of the kind. Just you wait here till I see the inspector. A bonny watch *you* keep on a gentleman's things.'

But Dickson did not interview the railway authorities. Instead he hurried to the left-luggage office. 'I deposited a small box here a short time ago. I mind the number. Is it there still?'

The attendant glanced at the shelf. 'A wee deal box with iron bands. It was took out ten minutes syne. A man brought the ticket and took it away on his shoulder.'

'Thank you. There's been a mistake, but the blame's mine. My man mistook my orders.'

Then he returned to the now nervous taxi-driver. 'I've taken it up with the station-master and he's putting the police on. You'll likely be wanted, so I gave him your number. It's a fair disgrace that there should be so many thieves about this station. It's not the first time I've lost things. Drive me to West George Street and look sharp.' And he slammed the door with the violence of an angry man.

But his reflexions were not violent, for he smiled to himself. 'That was pretty neat. They'll take some time to get the kist open, for I dropped the key out of the train after we left Kirkmichael. That gives me a fair start. If I hadn't thought of that, they'd have found some way to grip me and ripe me long before I got to the Bank.' He shuddered as he thought of the dangers he had escaped. 'As it is, they're off the track for half an hour at least, while they're rummaging among Auntie Phemie's scones.' At the thought he laughed heartily, and when he brought the taxi-cab to a standstill by rapping on the front window, he left it with a temper apparently restored. Obviously he had no grudge against the driver, who to his immense surprise was rewarded with ten shillings.

Three minutes later Mr McCunn might have been seen entering the head office of the Strathclyde Bank and inquiring for the manager. There was no hesitation about him now, for his foot was on his native heath. The chief cashier received him with deference in spite of his unorthodox garb, for he was not the least honoured of the bank's customers. As it chanced he had been talking about him that very morning to a gentleman from London. 'The strength of this city,' he had said, tapping his eyeglasses on his knuckles, 'does not lie in its dozen very rich men, but in the hundred or two homely folk who make no parade of wealth. Men like Dickson McCunn, for example, who live all their life in a semi-detached villa and die worth half a million.' And the Londoner had cordially assented.

So Dickson was ushered promptly into an inner room, and was warmly greeted by Mr Mackintosh, the patron of the Gorbals Die-Hards.

'I must thank you for your generous donation, McCunn. Those boys will get a little fresh air and quiet after the smoke and din of Glasgow. A little country peace to smooth out the creases in their poor little souls.'

'Maybe,' said Dickson, with a vivid recollection of Dougal as he had last seen him. Somehow he did not think that peace was likely to be the portion of that devoted band. 'But I've not come here to speak about that.'

He took off his waterproof; then his coat and waistcoat; and showed himself a strange figure with sundry bulges about the middle. The manager's eyes grew very round. Presently these excrescences were revealed as linen bags sewn on to his shirt, and fitting into the hollow between ribs and hip. With some difficulty he slit the bags and extracted three hide-bound packages.

'See here, Mackintosh,' he said solemnly. 'I hand you over these parcels, and you're to put them in the innermost corner of your strong room. You needn't open them. Just put them away as they are, and write me a receipt for them. Write it now.'

Mr Mackintosh obediently took pen in hand.

'What'll I call them?' he asked.

'Just the three leather parcels handed to you by Dickson McCunn, Esq., naming the date.'

Mr Mackintosh wrote. He signed his name with his usual flourish and handed the slip to his client.

'Now,' said Dickson, 'you'll put that receipt in the strong box where you keep my securities, and you'll give it up to nobody but me in person and you'll surrender the parcels only on presentation of the receipt. D'you understand?'

'Perfectly. May I ask any questions?'

'You'd better not if you don't want to hear lees.'

'What's in the packages?' Mr Mackintosh weighed them in his hand.

'That's asking,' said Dickson. 'But I'll tell ye this much. It's jools.'

'Your own?'

'No, but I'm their trustee.'

'Valuable?'

'I was hearing they were worth more than a million pounds.'

'God bless my soul,' said the startled manager. 'I don't like this kind of business, McCunn.'

'No more do I. But you'll do it to oblige an old friend and a good customer. If you don't know much about the packages you know all about me. Now, mind, I trust you.'

Mr Mackintosh forced himself to a joke. 'Did you maybe steal them?'

Dickson grinned. 'Just what I did. And that being so, I want you to let me out by the back door.'

When he found himself in the street he felt the huge relief of a boy who had emerged with credit from the dentist's chair. Remembering that there would be no midday dinner for him at home, his first step was to feed heavily at a restaurant. He had, so far as he could see, surmounted all his troubles, his one regret being that he had lost his pack, which contained among other things his Izaak Walton and his safety razor. He bought another razor and a new Walton, and mounted an electric tram-car *en route* for home.

Very contented with himself he felt as the car swung across the Clyde bridge. He had done well – but of that he did not want to think, for the whole beastly thing was over. He was going to bury that memory, to be resurrected perhaps on a later day when the unpleasantness had been forgotten. Heritage had his address, and knew where to come when it was time to claim the jewels. As for the watchers, they must have ceased to suspect him, when they discovered the innocent contents of his knapsack and Mrs Morran's box. Home for him, and a luxurious tea by his own fire-side; and then an evening with his books, for Heritage's nonsense had stimulated his literary fervour. He would dip into his old favourites again to confirm his faith. Tomorrow he would go for a jaunt somewhere – perhaps down the Clyde, or to the South of England, which he had heard was a pleasant, thickly peopled country. No more lonely inns and deserted villages for him; henceforth he would make certain of comfort and peace.

The rain had stopped, and, as the car moved down the dreary vista of Eglinton Street, the sky opened into fields of blue and the April sun silvered the puddles. It was in such place and under such weather that Dickson suffered an overwhelming experience.

It is beyond my skill, being all unlearned in the game of psycho-analysis, to explain how this thing happened, I concern myself only with facts. Suddenly the pretty veil of self-satisfaction was rent from top to bottom, and Dickson saw a figure of himself within, a smug leaden little figure which simpered and preened itself and was hollow as a rotten nut. And he hated it.

The horrid truth burst on him that Heritage had been right. He only played with life. That imbecile image was a mere spectator, content to applaud, but shrinking from the contact of reality. It had been all right as a provision merchant, but when it fancied itself capable of higher things it had deceived itself. Foolish little image with its brave dreams and its swelling words from Browning! All make-believe of the feeblest. He was a coward, running away at the first threat of danger. It was as if he were watching a tall stranger with a wand pointing to the embarrassed phantom that was himself, and ruthlessly exposing its frailties! And yet the pitiless showman was himself too – himself as he wanted to be, cheerful, brave, resourceful, indomitable.

Dickson suffered a spasm of mortal agony. 'Oh, I'm surely not so bad as all that,' he groaned. But the hurt was not only in his pride. He saw himself being forced to new decisions, and each alternative was of the blackest. He fairly shivered with the horror of it. The car slipped past a suburban station from which passengers were emerging – comfortable black-coated men such as he had once been. He was bitterly angry with Providence for picking him out of the great crowd of sedentary folk for this sore ordeal. 'Why was I tethered to sich a conscience?' was his moan. But there was that stern inquisitor with his pointer exploring his soul. 'You flatter yourself you have done your share,' he was saying. 'You will make pretty stories about it to yourself, and some day you may tell your friends, modestly disclaiming any special credit. But you will be a liar, for you know you are afraid. You are running away when the work is scarcely begun, and leaving it to a few boys and a poet whom you had the impudence the other day to despise. I think you are worse than a coward. I think you are a cad.'

His fellow-passengers on the top of the car saw an absorbed middle-aged gentleman who seemed to have something the matter with his bronchial tubes. They could not guess at the tortured soul. The decision was coming nearer, the alternatives loomed up dark and inevitable. On one side was submission to ignominy, on the other a return to that place which he detested, and yet loathed himself for detesting. 'It seems I'm not likely to have much peace either way,' he reflected dismally.

How the conflict would have ended had it continued on these lines I cannot say. The soul of Mr McCunn was being assailed by moral and metaphysical adversaries with which he had not been trained to deal. But suddenly it leapt from negatives to positives. He saw the face of the girl in the shuttered House, so fair and young and yet so haggard. It seemed to be appealing to him to rescue it from a great loneliness and fear. Yes, he had been right, it had a strange look of his Janet – the wide-open eyes, the solemn mouth. What was to become of that child if he failed her in her need?

Now Dickson was a practical man, and this view of the case brought him into a world which he understood. 'It's fair ridiculous,' he reflected. 'Nobody there to take a grip of things. Just a wheen Gorbals keelies and the lad Heritage. Not a business man among the lot.'

The alternatives, which hove before him like two great banks of cloud, were altering their appearance. One was becoming faint and tenuous; the other, solid as ever, was just a shade less black. He lifted his eyes and saw in the near distance the corner of the road which led to his home. 'I must decide before I reach that corner,' he told himself.

Then his mind became apathetic. He began to whistle dismally through his teeth, watching the corner as it came nearer. The car stopped with a jerk. 'I'll go back,' he said aloud, clambering down the steps. The truth was he had decided five minutes before when he first saw Janet's face.

He walked briskly to his house, entirely refusing to waste any more energy on reflexion. 'This is a business proposition,' he told himself, 'and I'm going to handle it as sich.' Tibby was surprised to see him and offered him tea in vain. 'I'm just back for a few minutes. Let's see the letters.'

There was one from his wife. She proposed to stay another week at the Neuk Hydropathic and suggested that he might join her and bring her home. He sat down and wrote a long affectionate reply, declining, but expressing his delight that she was soon returning. 'That's very likely the last time Mamma will hear from me,' he reflected, but – oddly enough – without any great fluttering of the heart.

Then he proceeded to be furiously busy. He sent out Tibby to buy another knapsack and to order a cab and to cash a considerable cheque. In the knapsack he packed a fresh change of clothing and the new safety razor, but no books, for he was past the need of them. That done, he drove to his solicitors.

'What like a firm are Glendonan and Speirs in Edinburgh?' he asked the senior partner.

'Oh, very respectable. Very respectable indeed. Regular Edinburgh W.S. lot. Do a lot of factoring.'

'I want you to telephone through to them and inquire about a place in Carrick called Huntingtower, near the village of Dalquharter. I understand it's to let, and I'm thinking of taking a lease of it.'

The senior partner after some delay got through to Edinburgh, and was presently engaged in the feverish dialectic which the long-distance telephone involves. 'I want to speak to Mr Glendonan himself . . . Yes, yes, Mr Caw of Paton and Linklater . . . Good afternoon . . . Huntingtower. Yes, in Carrick. Not to let? But I understand it's been in the market for some months. You say you've an idea it has just been let. But my client is positive that you're mistaken, unless the agreement was made this morning . . . You'll inquire? Oh, I see. The actual factoring is done by your local agent, Mr James Loudon, in Auchenlochan. You think my client had better get into touch with him at once. Just wait a minute, please.'

He put his hand over the receiver. 'Usual Edinburgh way of doing business,' he observed caustically. 'What do you want done?'

'I'll run down and see this Loudon. Tell Glendonan and Spiers to advise him to expect me, for I'll go this very day.'

Mr Caw resumed his conversation. 'My client would like a telegram sent at once to Mr Loudon introducing him. He's Mr

Dickson McCunn of Mearns Street – the great provision merchant, you know. Oh, yes! Good for any rent. Refer if you like to the Strathclyde Bank, but you can take my word for it. Thank you. Then that's settled. Goodbye.'

Dickson's next visit was to a gunmaker who was a fellow-elder with him in the Guthrie Memorial Kirk.

'I want a pistol and a lot of cartridges,' he announced. 'I'm not caring what kind it is, so long as it is a good one and not too big.'

'For yourself?' the gunmaker asked. 'You must have a licence, I doubt, and there's a lot of new regulations.'

'I can't wait on a licence. It's for a cousin of mine who's off to Mexico at once. You've got to find some way of obliging an old friend, Mr McNair.'

Mr McNair scratched his head. 'I don't see how I can sell you one. But I'll tell you what I'll do – I'll lend you one. It belongs to my nephew, Peter Tait, and has been lying in a drawer ever since he came back from the front. He has no use for it now that he's a placed minister.'

So Dickson bestowed in the pockets of his waterproof a service revolver and fifty cartridges, and bade his cab take him to the shop in Mearns Street. For a moment the sight of the familiar place struck a pang to his breast, but he choked down unavailing regrets. He ordered a great hamper of foodstuffs – the most delicate kind of tinned goods, two perfect hams, tongues, Strassburg pies, chocolate, cakes, biscuits, and, as a last thought, half a dozen bottles of old liqueur brandy. It was to be carefully packed, addressed to Mrs Morran, Dalquharter Station, and delivered in time for him to take down by the 7.33 train. Then he drove to the terminus and dined with something like a desperate peace in his heart.

On this occasion he took a first-class ticket, for he wanted to be alone. As the lights began to be lit in the wayside stations and the clear April dusk darkened into night, his thoughts were sombre yet resigned. He opened the window and let the sharp air of the Renfrewshire uplands fill the carriage. It was fine weather again after the rain, and a bright constellation – perhaps Dougal's friend O'Brien – hung in the western sky. How happy he would have been a week ago had he been starting thus for a country holiday! He could sniff the faint scent of moor-burn and ploughed earth which had always been his first reminder of spring. But he had been pitchforked out of that old happy world and could never enter it again. Alas! for the roadside fire, the cosy inn, the *Compleat Angler*, the Chavender or Chub!

And yet – and yet! He had done the right thing, though the Lord alone knew how it would end. He began to pluck courage from his very melancholy, and hope from his reflexions upon the transitoriness of life. He was austerely following Romance as he conceived it, and if that capricious lady had taken one dream from him she might yet reward him with a better. Tags of poetry came into his head which seemed to favour this philosophy – particularly some lines of Browning on which he used to discourse to his Kirk Literary Society. Uncommon silly, he considered, these homilies of his must have been, mere twitterings of the unfledged. But now he saw more in the lines, a deeper interpretation which he had earned the right to make.

> *Oh world, where all things change and nought abides,*
> *Oh life, the long mutation – is it so?*
> *Is it with life as with the body's change?–*
> *Where, e'en tho' better follow, good must pass.*

That was as far as he could get, though he cudgelled his memory to continue. Moralizing thus, he became drowsy, and was almost asleep when the train drew up at the station of Kirkmichael.

SEVEN

Sundry Doings in the Mirk

FROM Kirkmichael on the train stopped at every station, but no passenger seemed to leave or arrive at the little platforms white in the moon. At Dalquharter the case of provisions was safely transferred to the porter with instructions to take charge of it till it was sent for. During the next ten minutes Dickson's mind began to work upon his problem with a certain briskness. It was all nonsense that the law of Scotland could not be summoned to the defence. The jewels had been safely got rid of, and who was to dispute their possession? Not Dobson and his crew, who had no sort of title, and were out for naked robbery. The girl had spoken of greater dangers from new enemies – kidnapping, perhaps. Well, that was felony, and the police must be brought in. Probably if all were known the three watchers had criminal records, pages long, filed at Scotland Yard. The man to deal with that side of the business was Loudon the factor, and to him he was bound in the first place. He had made a clear picture in his head of this Loudon – a derelict old country writer, formal, pedantic, lazy, anxious only to get an unprofitable business off his hands with the least possible trouble, never going near the place himself, and ably supported in his lethargy by conceited Edinburgh Writers to the Signet. 'Sich notions of business!' he murmured. 'I wonder that there's a single county family in Scotland no' in the bankruptcy court!' It was his mission to wake up Mr James Loudon.

Arrived at Auchenlochan he went first to the Salutation Hotel, a pretentious place sacred to golfers. There he engaged a bedroom for the night and, having certain scruples, paid for it in advance. He also had some sandwiches prepared which he stowed in his pack, and filled his flask with whisky. 'I'm going home to Glasgow by the first train tomorrow,' he told the landlady, 'and now I've got to see a friend. I'll not be back till late.' He was assured that there would be no difficulty about his admittance at any hour, and directed how to find Mr Loudon's dwelling.

It was an old house fronting direct on the street, with a fanlight above the door and a neat brass plate bearing the legend 'Mr James Loudon, Writer'. A lane ran up one side leading apparently to a garden, for the moonlight showed the dusk of trees. In front was the main street of Auchenlochan, now deserted save for a single roisterer, and opposite stood the ancient town house, with arches where the country folk came at the spring and autumn hiring fairs. Dickson rang the antiquated bell, and was presently admitted to a dark hall floored with oilcloth, where a single gas-jet showed that on one side was the business office and on the other the living-rooms. Mr Loudon was at supper, he was told, and he sent in his card. Almost at once the door at the end on the left side was flung open and a large figure appeared flourishing a napkin. 'Come in, sir, come in,' it cried. 'I've just finished a bite of meat. Very glad to see you. Here, Maggie, what d'you mean by keeping the gentleman standing in that outer darkness?'

The room into which Dickson was ushered was small and bright, with a red paper on the walls, a fire burning, and a big oil lamp in the centre of a table. Clearly Mr Loudon had no wife, for it was a bachelor's den in every line of it. A cloth was laid on a corner of the table, in which stood the remnants of a meal. Mr Loudon seemed to have been about to make a brew of punch, for a kettle simmered by the fire, and lemons and sugar flanked a pot-bellied whisky decanter of the type that used to be known as a 'mason's mell'.

The sight of the lawyer was a surprise to Dickson and dissipated his notions of an aged and lethargic incompetent. Mr Loudon was a strongly built man who could not be a year over fifty. He had a ruddy face, clean shaven except for a grizzled moustache; his grizzled hair was thinning round the temples; but his skin was unwrinkled and his eyes had all the vigour of youth. His tweed suit was well cut, and the buff waistcoat with flaps and pockets and the plain leather watchguard hinted at the sportsman, as did the half-dozen racing prints on the wall. A pleasant high-coloured figure he made; his voice had the frank ring due to much use out of doors; and his expression had the singular candour which comes from grey eyes with large pupils and a narrow iris.

'Sit down, Mr McCunn. Take the arm-chair by the fire. I've had a wire from Glendonan and Speirs about you. I was just going to have a glass of toddy – a grand thing for these uncertain April nights. You'll join me? No? Well, you'll smoke anyway. There's cigars at your elbow. Certainly, a pipe if you like. This is Liberty Hall.'

Dickson found some difficulty in the part for which he had cast himself. He had expected to condescend upon an elderly inept and give him sharp instructions; instead he found himself faced with a jovial, virile figure which certainly did not suggest incompetence. It has been mentioned already that he had always great difficulty in looking any one in the face, and this difficulty was intensified when he found himself confronted with bold and candid eyes. He felt abashed and a little nervous.

'I've come to see you about Huntingtower House,' he began.

'I know. So Glendonans informed me. Well, I'm very glad to hear it. The place has been standing empty far too long, and that is worse for a new house than an old house. There's not much money to spend on it either, unless we can make sure of a good tenant. How did you hear about it?'

'I was taking a bit holiday and I spent a night at Dalquharter with an old auntie of mine. You must understand I've just retired from business, and I'm thinking of finding a country place. I used to have the big provision shop in Mearns Street – now the United Supply Stores, Limited. You've maybe heard of it?'

The other bowed and smiled. 'Who hasn't? The name of Dickson McCunn is known far beyond the city of Glasgow.'

Dickson was not insensible of the flattery, and he continued with more freedom. 'I took a walk and got a glisk of the House, and I liked the look of it. You see, I want a quiet bit a good long way from a town, and at the same time a house with all modern conveniences. I suppose Huntingtower has that?'

'When it was built fifteen years ago it was considered a model – six bathrooms, its own electric light plant, steam heating, and independent boiler for hot water, the whole bag of tricks. I won't say but what some of these contrivances will want looking to, for the place has been some time empty, but there can be nothing very far wrong, and I can guarantee that the bones of the house are good.'

'Well, that's all right,' said Dickson. 'I don't mind spending a little money myself if the place suits me. But of that, of course, I'm not yet certain, for I've only had a glimpse of the outside. I wanted to get into the policies, but a man at the lodge wouldn't let me. They're a mighty uncivil lot down there.'

'I'm very sorry to hear that,' said Mr Loudon in a tone of concern.

'Ay, and if I take the place I'll stipulate that you get rid of the lodgekeepers.'

'There won't be the slightest difficulty about that, for they are only weekly tenants. But I'm vexed to hear they were uncivil. I was glad to get any tenant that offered, and they were well recommended to me.'

'They're foreigners.'

'One of them is – a Belgian refugee that Lady Morewood took an interest in. But the other – Spittal, they call him – I thought he was Scotch.'

'He's not that. And I don't like the innkeeper either. I would want him shifted.'

Mr Loudon laughed. 'I dare say Dobson is a rough diamond. There's worse folk in the world all the same, but I don't think he will want to stay. He only went there to pass the time till he heard from his brother in Vancouver. He's a roving spirit, and will be off overseas again.'

'That's all right!' said Dickson, who was beginning to have horrid suspicions that he might be on a wild-goose chase after all. 'Well, the next thing is for me to see over the House.'

'Certainly. I'd like to go with you myself. What day would suit you? Let me see. This is Friday. What about this day week?'

'I was thinking of tomorrow. Since I'm down in these parts I may as well get the job done.'

Mr Loudon looked puzzled. 'I quite see that. But I don't think it's possible. You see, I have to consult the owners and get their consent to a lease. Of course they have the general purpose of letting, but – well, they're queer folk the Kennedys,' and his face wore the half-embarrassed smile of an honest man preparing to make confidences. 'When poor Mr Quentin died, the place went to his two sisters in joint ownership. A very bad arrangement, as you can imagine. It isn't entailed, and I've always been pressing them to sell, but so far they won't hear of it. They both married Englishmen, so it will take a day or two to get in touch with them. One, Mrs Stukely, lives in Devonshire. The other – Miss Katie that was – married Sir Francis Morewood, the general, and I hear that she's expected back in London next Monday from the Riviera. I'll wire and write first thing tomorrow morning. But you must give me a day or two.'

Dickson felt himself waking up. His doubts about his own sanity were dissolving, for, as his mind reasoned, the factor was prepared to do anything he asked – but only after a week had gone. What he was concerned with was the next few days.

'All the same I would like to have a look at the place tomorrow, even if nothing comes of it.'

Mr Loudon looked seriously perplexed. 'You will think me absurdly fussy, Mr McCunn, but I must really beg of you to give up the idea. The Kennedys, as I have said, are – well, not exactly like other people, and I have the strictest orders not to let any one visit the house without their express leave. It sounds a ridiculous rule, but I assure you it's as much as my job is worth to disregard it.'

'D'you mean to say not a soul is allowed inside the House?'

'Not a soul.'

'Well, Mr Loudon, I'm going to tell you a queer thing, which I think you ought to know. When I was taking a walk the other night – your Belgian wouldn't let me into the policies, but I went down the glen – what's that they call it? the Garple Dean – I got round the back where the old ruin stands and I had a good look at the House. I tell you there was somebody in it.'

'It would be Spittal, who acts as caretaker.'

'It was not. It was a woman. I saw her on the veranda.'

The candid grey eyes were looking straight at Dickson, who managed to bring his own shy orbs to meet them. He thought that he detected a shade of hesitation. Then Mr Loudon got up from his chair and stood on the hearthrug looking down at his visitor. He laughed, with some embarrassment, but ever so pleasantly.

'I really don't know what you will think of me, Mr McCunn. Here are you, coming to do us all a kindness, and lease that infernal white elephant, and here have I been steadily hoaxing you for the last five minutes. I humbly ask your pardon. Set it down to the loyalty of an old family lawyer. Now, I am going to tell you the truth and take you into our confidence, for I know we are safe with you. The Kennedys are – always have been – just a wee bit queer. Old inbred stock, you know. They will produce somebody like poor Mr Quentin, who was as sane as you or me, but as a rule in every generation there is one member of the family – or more – who is just a little bit –' and he tapped his forehead. 'Nothing violent, you understand, but just not quite "wise and world-like", as the old folk say. Well, there's a certain old lady, an aunt of Mr Quentin and his sisters, who has always been about tenpence in the shilling. Usually she lives at Bournemouth, but one of her crazes is a passion for Huntingtower, and the Kennedys have always humoured her and had her to stay every spring. When the House was shut up that became impossible, but this year she took such a craving to come back, that Lady Morewood asked me to arrange it. It had to be kept very quiet, but the poor old thing is perfectly harm-less, and just sits and knits with her maid and looks out of the seaward windows. Now you see why I can't take you there tomorrow. I have to get rid of the old lady, who in any case was travelling south early next week. Do you understand?'

'Perfectly,' said Dickson with some fervour. He had learned exactly what he wanted. The factor was telling him lies. Now he knew where to place Mr Loudon.

He always looked back upon what followed as a very credita-ble piece of play-acting for a man who had small experience in that line.

'Is the old lady a wee wizened body, with a black cap and something like a white cashmere shawl round her shoulders?'

'You describe her exactly,' Mr Loudon replied eagerly.

'That would explain the foreigners.'

'Of course. We couldn't have natives who would make the thing the clash of the countryside.'

'Of course not. But it must be a difficult job to keep a busi-ness like that quiet. Any wandering policeman might start inquiries. And supposing the lady became violent?'

'Oh, there's no fear of that. Besides, I've a position in this country – Deputy Fiscal and so forth – and a friend of the Chief Constable. I think I may be trusted to do a little private explain-ing if the need arose.'

'I see,' said Dickson. He saw, indeed, a great deal which would give him food for furious thought. 'Well, I must just possess my soul in patience. Here's my Glasgow address, and I look to you to send me a telegram whenever you're ready for me. I'm at the Salutation tonight, and go home tomorrow with the first train. Wait a minute' – and he pulled out his watch – 'there's a train stops at Auchenlochan at 10.17. I think I'll catch that . . . Well, Mr Loudon, I'm very much obliged to you, and I'm glad to think that it'll no' be long till we renew our acquaintance.'

The factor accompanied him to the door, diffusing geniality. 'Very pleased indeed to have met you. A pleasant journey and a quick return.'

The street was still empty. Into a corner of the arches opposite the moon was shining, and Dickson retired thither to
consult his map of the neighbourhood. He found what he
wanted, and, as he lifted his eyes, caught sight of a man coming
down the causeway. Promptly he retired into the shadow and
watched the newcomer. There could be no mistake about the
figure; the bulk, the walk, the carriage of the head marked it for
Dobson. The innkeeper went slowly past the factor's house;
then halted and retraced his steps; then, making sure that the
street was empty, turned into the side lane which led to the
garden.

This was what sailors call a cross-bearing, and strengthened
Dickson's conviction. He delayed no longer, but hurried down
the side street by which the north road leaves the town.

He had crossed the bridge of Lochan and was climbing the
steep ascent which led to the heathy plateau separating the
stream from the Garple before he had got his mind quite clear
on the case. *First*, Loudon was in the plot, whatever it was;
responsible for the details of the girl's imprisonment, but not
the main author. That must be the Unknown who was still to
come, from whom Spidel took his orders. Dobson was probably
Loudon's special henchman, working directly under him.
Secondly, the immediate object had been the jewels, and they
were happily safe in the vaults of the incorruptible Mackintosh.
But, *third* – and this only on Saskia's evidence – the worst
danger to her began with the arrival of the Unknown. What
could that be? Probably, kidnapping. He was prepared to believe
anything of people like Bolsheviks. And, *fourth*, this danger was
due within the next day or two. Loudon had been quite willing
to let him into the house and to sack all the watchers within a
week from that date. The natural and right thing was to summon
the aid of the law, but, *fifth*, that would be a slow business with
Loudon able to put spokes in the wheels and befog the authorities, and the mischief would be done before a single policeman
showed his face in Dalquharter. Therefore, *sixth*, he and
Heritage must hold the fort in the meantime, and he would

send a wire to his lawyer, Mr Caw, to get to work with the constabulary. *Seventh*, he himself was probably free from suspicion in both Loudon's and Dobson's minds as a harmless fool. But that freedom would not survive his reappearance in Dalquharter. He could say, to be sure, that he had come back to see his auntie, but that would not satisfy the watchers, since, so far as they knew, he was the only man outside the gang who was aware that people were dwelling in the House. They would not tolerate his presence in the neighbourhood.

He formulated his conclusions as if it were an ordinary business deal, and rather to his surprise was not conscious of any fear. As he pulled together the belt of his waterproof he felt the reassuring bulges in its pockets which were his pistol and cartridges. He reflected that it must be very difficult to miss with a pistol if you fired it at, say, three yards, and if there was to be shooting that would be his range. Mr McCunn had stumbled on the precious truth that the best way to be rid of quaking knees is to keep a busy mind.

He crossed the ridge of the plateau and looked down on the Garple glen. There were the lights of Dalquharter – or rather a single light, for the inhabitants went early to bed. His intention was to seek quarters with Mrs Morran, when his eye caught a gleam in a hollow of the moor a little to the east. He knew it for the camp-fire around which Dougal's warriors bivouacked. The notion came to him to go there instead, and hear the news of the day before entering the cottage. So he crossed the bridge, skirted a plantation of firs, and scrambled through the broom and heather in what he took to be the right direction.

The moon had gone down, and the quest was not easy. Dickson had come to the conclusion that he was on the wrong road, when he was summoned by a voice which seemed to arise out of the ground.

'Who goes there?'

'What's that you say?'

'Who goes there?' The point of a pole was held firmly against his chest.

'I'm Mr McCunn, a friend of Dougal's.'

'Stand, friend.' The shadow before him whistled and another shadow appeared. 'Report to the Chief that there's a man here, name o' McCunn, seekin' for him.'

Presently the messenger returned with Dougal and a cheap lantern which he flashed in Dickson's face.

'Oh, it's you,' said that leader, who had his jaw bound up as if he had the toothache. 'What are ye doing back here?'

'To tell the truth, Dougal,' was the answer, 'I couldn't stay away. I was fair miserable when I thought of Mr Heritage and you laddies left to yourselves. My conscience simply wouldn't let me stop at home, so here I am.'

Dougal grunted, but clearly he approved, for from that moment he treated Dickson with a new respect. Formerly when he had referred to him at all it had been as 'auld McCunn'. Now it was 'Mister McCunn'. He was given rank as a worthy civilian ally.

The bivouac was a cheerful place in the wet night. A great fire of pine roots and old paling posts hissed in the fine rain, and around it crouched several urchins busy making oatmeal cakes in the embers. On one side a respectable lean-to had been constructed by nailing a plank to two fir-trees, running sloping poles thence to the ground, and thatching the whole with spruce branches and heather. On the other side two small dilapidated home-made tents were pitched. Dougal motioned his companion into the lean-to, where they had some privacy from the rest of the band.

'Well, what's your news?' Dickson asked. He noticed that the Chieftain seemed to have been comprehensively in the wars, for apart from the bandage on his jaw, he had numerous small cuts on his brow, and a great rent in one of his shirt sleeves. Also he appeared to be going lame, and when he spoke a new gap was revealed in his large teeth.

'Things,' said Dougal solemnly, 'has come to a bonny cripus. This very night we've been in a battle.'

He spat fiercely, and the light of war burned in his eyes.

'It was the tinklers from the Garple Dean. They yokit on us about seven o'clock, just at the darkenin'. First they tried to bounce us. We weren't wanted here, they said, so we'd better clear. I told them that it was them that wasn't wanted. "Awa' to Finnick," said I. "D'ye think we take our orders from dirty ne'er-do-weels like you?" "By God," says they, "we'll cut your lights out," and then the battle started.'

'What happened?' Dickson asked excitedly.

'They were four muckle men against six laddies, and they thought they had an easy job! Little they kenned the Gorbals Die-Hards! I had been expectin' something of the kind, and had made my plans. They first tried to pu' down our tents and burn them. I let them get within five yards, reservin' my fire. The first volley – stones from our hands and our catties – halted them, and before they could recover three of us had got hold o' burnin' sticks frae the fire and were lammin' into them. We kinnled their claes, and they fell back swearin' and stampin' to get the fire out. Then I gave the word and we were on them wi' our poles, usin' the points accordin' to instructions. My orders was to keep a good distance, for if they had grippit one o' us he'd ha' been done for. They were roarin' mad by now, and twae had out their knives, but they couldn't do muckle, for it was gettin' dark, and they didn't ken the ground like us, and were aye trippin' and tumblin'. But they pressed us hard, and one o' them landed me an awful clype on the jaw. They were still aiming at our tents, and I saw that if they got near the fire again it would be the end o' us. So I blew my whistle for Thomas Yownie, who was in command o' the other half of us, with instructions to fall upon their rear. That brought Thomas up, and the tinklers had to face round about and fight a battle on two fronts. We charged them and they broke, and the last seen o' them they were coolin' their burns in the Garple.'

'Well done, man. Had you many casualties?'

'We're a' a wee thing battered, but nothing to hurt. I'm the worst, for one o' them had a grip o' me for about three seconds, and Gosh! he was fierce.'

Huntingtower

'They're beaten off for the night, anyway?'

'Ay, for the night. But they'll come back, never fear. That's why I said that things had come to a cripus.'

'What's the news from the House?'

'A quiet day, and no word o' Lean or Dobson.'

Dickson nodded. 'They were hunting me.'

'Mr Heritage has gone to bide in the Hoose. They were watchin' the Garple Dean, so I took him round by the Laver foot and up the rocks. He's a soople yin, yon. We fund a road up the rocks and got in by the verandy. Did ye ken that the lassie had a pistol? Well, she has, and it seems that Mr Heritage is a good shot wi' a pistol, so there's some hope thereaways . . . Are the jools safe?'

'Safe in the bank. But the jools were not the main thing.'

Dougal nodded. 'So I was thinkin'. The lassie wasn't muckle the easier for gettin' rid o' them. I didn't just quite understand what she said to Mr Heritage, for they were aye wanderin' into foreign langwidges, but it seems she's terrible feared o' somebody that may turn up any moment. What's the reason I can't say. She's maybe got a secret, or maybe it's just that she's ower bonny.'

'That's the trouble,' said Dickson, and proceeded to recount his interview with the factor, to which Dougal gave close attention. 'Now the way I read the thing is this. There's a plot to kidnap that lady for some infernal purpose, and it depends on the arrival of some person or persons, and it's due to happen in the next day or two. If we try to work it through the police alone, they'll beat us, for Loudon will manage to hang the business up till it's too late. So we must take on the job ourselves. We must stand a siege, Mr Heritage and me and you laddies, and for that purpose we'd better all keep together. It won't be extra easy to carry her off from all of us, and if they do manage it we'll stick to their heels . . . Man, Dougal, isn't it a queer thing that whiles law-abiding folk have to make their own laws? . . . So my plan is that the lot of us get into the House and form a garrison. If you don't, the tinklers will come back and you'll no' beat them in the daylight.'

'I doubt no',' said Dougal. 'But what about our meat?'

'We must lay in provisions. We'll get what we can from Mrs Morran, and I've left a big box of fancy things at Dalquharter station. Can you laddies manage to get it down here?'

Dougal reflected. 'Ay, we can hire Mrs Sempill's powny, the same that fetched our kit.'

'Well, that's your job tomorrow. See, I'll write you a line to the station-master. And will you undertake to get it some way into the House?'

'There's just the one road open – by the rocks. It'll have to be done. It *can* be done.'

'And I've another job. I'm writing this telegram to a friend in Glasgow who will put a spoke in Mr Loudon's wheel. I want one of you to go to Kirkmichael to send it from the telegraph office there.'

Dougal placed the wire to Mr Caw in his bosom. 'What about yourself? We want somebody outside to keep his eyes open. It's bad strawtegy to cut off your communications.'

Dickson thought for a moment. 'I believe you're right. I believe the best plan for me is to go back to Mrs Morran's as soon as the old body's like to be awake. You can always get at me there, for it's easy to slip into her back kitchen without anybody in the village seeing you . . . Yes, I'll do that, and you'll come and report developments to me. And now I'm for a bite and a pipe. It's hungry work travelling the country in the small hours.'

'I'm going to introjuice ye to the rest o' us,' said Dougal. 'Here, men!' he called, and four figures rose from the side of the fire. As Dickson munched a sandwich he passed in review the whole company of the Gorbals Die-Hards, for the pickets were also brought in, two others taking their places. There was Thomas Yownie, the Chief of Staff, with a wrist wound up in the handkerchief which he had borrowed from his neck. There was a burly lad who wore trousers much too large for him, and who was known as Peer Pairson, a contraction presumably for Peter Paterson. After him came a lean tall boy who answered to the name of Napoleon. There was a midget of a child, desperately sooty in the face either from battle or from fire-tending, who was presented as Wee Jaikie. Last came the picket who had held his pole at Dickson's chest, a sandy-haired warrior with a snub nose and the mouth and jaw of a pug-dog. He was Old Bill, or, in Dougal's parlance, 'Auld Bull'.

The Chieftain viewed his scarred following with a grim content. 'That's a tough lot for ye, Mr McCunn. Used a' their days wi' sleepin' in coalrees and dunnies and dodgin' the polis. Ye'll no beat the Gorbals Die-Hards.'

'You're right, Dougal,' said Dickson. 'There's just the six of you. If there were a dozen, I think this country would be needing some new kind of a government.'

EIGHT

How a Middle-Aged Crusader
Accepted a Challenge

THE first cocks had just begun to crow and the clocks had not yet struck five when Dickson presented himself at Mrs Morran's back door. That active woman had already been half an hour out of bed, and was drinking her morning cup of tea in the kitchen. She received him with cordiality, nay, with relief.

'Eh, sir, but I'm glad to see ye back. Guid kens what's gaun on at the Hoose thae days. Mr Heritage left here yestreen, creepin' round by dyke-sides and berry-busses like a wheasel. It's a mercy to get a responsible man in the place. I aye had a notion ye wad come back, for, thinks I, nevoy Dickson is no the yin to desert folk in trouble . . . Whaur's my wee kist? . . . Lost, ye say. That's a peety, for it's been my cheese-box thae thirty year.'

Dickson ascended to the loft, having announced his need of at least three hours' sleep. As he rolled into bed his mind was curiously at ease. He felt equipped for any call that might be made on him. That Mrs Morran should welcome him back as a resource in need gave him a new assurance of manhood.

He woke between nine and ten to the sound of rain lashing against the garret window. As he picked his way out of the mazes of sleep and recovered the skein of his immediate past, he found to his disgust that he had lost his composure. All the flock of fears, that had left him when on the top of the Glasgow tram-car he had made the great decision, had flown back again and settled like black crows on his spirit. He was running a horrible risk and all for a whim. What business had he to be mixing himself up in things he did not understand? It might be a huge mistake, and then he would be a laughing stock; for a moment he repented his telegram to Mr Caw. Then he recanted that suspicion; there could be no mistake, except the fatal one that he had taken on a job too big for him. He sat on the edge of his bed and shivered with his eyes on the grey drift of rain. He would have felt more stout-hearted had the sun been shining.

He shuffled to the window and looked out. There in the village street was Dobson, and Dobson saw him. That was a bad blunder, for his reason told him that he should have kept his presence in Dalquharter hid as long as possible.

There was a knock at the cottage door, and presently Mrs Morran appeared.

'It's the man frae the inn,' she announced. 'He's wantin' a word wi' ye. Speakin' verra ceevil, too.'

'Tell him to come up,' said Dickson. He might as well get the interview over. Dobson had seen Loudon and must know of their conversation. The sight of himself back again when he had pretended to be off to Glasgow would remove him effectually from the class of the unsuspected. He wondered just what line Dobson would take.

The innkeeper obtruded his bulk through the low door. His face was wrinkled into a smile, which nevertheless left the small eyes ungenial. His voice had a loud vulgar cordiality. Suddenly Dickson was conscious of a resemblance, a resemblance to somebody whom he had recently seen. It was Loudon. There was the same thrusting of the chin forward, the same odd cheek-bones, the same unctuous heartiness of speech. The innkeeper, well washed and polished and dressed, would be no bad copy of the factor. They must be near kin, perhaps brothers.

'Good morning to you, Mr McCunn. Man, it's pitifu' weather, and just when the farmers are wanting a dry seed-bed. What brings ye back here? Ye travel the country like a drover.'

'Oh, I'm a free man now and I took a fancy to this place. An idle body has nothing to do but please himself.'

'I hear ye're taking a lease of Huntingtower?'

'Now who told you that?'

'Just the clash of the place. Is it true?'

Dickson looked sly and a little annoyed.

'I maybe had half a thought of it, but I'll thank you not to repeat the story. It's a big house for a plain man like me, and I haven't properly inspected it.'

'Oh, I'll keep mum, never fear. But if ye've that sort of notion, I can understand you not being able to keep away from the place.'

'That may be the fact,' Dickson admitted.

'Well! It's just on that point I want a word with you.' The innkeeper seated himself unbidden on the chair which held Dickson's modest raiment. He leaned forward and with a coarse forefinger tapped Dickson's pyjama-clad knees. 'I can't have ye wandering about the place. I'm very sorry, but I've got my orders from Mr Loudon. So if you think that by bidin' here you can see more of the House and the policies, ye're wrong, Mr McCunn. It can't be allowed, for we're no' ready for ye yet. D'ye understand? That's Mr Loudon's orders . . . Now, would it not be a far better plan if ye went back to Glasgow and came back in a week's time? I'm thinking of your own comfort, Mr McCunnn.'

Dickson was cogitating hard. This man was clearly instructed to get rid of him at all costs for the next few days. The neighbourhood had to be cleared for some black business. The tinklers had been deputed to drive out the Gorbals Die-Hards, and as for Heritage they seemed to have lost track of him. He, Dickson, was now the chief object of their care. But what could Dobson do if he refused? He dared not show his true hand. Yet he might, if sufficiently irritated. It became Dickson's immediate object to get the innkeeper to reveal himself by rousing his temper. He did not stop to consider the policy of this course; he imperatively wanted things cleared up and the issue made plain.

'I'm sure I'm much obliged to you for thinking so much about my comfort,' he said in a voice into which he hoped he had insinuated a sneer. 'But I'm bound to say you're awful suspicious folk about here. You needn't be feared for your old policies. There's plenty of nice walks about the roads, and I want to explore the sea-coast.'

The last words seemed to annoy the innkeeper. 'That's no' allowed either,' he said. 'The shore's as private as the policies . . . Well, I wish ye joy tramping the roads in the glaur.'

'It's a queer thing,' said Dickson meditatively, 'that you should keep a hotel and yet be set on discouraging people from visiting this neighbourhood. I tell you what, I believe that hotel of yours is all sham. You've some other business, you and these lodgekeepers, and in my opinion it's not a very creditable one.'

'What d'ye mean?' asked Dobson sharply.

'Just what I say. You must expect a body to be suspicious, if you treat him as you're treating me.' Loudon must have told this man the story with which he had been fobbed off about the half-witted Kennedy relative. Would Dobson refer to that?

The innkeeper had an ugly look on his face, but he controlled his temper with an effort.

'There's no cause for suspicion,' he said. 'As far as I'm concerned it's all honest and above-board.'

'It doesn't look like it. It looks as if you were hiding something up in the House which you don't want me to see.'

Dobson jumped from his chair, his face pale with anger. A man in pyjamas on a raw morning does not feel at his bravest, and Dickson quailed under the expectation of assault. But even in his fright he realized that Loudon could not have told Dobson the tale of the half-witted lady. The last remark had cut clean through all camouflage and reached the quick.

'What the hell d'ye mean?' he cried. 'Ye're a spy, are ye? Ye fat little fool, for two cents I'd wring your neck.'

Now it is an odd trait of certain mild people that a suspicion of threat, a hint of bullying, will rouse some unsuspected obstinacy deep down in their souls. The insolence of the man's speech woke a quiet but efficient little devil in Dickson.

'That's a bonny tone to adopt in addressing a gentleman. If you've nothing to hide what way are you so touchy? I can't be a spy unless there's something to spy on.'

The innkeeper pulled himself together. He was apparently acting on instructions, and had not yet come to the end of them. He made an attempt at a smile.

'I'm sure I beg your pardon if I spoke too hot. But it nettled me to hear ye say that . . . I'll be quite frank with ye, Mr McCunn, and, believe me, I'm speaking in your best interests. I give ye my word there's nothing wrong up at the House. I'm on the side of the law, and when I tell ye the whole story ye'll admit it. But I can't tell it ye yet . . . This is a wild, lonely bit, and very few folk bide in it. And these are wild times, when a lot of queer things happen that never get into the papers. I tell ye it's for your own good to leave Dalquharter for the present. More I can't say, but I ask ye to look at it as a sensible man. Ye're one that's accustomed to a quiet life and no' meant for rough work. Ye'll do no good if you stay, and, maybe, ye'll land yourself in bad trouble.'

'Mercy on us!' Dickson exclaimed. 'What is it you're expecting? Sinn Fein?'

The innkeeper nodded. 'Something like that.'

'Did you ever hear the like? I never did think much of the Irish.'

'Then ye'll take my advice and go home? Tell ye what, I'll drive ye to the station.'

Dickson got up from the bed, found his new safety-razor and began to strop it. 'No, I think I'll bide. If you're right there'll be more to see than glaury roads.'

'I'm warning ye, fair and honest. Ye . . . can't . . . be . . . allowed . . . to . . . stay . . . here!'

'Well, I never!' said Dickson. 'Is there any law in Scotland, think you, that forbids a man to stop a day or two with his auntie?'

'Ye'll stay?'

'Ay, I'll stay.'

'By God, we'll see about that.'

For a moment Dickson thought that he would be attacked, and he measured the distance that separated him from the peg

whence hung his waterproof with the pistol in its pocket. But
the man restrained himself and moved to the door. There he
stood and cursed him with a violence and a venom which
Dickson had not believed possible. The full hand was on the
table now.

'Ye wee pot-bellied, pig-heided Glasgow grocer' (I para-
phrase), 'would *you* set up to defy me? I tell ye, I'll make ye rue
the day ye were born.' His parting words were a brilliant sketch
of the maltreatment in store for the body of the defiant one.

'Impident dog,' said Dickson without heat. He noted with
pleasure that the innkeeper hit his head violently against the
low lintel, and, missing a step, fell down the loft stairs into the
kitchen, where Mrs Morran's tongue could be heard speeding
him trenchantly from the premises.

Left to himself, Dickson dressed leisurely, and by and by went
down to the kitchen and watched his hostess making broth. The
fracas with Dobson had done him all the good in the world, for
it had cleared the problem of dubieties and had put an edge on
his temper. But he realized that it made his continued stay in
the cottage undesirable. He was now the focus of all suspicion,
and the innkeeper would be as good as his word and try to drive
him out of the place by force. Kidnapping, most likely, and that
would be highly unpleasant, besides putting an end to his
usefulness. Clearly he must join the others. The soul of Dickson
hungered at the moment for human companionship. He felt
that his courage would be sufficient for any team-work, but
might waver again if he were left to play a lone hand.

He lunched nobly off three plates of Mrs Morran's kail – an
early lunch, for that lady, having breakfasted at five, partook of
the midday meal about eleven. Then he explored her library,
and settled himself by the fire with a volume of Covenanting
tales, entitled *Gleanings among the Mountains*. It was a most
practical work for one in his position, for it told how various
eminent saints of that era escaped the attention of Claverhouse's
dragoons. Dickson stored up in his memory several of the inci-
dents in case they should come in handy. He wondered if any of

his forbears had been Covenanters; it comforted him to think that some old progenitor might have hunkered behind turf walls and been chased for his life in the heather. 'Just like me,' he reflected. 'But the dragoons weren't foreigners, and there was a kind of decency about Claverhouse too.'

About four o'clock Dougal presented himself in the back kitchen. He was an even wilder figure than usual, for his bare legs were mud to the knees, his kilt and shirt clung sopping to his body, and, having lost his hat, his wet hair was plastered over his eyes. Mrs Morran said, not unkindly, that he looked 'like a wull-cat glowerin' through a whin-buss.'

'How are you, Dougal?' Dickson asked genially. 'Is the peace of nature smoothing out the creases in your poor little soul?'

'What's that ye say?'

'Oh, just what I heard a man say in Glasgow. How have you got on?'

'No' so bad. Your telegram was sent this mornin'. Old Bill took it in to Kirkmichael. That's the first thing. Second, Thomas Yownie has took a party to get down the box from the station. He got Mrs Sempill's powny, and he took the box ayont the Laver by the ford at the herd's hoose and got it on to the shore maybe a mile ayont Laverfoot. He managed to get the machine up as far as the water, but he could get no farther, for ye'll no' get a machine over the wee waterfa' just before the Laver ends in the sea. So he sent one o' the men back with it to Mrs Sempill, and, since the box was ower heavy to carry, he opened it and took the stuff across in bits. It's a' safe in the hole at the foot o' the Huntingtower rocks, and he reports that the rain has done it no harm. Thomas has made a good job of it. Ye'll no' fickle Thomas Yownie.'

'And what about your camp on the moor?'

'It was broke up afore daylight. Some of our things we've got with us, but most is hid near at hand. The tents are in the auld wife's hen-hoose,' and he jerked his disreputable head in the direction of the back door.

'Have the tinklers been back?'

'Aye. They turned up about ten o'clock, no doubt intendin'
murder. I left Wee Jaikie to watch developments. They fund him
sittin' on a stone, greetin' sore. When he saw them, he up and
started to run, and they cried on him to stop, but he wouldn't
listen. Then they cried out where were the rest, and he telled
them they were feared for their lives and had run away. After
that they offered to catch him, but ye'll no' catch Jaikie in a
hurry. When he had run round about them till they were wappit,
he out wi' his catty and got one o' them on the lug. Syne he
made for the Laverfoot and reported.'

'Man, Dougal, you've managed fine. Now I've something to
tell you,' and Dickson recounted his interview with the
innkeeper. 'I don't think it's safe for me to bide here, and if I did,
I wouldn't be any use, hiding in cellars and such like, and not
daring to stir a foot. I'm coming with you to the House. Now tell
me how to get there.'

Dougal agreed to this view. 'There's been nothing doing at
the Hoose the day, but they're keepin' a close watch on the policies. The cripus may come any moment. There's no doubt, Mr
McCunn, that ye're in danger, for they'll serve you as the tinklers
tried to serve us. Listen to me. Ye'll walk up the station road, and
take the second turn on your left, a wee grass road that'll bring
ye to the ford at the herd's hoose. Cross the Laver – there's a
plank bridge – and take straight across the moor in the direction
of the peakit hill they call Grey Carrick. Ye'll come to a big burn,
which ye must follow till ye get to the shore. Then turn south,
keepin' the water's edge till ye reach the Laver, where you'll find
one o' us to show ye the rest of the road . . . I must be off now,
and I advise ye not to be slow of startin', for wi' this rain the
water's risin' quick. It's a mercy it's such coarse weather, for it
spoils the veesibility.'

'Auntie Phemie,' said Dickson a few minutes later, 'will you
oblige me by coming for a short walk?'

'The man's daft,' was the answer.

'I'm not. I'll explain if you'll listen . . . You see,' he concluded,
'the dangerous bit for me is just the mile out of the village.

They'll no' be so likely to try violence if there's somebody with me that could be a witness. Besides, they'll maybe suspect less if they just see a decent body out for a breath of air with his auntie.'

Mrs Morran said nothing, but retired, and returned presently equipped for the road. She had indued her feet with galoshes and pinned up her skirts till they looked like some demented Paris mode. An ancient bonnet was tied under her chin with strings, and her equipment was completed by an exceedingly smart tortoiseshell-handled umbrella, which, she explained, had been a Christmas present from her son.

'I'll convoy ye as far as the Laverfoot herd's,' she announced. 'The wife's a freend o' mine and will set me a bit on the road back. Ye needna fash for me. I'm used to a' weathers.'

The rain had declined to a fine drizzle, but a tearing wind from the south-west scoured the land. Beyond the shelter of the trees the moor was a battle-ground of gusts which swept the puddles into spindrift and gave to the stagnant bog-pools the appearance of running water. The wind was behind the travellers, and Mrs Morran, like a full-rigged ship, was hustled before it, so that Dickson who had linked arms with her, was sometimes compelled to trot.

'However will you get home, mistress?' he murmured anxiously.

'Fine. The wind will fa' at the darkenin'. This'll be a sair time for ships at sea.'

Not a soul was about, as they breasted the ascent of the station road and turned down the grassy bypath to the Laverfoot herd's. The herd's wife saw them from afar and was at the door to receive them.

'Megsty! Phemie Morran!' she shrilled. 'Wha wad ettle to see ye on a day like this? John's awa' at Dumfries, buyin' tups. Come in, the baith o' ye. The kettle's on the boil.'

'This is my nevoy Dickson,' said Mrs Morran. 'He's gaun to stretch his legs ayont the burn, and come back by the Ayr road. But I'll be blithe to tak' my tea wi' ye, Elspeth . . . Now, Dickson, I'll expect ye hame on the chap o' seeven.'

He crossed the rising stream on a swaying plank and struck into the moorland, as Dougal had ordered, keeping the bald top of Grey Carrick before him. In that wild place with the tempest battling overhead he had no fear of human enemies. Steadily he covered the ground, till he reached the west-flowing burn, that was to lead him to the shore. He found it an entertaining companion, swirling into black pools, foaming over little falls, and lying in dark canal-like stretches in the flats. Presently it began to descend steeply in a narrow green gully, where the going was bad, and Dickson, weighted with pack and water-proof, had much ado to keep his feet on the sodden slopes. Then, as he rounded a crook of hill, the ground fell away from his feet, the burn swept in a water-slide to the boulders of the shore, and the storm-tossed sea lay before him.

It was now that he began to feel nervous. Being on the coast again seemed to bring him inside his enemies' territory, and had not Dobson specifically forbidden the shore? It was here that they might be looking for him. He felt himself out of condition, very wet and very warm, but he attained a creditable pace, for he struck a road which had been used by manure-carts collecting seaweed. There were faint marks on it, which he took to be the wheels of Dougal's 'machine' carrying the provision-box. Yes. On a patch of gravel there was a double set of tracks, which showed how it had returned to Mrs Sempill. He was exposed to the full force of the wind, and the strenuousness of his bodily exertions kept his fears quiescent, till the cliffs on his left sunk suddenly and the valley of the Laver lay before him.

A small figure rose from the shelter of a boulder, the warrior who bore the name of Old Bill. He saluted gravely.

'Ye're just in time. The water has rose three inches since I've been here. Ye'd better strip.'

Dickson removed his boots and socks. 'Breeks too,' commanded the boy; 'there's deep holes ayont thae stanes.'

Dickson obeyed, feeling very chilly, and rather improper. 'Now follow me,' said the guide. The next moment he was stepping delicately on very sharp pebbles, holding on to the end of the scout's pole, while an icy stream ran to his knees.

The Laver as it reaches the sea broadens out to the width of fifty or sixty yards and tumbles over little shelves of rock to meet the waves. Usually it is shallow, but now it was swollen to an average depth of a foot or more, and there were deeper pockets. Dickson made the passage slowly and miserably, sometimes crying out with pain as his toes struck a sharper flint, once or twice sitting down on a boulder to blow like a whale, once slipping on his knees and wetting the strange excrescence about his middle, which was his tucked-up waterproof. But the crossing was at length achieved, and on a patch of sea-pinks he dried himself perfunctorily and hastily put on his garments. Old Bill, who seemed to be regardless of wind or water, squatted beside him and whistled through his teeth.

Above them hung the sheer cliffs of the Huntingtower cape, so sheer that a man below was completely hidden from any watcher on the top. Dickson's heart fell, for he did not profess to be a cragsman and had indeed a horror of precipitous places. But as the two scrambled along the foot, they passed deep-cut gullies and fissures, most of them unclimbable, but offering something more hopeful than the face. At one of these Old Bill halted, and led the way up and over a chaos of fallen rock and loose sand. The grey weather had brought on the dark prematurely, and in the half-light it seemed that this ravine was blocked by an unscalable nose of rock. Here Old Bill whistled, and there was a reply from above. Round the corner of the nose came Dougal.

'Up here,' he commanded. 'It was Mr Heritage that fund this road.'

Dickson and his guide squeezed themselves between the nose and the cliff up a spout of stones, and found themselves in an upper storey of the gulley, very steep, but practicable even for one who was no cragsman. This in turn ran out against a wall up which there led only a narrow chimney. At the foot of this were two of the Die-Hards, and there were others above, for a rope hung down, by the aid of which a package was even now ascending.

'That's the top,' said Dougal, pointing to the rim of sky, 'and that's the last o' the supplies.' Dickson noticed that he spoke in a whisper, and that all the movements of the Die-Hards were judicious and stealthy. 'Now, it's your turn. Take a good grip o' the rope, and ye'll find plenty holes for your feet. It's no more than ten yards and ye're well held above.'

Dickson made the attempt and found it easier than he expected. The only trouble was his pack and waterproof, which had a tendency to catch on jags of rock. A hand was reached out to him, he was pulled over the edge, and then pushed down on his face.

When he lifted his head Dougal and the others had joined him, and the whole company of the Die-Hards was assembled on a patch of grass which was concealed from the landward view by a thicket of hazels. Another, whom he recognized as Heritage, was coiling up the rope.

'We'd better get all the stuff into the old Tower for the present,' Heritage was saying. 'It's too risky to move it into the House now. We'll need the thickest darkness for that, after the moon is down. Quick, for the beastly thing will be rising soon, and before that we must all be indoors.'

Then he turned to Dickson and gripped his hand. 'You're a high class of sportsman, Dogson. And I think you're just in time.'

'Are they due tonight?' Dickson asked in an excited whisper, faint against the wind.

'I don't know about They. But I've got a notion that some devilish queer things will happen before tomorrow morning.'

NINE

The First Battle of the Cruives

THE old keep of Huntingtower stood some three hundred yards from the edge of the cliffs, a gnarled wood of hazels and oaks protecting it from the sea-winds. It was still in fair preservation, having till twenty years before been an adjunct of the house of Dalquharter, and used as kitchen, buttery, and servants' quarters. There had been residential wings attached, dating from the mid-eighteenth century, but these had been pulled down and used for the foundations of the new mansion. Now it stood a lonely shell, its three storeys, each a single great room connected by a spiral stone staircase, being dedicated to lumber and the storage of produce. But it was dry and intact, its massive oak doors defied any weapon short of artillery, its narrow unglazed windows would scarcely have admitted a cat – a place portentously strong, gloomy, but yet habitable.

Dougal opened the main door with a massy key. 'The lassie fund it,' he whispered to Dickson, 'somewhere about the kitchen – and I guessed it was the key o' this castle. I was thinkin' that if things got ower hot it would be a good plan to flit here. Change our base, like.' The Chieftain's occasional studies in war had trained his tongue to a military jargon.

In the ground room lay a fine assortment of oddments, including old bedsteads and servants' furniture, and what looked like ancient discarded deerskin rugs. Dust lay thick over everything, and they heard the scurry of rats. A dismal place, indeed, but Dickson felt only its strangeness. The comfort of being back again among allies had quickened his spirit to an adventurous mood. The old lords of Huntingtower had once quarrelled and revelled and plotted here, and now here he was at the same game. Present and past joined hands over the gulf of years. The saga of Huntingtower was not ended.

The Die-Hards had brought with them their scanty bedding, their lanterns, and camp-kettles. These and the provisions from Mearns Street were stowed away in a corner.

'Now for the Hoose, men,' said Dougal. They stole over the downs to the shrubbery, and Dickson found himself almost in the same place as he had lain in three days before, watching a dusky lawn, while the wet earth soaked through his trouser knees and the drip from the azaleas trickled over his spine. Two of the boys fetched the ladder and placed it against the veranda wall. Heritage first, then Dickson, darted across the lawn and made the ascent. The six scouts followed, and the ladder was pulled up and hidden among the veranda litter. For a second the whole eight stood still and listened. There was no sound except the murmur of the now falling wind and the melancholy hooting of owls. The garrison had entered the Dark Tower.

A council in whispers was held in the garden-room.

'Nobody must show a light,' Heritage observed. 'It mustn't be known that we're here. Only the Princess will have a lamp. Yes' – this in answer to Dickson – 'she knows that we're coming – you too. We'll hunt for quarters later upstairs. You scouts, you must picket every possible entrance. The windows are safe, I think, for they are locked from the inside. So is the main door. But there's the veranda door, of which they have a key, and the back door beside the kitchen, and I'm not at all sure that there's not a way in by the boiler-house. You understand. We're holding this place against all comers. We must barricade the danger points. The headquarters of the garrison will be in the hall, where a scout must be always on duty. You've all got whistles? Well, if there's an attempt on the veranda door the picket will whistle once, if at the back door twice, if anywhere else three times, and it's everybody's duty, except the picket who whistles, to get back to the hall for orders.'

'That's so,' assented Dougal.

'If the enemy forces an entrance we must overpower him. Any means you like. Sticks or fists, and remember if it's a scrap in the dark to make for the man's throat. I expect you little devils have eyes like cats. The scoundrels must be kept away from the ladies at all costs. If the worst comes to the worst, the Princess has a revolver.'

'So have I,' said Dickson. 'I got it in Glasgow.'

'The deuce you have! Can you use it?'

'I don't know.'

'Well, you can hand it over to me, if you like. But it oughtn't to come to shooting, if it's only the three of them. The eight of us should be able to manage three and one of them lame. If the others turn up – well, God help us all! But we've got to make sure of one thing, that no one lays hands on the Princess so long as there's one of us left alive to hit out.'

'Ye needn't be feared for that,' said Dougal. There was no light in the room, but Dickson was certain that the morose face of the Chieftain was lit with unholy joy.

'Then off with you. Mr McCunn and I will explain matters to the ladies.'

When they were alone, Heritage's voice took a different key. 'We're in for it, Dogson, old man. There's no doubt these three scoundrels expect reinforcements at any moment, and with them will be one who is the devil incarnate. He's the only thing on earth that that brave girl fears. It seems he is in love with her and has pestered her for years. She hated the sight of him, but he wouldn't take no, and being a powerful man – rich and well-born and all the rest of it – she had a desperate time. I gather he was pretty high in favour with the old Court. Then when the Bolsheviks started he went over to them, like plenty of other grandees, and now he's one of their chief brains – none of your callow revolutionaries, but a man of the world, a kind of genius, she says, who can hold his own anywhere. She believes him to be in this country, and only waiting the right moment to turn up. Oh, it sounds ridiculous, I know, in Britain in the twentieth century, but I learned in the war that civilization anywhere is a very thin crust. There are a hundred ways by which that kind of fellow could bamboozle all our law and police and spirit her away. That's the kind of crowd we have to face.'

'Did she say what he was like in appearance?'

'A face like an angel – a lost angel, she says.'

Dickson suddenly had an inspiration.

'D'you mind the man you said was an Australian – at Kirkmichael? I thought myself he was a foreigner. Well, he was asking for a place he called Darkwater, and there's no sich place in the countryside. I believe he meant Dalquharter. I believe he's the man she's feared of.'

A gasped 'By Jove!' came from the darkness. 'Dogson, you've hit it. That was five days ago, and he must have got on the right trail by this time. He'll be here tonight. That's why the three have been lying so quiet today. Well, we'll go through with it, even if we haven't a dog's chance! Only I'm sorry that you should be mixed up in such a hopeless business.'

'Why me more than you?'

'Because it's all pure pride and joy for me to be here. Good God, I wouldn't be elsewhere for worlds. It's the great hour of my life. I would gladly die for her.'

'Tuts, that's no' the way to talk, man. Time enough to speak about dying when there's no other way out. I'm looking at this thing in a business way. We'd better be seeing the ladies.'

They groped into the pitchy hall, somewhere in which a Die-Hard was on picket, and down the passage to the smoking-room. Dickson blinked in the light of a very feeble lamp and Heritage saw that his hands were cumbered with packages. He deposited them on a sofa and made a ducking bow.

'I've come back, Mem, and glad to be back. Your jools are in safe keeping, and not all the blagyirds in creation could get at them. I've come to tell you to cheer up – a stout heart to a stey brae, as the old folk say. I'm handling this affair as a business proposition, so don't be feared, Mem. If there are enemies seeking you, there's friends on the road too . . . Now, you'll have had your dinner, but you'd maybe like a little dessert.'

He spread before them a huge box of chocolates, the best that Mearns Street could produce, a box of candied fruits, and another of salted almonds. Then from his hideously over-crowded pockets he took another box, which he offered rather shyly. 'That's some powder for your complexion. They tell me that ladies find it useful whiles.'

The girl's strained face watched him at first in mystification, and then broke slowly into a smile. Youth came back to it, the smile changed to a laugh, a low rippling laugh like far-away bells. She took both his hands.

'You are kind,' she said, 'you are kind and brave. You are a dear.'

And then she kissed him.

Now, as far as Dickson could remember, no one had ever kissed him except his wife. The light touch of her lips on his forehead was like the pressing of an electric button which explodes some powerful charge and alters the face of a country-side. He blushed scarlet; then he wanted to cry; then he wanted to sing. An immense exhilaration seized him, and I am certain that if at that moment the serried ranks of Bolshevy had appeared in the doorway, Dickson would have hurled himself upon them with a joyful shout.

Cousin Eugénie was earnestly eating chocolates, but Saskia had other business.

'You will hold the house?' she asked.

'Please God, yes,' said Heritage. 'I look at it this way. The time is very near when your three gaolers expect the others, their masters. They have not troubled you in the past two days as they threatened, because it was not worth while. But they won't want to let you out of their sight in the final hours, so they will almost certainly come here to be on the spot. Our object is to keep them out and confuse their plans. Somewhere in this neighbourhood, probably very near, is the man you fear most. If we nonplus the three watchers, they'll have to revise their policy, and that means a delay, and every hour's delay is a gain. Mr McCunn has found out that the factor Loudon is in the plot, and he has purchase enough, it seems, to blanket for a time any appeal to the law. But Mr McCunn has taken steps to circumvent him, and in twenty-four hours we should have help here.'

'I do not want the help of your law,' the girl interrupted. 'It will entangle me.'

'Not a bit of it,' said Dickson cheerfully. 'You see, Mem, they've clean lost track of the jools, and nobody knows where they are but me. I'm a truthful man, but I'll lie like a packman if I'm asked questions. For the rest, it's a question of kidnapping, I understand, and that's a thing that's not to be allowed. My advice is to go to our beds and get a little sleep while there's a chance of it. The Gorbals Die-Hards are grand watchdogs.'

This view sounded so reasonable that it was at once acted upon. The ladies' chamber was next door to the smoking-room – what had been the old schoolroom. Heritage arranged with Saskia that the lamp was to be kept burning low, and that on no account were they to move unless summoned by him. Then he and Dickson made their way to the hall, where there was a faint glimmer from the moon in the upper unshuttered windows – enough to reveal the figure of Wee Jaikie on duty at the foot of the staircase. They ascended to the second floor, where, in a large room above the hall, Heritage had bestowed his pack. He had managed to open a fold of the shutters, and there was sufficient light to see two big mahogany bedsteads without mattresses or bedclothes, and wardrobes and chests of drawers sheeted in holland. Outside the wind was rising again, but the rain had stopped. Angry watery clouds scurried across the heavens.

Dickson made a pillow of his waterproof, stretched himself on one of the bedsteads, and, so quiet was his conscience and so weary his body from the buffetings of the past days, was almost instantly asleep. It seemed to him that he had scarcely closed his eyes when he was awakened by Dougal's hand pinching his shoulder. He gathered that the moon was setting, for the room was pitchy dark.

'The three o' them is approachin' the kitchen door,' whispered the Chieftain. 'I seen them from a spy-hole I made out o' a ventilator.'

'Is it barricaded?' asked Heritage, who had apparently not been asleep.

'Aye, but I've thought o' a far better plan. Why should we keep them out? They'll be safer inside. Listen! We might manage to get them in one at a time. If they can't get in at the kitchen door, they'll send one o' them round to get in by another door and open to them. That gives us a chance to get them separated, and lock them up. There's walth o' closets and hidy-holes all over the place, each with good doors and good keys to them. Supposin' we get the three o' them shut up – the others, when they come, will have nobody to guide them. Of course some time or other the three will break out, but it may be ower late for them. At present we're besieged and they're roamin' the country. Would it no' be far better if they were the ones lockit up and we were goin' loose?'

'Supposing they don't come in one at a time?' Dickson objected.

'We'll make them,' said Dougal firmly. 'There's no time to waste. Are ye for it?'

'Yes,' said Heritage. 'Who's at the kitchen door?'

'Peter Paterson. I told him no' to whistle, but to wait on me ... Keep your boots off. Ye're better in your stockin' feet. Wait you in the hall and see ye're well hidden, for likely whoever comes in will have a lantern. Just you keep quiet unless I give ye a cry. I've planned it a' out, and we're ready for them.'

Dougal disappeared, and Dickson and Heritage, with their boots tied round their necks by their laces, crept out to the upper landing. The hall was impenetrably dark, but full of voices, for the wind was talking in the ceiling beams, and murmuring through the long passages. The walls creaked and muttered and little bits of plaster fluttered down. The noise was an advantage for the game of hide-and-seek they proposed to play, but it made it hard to detect the enemy's approach. Dickson, in order to get properly wakened, adventured as far as the smoking-room. It was black with night, but below the door of the adjacent room a faint line of light showed where the Princess's lamp was burning. He advanced to the window, and heard distinctly a foot on the gravel path that led to the veranda. This sent him back to the hall in search of Dougal, whom he encountered in the passage. That boy could certainly see in the dark, for he caught Dickson's wrist without hesitation.

'We've got Spittal in the wine-cellar,' he whispered triumphantly. 'The kitchen door was barricaded, and when they tried it, it wouldn't open. "Bide here," says Dobson to Spittal, "and we'll go round by another door and come back and open to ye." So off they went, and by that time Peter Paterson and me had the barricade down. As we expected, Spittal tries the key again and it opens quite easy. He comes in and locks it behind him, and, Dobson having took away the lantern, he gropes his way very carefu' towards the kitchen. There's a point where the wine-cellar door and the scullery door are aside each other. He should have taken the second, but I had it shut so he takes the first. Peter Paterson gave him a wee shove and he fell down the two-three steps into the cellar, and we turned the key on him. Yon cellar has a grand door and no windies.'

'And Dobson and Léon are at the veranda door? With a light?'

'Thomas Yownie's on duty there. Ye can trust him. Ye'll no fickle Thomas Yownie.'

The next minutes were for Dickson a delirium of excitement not unpleasantly shot with flashes of doubt and fear. As a child he had played hide-and-seek, and his memory had always cherished the delights of the game. But how marvellous to play it thus in a great empty house, at dark of night, with the heaven filled with tempest, and with death or wounds as the stakes!

He took refuge in a corner where a tapestry curtain and the side of a Dutch awmry gave him shelter, and from where he stood he could see the garden-room and the beginning of the tiled passage which led to the veranda door. That is to say, he could have seen these things if there had been any light, which there was not. He heard the soft flitting of bare feet, for a delicate sound is often audible in a din when a loud noise is obscured. Then a gale of wind blew towards him, as from an open door, and far away gleamed the flickering light of a lantern.

Suddenly the light disappeared and there was a clatter on the floor and a breaking of glass. Either the wind or Thomas Yownie.

The veranda door was shut, a match spluttered and the lantern was relit. Dobson and Léon came into the hall, both clad in long mackintoshes which glistened from the weather. Dobson halted and listened to the wind howling in the upper spaces. He cursed it bitterly, looked at his watch, and then made an observation which woke the liveliest interest in Dickson lurking beside the awmry and Heritage ensconced in the shadow of a window-seat.

'He's late. He should have been here five minutes syne. It would be a dirty road for his car.'

So the Unknown was coming that night. The news made Dickson the more resolved to get the watchers under lock and key before reinforcements arrived, and so put grit in their wheels. Then his party must escape – flee anywhere so long as it was far from Dalquharter.

'You stop here,' said Dobson, 'I'll go down and let Spidel in. We want another lamp. Get the one that the women use, and for God's sake get a move on.'

The sound of his feet died in the kitchen passage and then rung again on the stone stairs. Dickson's ear of faith heard also the soft patter of naked feet as the Die-Hards preceded and followed him. He was delivering himself blind and bound into their hands.

For a minute or two there was no sound but the wind, which had found a loose chimney cowl on the roof and screwed out of it an odd sound like the drone of a bagpipe. Dickson, unable to remain any longer in one place, moved into the centre of the hall, believing that Léon had gone to the smoking-room. It was a dangerous thing to do, for suddenly a match was lit a yard from him. He had the sense to drop low, and so was out of the main glare of the light. The man with the match apparently had no more, judging by his execrations. Dickson stood stock still, longing for the wind to fall so that he might hear the sound of the fellow's boots on the stone floor. He gathered that they were moving towards the smoking-room.

'Heritage,' he whispered as loud as he dared, but there was no answer.

Then suddenly a moving body collided with him. He jumped a step back and then stood at attention. 'Is that you, Dobson?' a voice asked.

Now behold the occasional advantage of a nickname. Dickson thought he was being addressed as 'Dogson' after the Poet's fashion. Had he dreamed it was Léon he would not have replied, but fluttered off into the shadows, and so missed a piece of vital news.

'Ay, it's me,' he whispered.

His voice and accent were Scotch, like Dobson's, and Léon suspected nothing.

'I do not like this wind,' he grumbled. 'The Captain's letter said at dawn, but there is no chance of the Danish brig making your little harbour in this weather. She must lie off and land the men by boats. That I do not like. It is too public.'

The news – tremendous news, for it told that the newcomers would come by sea, which had never before entered Dickson's head – so interested him that he stood dumb and ruminating. The silence made the Belgian suspect; he put out a hand and felt a waterproofed arm which might have been Dobson's. But the height of the shoulder proved that it was not the burly innkeeper. There was an oath, a quick movement, and Dickson went down with a knee on his chest and two hands at his throat.

'Heritage,' he gasped. 'Help!'

There was a sound of furniture scraped violently on the floor. A gurgle from Dickson served as a guide, and the Poet suddenly cascaded over the combatants. He felt for a head, found Léon's, and gripped the neck so savagely that the owner loosened his hold on Dickson. The last-named found himself being buffeted violently by heavy-shod feet which seemed to be manoeuvring before an unseen enemy. He rolled out of the road and encountered another pair of feet, this time unshod. Then came a sound of a concussion, as if metal or wood had struck some part of a human frame, and then a stumble and fall.

After that a good many things all seemed to happen at once. There was a sudden light, which showed Léon blinking with a short loaded life-preserver in his hand, and Heritage prone in front of him on the floor. It also showed Dickson the figure of Dougal, and more than one Die-Hard in the background. The light went out as suddenly as it had appeared. There was a whistle and a hoarse 'Come on, men,' and then for two seconds there was a desperate silent combat. It ended with Léon's head meeting the floor so violently that its possessor became oblivious of further proceedings. He was dragged into a cubby-hole, which had once been used for coats and rugs, and the door locked on him. Then the light sprang forth again. It revealed Dougal and five Die-Hards, somewhat the worse for wear; it revealed also Dickson squatted with outspread waterproof very like a sitting hen.

'Where's Dobson?' he asked.

'In the boiler-house,' and for once Dougal's gravity had laughter in it. 'Govery Dick! but yon was a fecht! Me and Peter Paterson and Wee Jaikie started it, but it was the whole company afore the end. Are ye better, Jaikie?'

'Ay, I'm better,' said a pallid midget.

'He kickit Jaikie in the stomach and Jaikie was seeck,' Dougal explained. 'That's the three accounted for. Now they're safe for five hours at the least. I think mysel' that Dobson will be the first to get out, but he'll have his work letting out the others. Now, I'm for flittin' to the old Tower. They'll no ken where we are for a long time, and anyway yon place will be far easier to defend. Without they kindle a fire and smoke us out, I don't see how they'll beat us. Our provisions are a' there, and there's a grand well o' water inside. Forbye there's the road down the rocks that'll keep our communications open ... But what's come to Mr Heritage?'

Dickson to his shame had forgotten all about his friend. The Poet lay very quiet with his head on one side and his legs crooked limply. Blood trickled over his eyes from an ugly scar on his forehead. Dickson felt his heart and pulse and found them faint but regular. The man had got a swinging blow and might have a slight concussion; for the present he was unconscious.

'All the more reason why we should flit,' said Dougal. 'What d'ye say, Mr McCunn?'

'Flit, of course, but further than the old Tower. What's the time?' He lifted Heritage's wrist and saw from his watch that it was half-past three. 'Mercy! It's nearly morning. Afore we put these blagyirds away, they were conversing, at least Léon and Dobson were. They said that they expected somebody every moment, but that the car would be late. We've still got that Somebody to tackle. Then Léon spoke to me in the dark, thinking I was Dobson, and cursed the wind, saying it would keep the Danish brig from getting in at dawn as had been intended. D'you see what that means? The worst of the lot, the ones the ladies are in terror of, are coming by sea. Ay, and they can return by sea. We thought that the attack would be by land, and that even if they succeeded we could hang on to their heels and follow them, till we got them stopped. But that's impossible! If they come in from the water, they can go out by the water, and there'll never be more heard tell of the ladies or of you or me.'

Dougal's face was once again sunk in gloom. 'What's your plan, then?'

'We must get the ladies away from here – away inland, far from the sea. The rest of us must stand a siege in the old Tower, so that the enemy will think we're all there. Please God we'll hold out long enough for help to arrive. But we mustn't hang about here. There's the man Dobson mentioned – he may come any second, and we want to be away first. Get the ladder, Dougal ... Four of you take Mr Heritage, and two come with me and carry the ladies' things. It's no' raining, but the wind's enough to take the wings off a seagull.'

Dickson roused Saskia and her cousin, bidding them be ready in ten minutes. Then with the help of the Die-Hards he proceeded to transport the necessary supplies – the stove, oil, dishes, clothes, and wraps; more than one journey was needed of small boys, hidden under clouds of baggage. When everything had gone he collected the keys, behind which, in various quarters of the house, three gaolers fumed impotently, and gave them to Wee Jaikie to dispose of in some secret nook. Then he led the two ladies to the veranda, the elder cross and sleepy, the younger alert at the prospect of movement.

'Tell me again,' she said. 'You have locked all the three up, and they are now the imprisoned?'

'Well, it was the boys that, properly speaking, did the locking up.'

'It is a great – how do you say? – a turning of the tables. Ah – what is that?'

At the end of the veranda there was a clattering down of pots which could not be due to the wind, since the place was sheltered. There was as yet only the faintest hint of light, and black night still lurked in the crannies. Followed another fall of pots, as from a clumsy intruder, and then a man appeared, clear against the glass door by which the path descended to the rock garden.

It was the fourth man, whom the three prisoners had awaited. Dickson had no doubt at all about his identity. He was that villain from whom all the others took their orders, the man whom the Princess shuddered at. Before starting he had loaded his pistol. Now he tugged it from his waterproof pocket, pointed it at the other and fired.

The man seemed to be hit, for he spun round and clapped a hand to his left arm. Then he fled through the door, which he left open.

Dickson was after him like a hound. At the door he saw him running and raised his pistol for another shot. Then he dropped it, for he saw something in the crouching, dodging figure which was familiar.

'A mistake,' he explained to Jaikie when he returned. 'But the shot wasn't wasted. I've just had a good try at killing the factor!'

TEN

Deals with an Escape and a Journey

FIVE scouts' lanterns burned smokily in the ground room of the keep when Dickson ushered his charges through its cavernous door. The lights flickered in the gusts that swept after them and whistled through the slits of windows, so that the place was full of monstrous shadows, and its accustomed odour of mould and disuse was changed to a salty freshness. Upstairs on the first floor Thomas Yownie had deposited the ladies' baggage, and was busy making beds out of derelict iron bedsteads and the wraps brought from their room. On the ground floor on a heap of litter covered by an old scout's blanket lay Heritage, with Dougal in attendance.

The Chieftain had washed the blood from the Poet's brow, and the touch of cold water was bringing back his senses. Saskia with a cry flew to him, and waved off Dickson who had fetched one of the bottles of liqueur brandy. She slipped a hand inside his shirt and felt the beating of his heart. Then her slim fingers ran over his forehead.

'A bad blow,' she muttered, 'but I do not think he is ill. There is no fracture. When I nursed in the Alexander Hospital I learnt much about head wounds. Do not give him cognac if you value his life.'

Heritage was talking now and with strange tongues. Phrases like 'lined digesters' and 'free sulphurous acid' came from his lips. He implored someone to tell him if 'the first cook' was finished, and he upbraided someone else for 'cooling off' too fast.

The girl raised her head. 'But I fear he has become mad,' she said.

'Wheesht, Mem,' said Dickson, who recognized the jargon. 'He's a paper-maker.'

Saskia sat down on the litter and lifted his head so that it rested on her breast. Dougal at her bidding brought a certain case from her baggage, and with swift, capable hands she made a bandage and rubbed the wound with ointment before tying it up. Then her fingers seemed to play about his temples and along his cheeks and neck. She was the professional nurse now, absorbed, sexless. Heritage ceased to babble, his eyes shut and he was asleep.

She remained where she was, so that the Poet, when a few minutes later he woke, found himself lying with his head in her lap. She spoke first, in an imperative tone: 'You are well now. Your head does not ache. You are strong again.'

'No. Yes,' he murmured. Then more clearly: 'Where am I? Oh, I remember, I caught a lick on the head. What's become of the brutes?'

Dickson, who had extracted food from the Mearns Street box and was pressing it on the others, replied through a mouthful of biscuit: 'We're in the old Tower. The three are lockit up in the House. Are you feeling better, Mr Heritage?'

The Poet suddenly realized Saskia's position and the blood came to his pale face. He got to his feet with an effort and held out a hand to the girl. 'I'm all right now, I think. Only a little dicky on my legs. A thousand thanks, Princess. I've given you a lot of trouble.'

She smiled at him tenderly. 'You say that when you have risked your life for me.'

'There's no time to waste,' the relentless Dougal broke in. 'Comin' over here, I heard a shot. What was it?'

'It was me,' said Dickson. 'I was shootin' at the factor.'

'Did ye hit him?'

'I think so, but I'm sorry to say not badly. When I last saw him he was running too quick for a sore hurt man. When I fired I thought it was the other man – the one they were expecting.'

Dickson marvelled at himself, yet his speech was not bravado, but the honest expression of his mind. He was keyed up to a mood in which he feared nothing very much, certainly not the laws of his country. If he fell in with the Unknown, he was entirely resolved, if his Maker permitted him, to do murder as being the simplest and justest solution. And if in the pursuit of this laudable intention he happened to wing lesser game it was no fault of his.

'Well, it's a pity ye didn't get him,' said Dougal, 'him being what we ken him to be . . . I'm for holding a council o' war, and considerin' the whole position. So far we haven't done that badly. We've shifted our base without serious casualties. We've got a far better position to hold, for there's too many ways into yon Hoose, and here there's just one. Besides, we've fickled the enemy. They'll take some time to find out where we've gone. But, mind you, we can't count on their staying long shut up. Dobson's no safe in the boiler-house, for there's a skylight far up and he'll see it when the light comes and maybe before. So we'd better get our plans ready. A word with ye, Mr McCunn,' and he led Dickson aside.

'D'ye ken what these blagyirds were up to?' he whispered fiercely in Dickson's ear. 'They were goin' to pushion the lassie. How do I ken, says you? Because Thomas Yownie heard Dobson say to Lean at the scullery door, 'Have ye got the dope?' he says, and Lean says, 'Aye.' Thomas mindit the word for he had heard about it at the picters.'

Dickson exclaimed in horror.

'What d'ye make o' that? I'll tell ye. They wanted to make sure of her, but they wouldn't have thought o' dope unless the men they expectit were due to arrive any moment. As I see it, we've to face a siege not by the three but by a dozen or more, and it'll no' be long till it starts. Now, isn't it a mercy we're safe in here?'

Dickson returned to the others with a grave face.

'Where d'you think the new folk are coming from?' he asked.

Heritage answered, 'From Auchenlochan, I suppose? Or perhaps down from the hills?'

'You're wrong.' And he told of Léon's mistaken confidences to him in the darkness. 'They are coming from the sea, just like the old pirates.'

'The sea,' Heritage repeated in a dazed voice.

'Ay, the sea. Think what that means. If they had been coming by the roads, we could have kept track of them, even if they beat us, and some of these laddies could have stuck to them and followed them up till help came. It can't be such an easy job to carry a young lady against her will along Scotch roads. But the sea's a different matter. If they've got a fast boat they could be out of the Firth and away beyond the law before we could wake up a single policeman. Ay, and even if the Government took it up and warned all the ports and ships at sea, what's to hinder them to find a hidy-hole about Ireland – or Norway? I tell you, it's a far more desperate business than I thought, and it'll no' do to wait on and trust that the Chief Constable will turn up afore the mischief's done.'

'The moral,' said Heritage, 'is that there can be no surrender. We've got to stick it out in this old place at all costs.'

'No,' said Dickson emphatically. 'The moral is that we must shift the ladies. We've got the chance while Dobson and his friends are locked up. Let's get them as far away as we can from the sea. They're far safer tramping the moors, and it's no' likely the new folk will dare to follow us.'

'But I cannot go.' Saskia, who had been listening intently, shook her head. 'I promised to wait till my friend came. If I leave I shall never find him.'

'If you stay you certainly never will, for you'll be away with the ruffians. Take a sensible view, Mem. You'll be no good to your friend or your friend to you if before night you're rocking in a ship.'

The girl shook her head again, gently but decisively. 'It was our arrangement. I cannot break it. Besides, I am sure that he will come in time, for he has never failed –'

There was a desperate finality about the quiet tones and the weary face with the shadow of a smile on it.

Then Heritage spoke. 'I don't think your plan will quite do, Dogson. Supposing we all break for the hinterland and the Danish brig finds the birds flown, that won't end the trouble. They will get on the Princess's trail, and the whole persecution will start again. I want to see things brought to a head here and now. If we can stick it out here long enough, we may trap the whole push and rid the world of a pretty gang of miscreants. Let them show their hand, and then, if the police are here by that time, we can jug the lot for piracy or something worse.'

'That's all right,' said Dougal, 'but we'd put up a better fight if we had the women off our mind. I've aye read that when a castle was going to be besieged the first thing was to get rid of the civilians.'

'Sensible to the last, Dougal,' said Dickson approvingly. 'That's just what I'm saying. I'm strong for a fight, but put the ladies in a safe bit first, for they're our weak point.'

'Do you think that if you were fighting my enemies I would consent to be absent?' came Saskia's reproachful question.

' 'Deed no, Mem,' said Dickson heartily. His martial spirit was with Heritage, but his prudence did not sleep, and he suddenly saw a way of placating both. 'Just you listen to what I propose. What do we amount to? Mr Heritage, six laddies, and myself – and I'm no more used to fighting than an old wife. We've seven desperate villains against us, and afore night they may be seventy. We've a fine old castle here, but for defence we want more than stone walls – we want a garrison. I tell you we must get help somewhere. Ay, but how, says you? Well, coming here I noticed a gentleman's house away up ayont the railway and close to the hills. The laird's maybe not at home, but there will be men there of some kind – gamekeepers and woodmen and such like. My plan is to go there at once and ask for help. Now, it's useless me going alone, for nobody would listen to me. They'd tell me to go back to the shop or they'd think me demented. But with you, Mem, it would be a different matter. They wouldn't disbelieve you. So I want you to come with me, and to come at once, for God knows how soon our need will be sore. We'll leave your cousin with Mrs Morran in the village, for bed's the place for her, and then you and me will be off on our business.'

The girl looked at Heritage, who nodded. 'It's the only way,' he said. 'Get every man jack you can raise, and if it's humanly possible get a gun or two. I believe there's time enough, for I don't see the brig arriving in broad daylight.'

'D'you not?' Dickson asked rudely. 'Have you considered what day this is? It's the Sabbath, the best of days for an ill deed. There's no kirk hereaways, and everybody in the parish will be sitting indoors by the fire.' He looked at his watch. 'In half an hour it'll be light. Haste you, Mem, and get ready. Dougal, what's the weather?'

The Chieftain swung open the door, and sniffed the air. The wind had fallen for the time being, and the surge of the tides below the rocks rose like the clamour of a mob. With the lull, mist and a thin drizzle had cloaked the world again.

To Dickson's surprise Dougal seemed to be in good spirits. He began to sing to a hymn tune a strange ditty.

> *Class-conscious we are, and class-conscious wull be*
> *Till our fit's on the neck o' the Boorjoyzee.*

'What on earth are you singing?' Dickson inquired.

Dougal grinned. 'Wee Jaikie went to a Socialist Sunday School last winter because he heard they were for fechtin' battles. Ay, and they telled him he was to jine a thing called an International, and Jaikie thought it was a fitba' club. But when he fund out there was no magic lantern or swaree at Christmas he gie'd it the chuck. They learned him a heap o' queer songs. That's one.'

'What does the last word mean?'

'I don't ken. Jaikie thought it was some kind of a draigon.'

'It's a daft-like thing anyway . . . When's high water?'

Dougal answered that to the best of his knowledge it fell between four and five in the afternoon.

'Then that's when we may expect the foreign gentry if they think to bring their boat in to the Garplefoot . . . Dougal, lad, I trust you to keep a most careful and prayerful watch. You had better get the Die-Hards out of the Tower and all round the place afore Dobson and Co get loose, or you'll no' get a chance later. Don't lose your mobility, as the sodgers say. Mr Heritage can hold the fort, but you laddies should be spread out like a screen.'

'That was my notion,' said Dougal. 'I'll detail two Die-Hards – Thomas Yownie and Wee Jaikie – to keep in touch with ye and watch for ye comin' back. Thomas ye ken already; ye'll no fickle Thomas Yownie. But don't be mistook about Wee Jaikie. He's terrible fond of greetin', but it's no fright with him but excitement. It's just a habit he's gotten. When ye see Jaikie begin to greet, ye may be sure that Jaikie's gettin' dangerous.'

The door shut behind them and Dickson found himself with his two charges in a world dim with fog and rain and the still lingering darkness. The air was raw, and had the sour smell which comes from soaked earth and wet boughs when the leaves are not yet fledged. Both the women were miserably equipped for such an expedition. Cousin Eugénie trailed heavy furs, Saskia's only wrap was a bright-coloured shawl about her shoulders, and both wore thin foreign shoes. Dickson insisted on stripping off his trusty waterproof and forcing it on the Princess, on whose slim body it hung very loose and very short. The elder woman stumbled and whimpered and needed the constant support of his arm, walking like a townswoman from the knees. But Saskia swung from the hips like a free woman, and Dickson had much ado to keep up with her. She seemed to delight in the bitter freshness of the dawn, inhaling deep breaths of it, and humming fragments of a tune.

Guided by Thomas Yownie they took the road which Dickson and Heritage had travelled the first evening, through the shrubberies on the north side of the House and the side avenue beyond which the ground fell to the Laver glen. On their right the House rose like a dark cloud, but Dickson had lost his terror of it. There were three angry men inside it, he remembered: long let them stay there. He marvelled at his mood, and also

rejoiced, for his worst fear had always been that he might prove
a coward. Now he was puzzled to think how he could ever be
frightened again, for his one object was to succeed, and in that
absorption fear seemed to him merely a waste of time. 'It all
comes of treating the thing as a business proposition,' he told
himself.

But there was far more in his heart than this sober resolution.
He was intoxicated with the resurgence of youth and felt a
rapture of audacity which he never remembered in his decorous
boyhood. 'I haven't been doing badly for an old man,' he reflected
with glee. What, oh what had become of the pillar of commerce,
the man who might have been a Bailie had he sought municipal
honours, the elder in the Guthrie Memorial Kirk, the instructor
of literary young men? In the past three days he had levanted
with jewels which had once been an Emperor's and certainly
were not his; he had burglariously entered and made free of a
strange house; he had played hide-and-seek at the risk of his
neck and had wrestled in the dark with a foreign miscreant; he
had shot at an eminent solicitor with intent to kill; and he was
now engaged in tramping the world with a fairy-tale Princess. I
blush to confess that of each of his doings he was unashamedly
proud, and thirsted for many more in the same line. 'Gosh, but
I'm seeing life,' was his unregenerate conclusion.

Without sight or sound of a human being, they descended to
the Laver, climbed again by the cart track, and passed the
deserted West Lodge and inn to the village. It was almost full
dawn when the three stood in Mrs Morran's kitchen.

'I've brought you two ladies, Auntie Phemie,' said Dickson.

They made an odd group in that cheerful place, where the
new-lit fire was crackling in the big grate – the wet undignified
form of Dickson, unshaven of cheek and chin and disreputable
in garb; the shrouded figure of Cousin Eugénie, who had sunk
into the arm-chair and closed her eyes; the slim girl, into whose
face the weather had whipped a glow like blossom; and the
hostess, with her petticoats kilted and an ancient mutch on her
head.

Mrs Morran looked once at Saskia, and then did a thing which she had not done since her girlhood. She curtseyed.

'I'm proud to see ye here, Mem. Off wi' your things, and I'll get ye dry claes. Losh, ye're fair soppin'. And your shoon! Ye maun change your feet . . . Dickson! Awa' up to the loft, and dinna you stir till I give ye a cry. The leddies will change by the fire. And you, Mem' – this to Cousin Eugénie – 'the place for you's your bed. I'll kinnle a fire ben the hoose in a jiffey. And syne ye'll have breakfast – ye'll hae a cup o' tea wi' me now, for the kettle's just on the boil. Awa' wi' ye, Dickson,' and she stamped her foot.

Dickson departed, and in the loft washed his face, and smoked a pipe on the edge of the bed, watching the mist eddying up the village street. From below rose the sounds of hospitable bustle, and when after some twenty minutes' vigil he descended, he found Saskia toasting stockinged toes by the fire in the great arm-chair, and Mrs Morran setting the table.

'Auntie Phemie, hearken to me. We've taken on too big a job for two men and six laddies, and help we've got to get, and that this very morning. D'you mind the big white house away up near the hills ayont the station and east of the Ayr road? It looked like a gentleman's shooting lodge. I was thinking of trying there. Mercy!'

The exclamation was wrung from him by his eyes settling on Saskia and noting her apparel. Gone were her thin foreign clothes, and in their place she wore a heavy tweed skirt cut very short, and thick homespun stockings, which had been made for someone with larger feet than hers. A pair of the coarse low-heeled shoes which country folk wear in the farmyard stood warming by the hearth. She still had her russet jumper, but round her neck hung a grey wool scarf, of the kind known as a 'comforter'. Amazingly pretty she looked in Dickson's eyes, but with a different kind of prettiness. The sense of fragility had fled, and he saw how nobly built she was for all her exquisiteness. She looked like a queen, he thought, but a queen to go gipsying through the world with.

'Ay, they're some o' Elspeth's things, rale guid furthy claes,' said Mrs Morran complacently. 'And the shoon are what she used to gang about the byres wi' when she was in the Castlewham dairy. The leddy was tellin' me she was for trampin' the hills, and thae things will keep her dry and warm . . . I ken the hoose ye mean. They ca' it the Mains of Garple. And I ken the man that bides in it. He's yin. Sir Erchibald Roylance. English, but his mither was a Dalziel. I'm no weel acquaint wi' his forbears, but I'm weel eneuch acquaint wi' Sir Erchie, and "better a guid coo than a coo o' a guid kind," as my mither used to say. He used to be an awfu' wild callant, a freend o' puir Maister Quentin, and up to ony deevilry. But they tell me he's a quieter lad since the war, and sair lamed by fa'in' oot o' an airyplane.'

'Will he be at the Mains just now?' Dickson asked.

'I wadna wonder. He has a muckle place in England, but he aye used to come here in the back-end for the shootin' and in April for birds. He's clean daft about birds. He'll be out a' day at the Craig watchin' solans, or lyin' a' mornin' i' the moss lookin' at bog-blitters.'

'Will he help, think you?'

'I'll wager he'll help. Onyway it's your best chance, and better a wee bush than nae bield. Now, sit in to your breakfast.'

It was a merry meal. Mrs Morran dispensed tea and gnomic wisdom. Saskia ate heartily, speaking little, but once or twice laying her hand softly on her hostess's gnarled fingers. Dickson was in such spirits that he gobbled shamelessly, being both hungry and hurried, and he spoke of the still unconquered enemy with ease and disrespect, so that Mrs Morran was moved to observe that there was 'naething sae bauld as a blind mear'. But when in a sudden return of modesty he belittled his usefulness and talked sombrely of his mature years he was told that he 'wad never be auld wi' sae muckle honesty'. Indeed it was very clear that Mrs Morran approved of her nephew.

They did not linger over breakfast, for both were impatient to be on the road. Mrs Morran assisted Saskia to put on Elspeth's shoes. ' "Even a young fit finds comfort in an auld bauchle," as my mother, honest woman, used to say.' Dickson's waterproof was restored to him, and for Saskia an old raincoat belonging to the son in South Africa was discovered, which fitted her better. 'Siccan weather,' said the hostess, as she opened the door to let in a swirl of wind. 'The deil's aye kind to his ain. Haste ye back, Mem, and be sure I'll tak' guid care o' your leddy cousin.'

The proper way to the Mains of Garple was either by the station and the Ayr road, or by the Auchenlochan highway, branching off half a mile beyond the Garple bridge. But Dickson, who had been studying the map and fancied himself as a path-finder, chose the direct route across the Long Muir as being at once shorter and more sequestered. With the dawn the wind had risen again, but it had shifted towards the north-west and was many degrees colder. The mist was furling on the hills like sails, the rain had ceased, and out at sea the eye covered a mile or two of wild water. The moor was drenching wet, and the peat bogs were brimming with inky pools, so that soon the travellers were soaked to the knees. Dickson had no fear of pursuit, for he calculated that Dobson and his friends, even if they had got out, would be busy looking for the truants in the vicinity of the House and would presently be engaged with the old Tower. But he realized, too, that speed on his errand was vital, for at any moment the Unknown might arrive from the sea.

So he kept up a good pace, half-running, half-striding, till they had passed the railway, and he found himself gasping with a stitch in his side, and compelled to rest in the lee of what had once been a sheepfold. Saskia amazed him. She moved over the rough heather like a deer, and it was her hand that helped him across the deeper hags. Before such youth and vigour he felt clumsy and old. She stood looking down at him as he recovered his breath, cool, unruffled, alert as Diana. His mind fled to Heritage, and it occurred to him suddenly that the Poet had set his affections very high. Loyalty drove him to speak a word for his friend.

'I've got the easy job,' he said. 'Mr Heritage will have the whole pack on him in that old Tower, and him with such a sore clout on his head. I've left him my pistol. He's a terrible brave man!'

She smiled.

'Ay, and he's a poet too.'

'So?' she said. 'I did not know. He is very young.'

'He's a man of very high ideels.'

She puzzled at the word, and then smiled. 'He is like many of our young men in Russia, the students – his mind is in a ferment and he does not know what he wants. But he is brave.'

This seemed to Dickson's loyal soul but a chilly tribute.

'I think he is in love with me,' she continued.

He looked up startled, and saw in her face that which gave him a view into a strange new world. He had thought that women blushed when they talked of love, but her eyes were as grave and candid as a boy's. Here was one who had gone through waters so deep that she had lost the foibles of sex. Love to her was only a word of ill omen, a threat on the lips of brutes, an extra battalion of peril in an army of perplexities. He felt like some homely rustic who finds himself swept unwittingly into the moonlight hunt of Artemis and her maidens.

'He is a romantic,' she said. 'I have known so many like him.'

'He's no' that,' said Dickson shortly. 'Why, he used to be aye laughing at me for being romantic. He's one that's looking for truth and reality, he says, and he's terrible down on the kind of poetry I like myself.'

She smiled. 'They all talk so. But you, my friend Dickson' (she pronounced the name in two staccato syllables ever so prettily), 'you are different. Tell me about yourself.'

'I'm just what you see – a middle-aged retired grocer.'

'Grocer?' she queried. 'Ah, yes, *épicier*. But you are a very remarkable *épicier*. Mr Heritage I understand, but you and those little boys – no. I am sure of one thing – you are not a romantic. You are too humorous and – and – I think you are like Ulysses, for it would not be easy to defeat you.'

Her eyes were kind, nay affectionate, and Dickson experienced a preposterous rapture in his soul, followed by a sinking, as he realized how far the job was still from being completed.

'We must be getting on, Mem,' he said hastily, and the two plunged again into the heather.

The Ayr road was crossed, and the fir wood around the Mains became visible, and presently the white gates of the entrance. A wind-blown spire of smoke beyond the trees proclaimed that the house was not untenanted. As they entered the drive the Scots firs were tossing in the gale, which blew fiercely at this altitude, but, the dwelling itself being more in the hollow, the daffodil clumps on the lawn were but mildly fluttered.

The door was opened by a one-armed butler who bore all the marks of the old regular soldier. Dickson produced a card and asked to see his master on urgent business. Sir Archibald was at home, he was told, and had just finished breakfast. The two were led into a large bare chamber which had all the chill and mustiness of a bachelor's drawing-room. The butler returned, and said Sir Archibald would see him. 'I'd better go myself first and prepare the way, Mem,' Dickson whispered, and followed the man across the hall.

He found himself ushered into a fair-sized room where a bright fire was burning. On a table lay the remains of breakfast, and the odour of food mingled pleasantly with the scent of peat. The horns and heads of big game, foxes' masks, the model of a gigantic salmon, and several bookcases adorned the walls, and books and maps were mixed with decanters and cigar-boxes on the long sideboard. After the wild out of doors the place seemed the very shrine of comfort. A young man sat in an arm-chair by the fire with a leg on a stool; he was smoking a pipe, and reading the *Field*, and on another stool at his elbow was a pile of new novels. He was a pleasant brown-faced young man, with remarkably smooth hair and a roving humorous eye.

'Come in, Mr McCunn. Very glad to see you. If, as I take it, you're the grocer, you're a household name in these parts. I get all my supplies from you, and I've just been makin' inroads on one of your divine hams. Now, what can I do for you?'

'I'm very proud to hear what you say, Sir Archibald. But I've not come on business. I've come with the queerest story you ever heard in your life and I've come to ask your help.'

'Go ahead. A good story is just what I want this vile mornin'.'

'I'm not here alone. I've a lady with me.'

'God bless my soul! A lady!'

'Aye, a princess. She's in the next room.'

The young man looked wildly at him and waved the book he had been reading.

'Excuse me, Mr McCunn, but are you quite sober? I beg your pardon. I see you are. But you know, it isn't done. Princesses don't as a rule come here after breakfast to pass the time of day. It's more absurd than this shocker I've been readin'.'

'All the same it's a fact. She'll tell you the story herself, and you'll believe her quick enough. But to prepare your mind I'll just give you a sketch of the events of the last few days.'

Before the sketch was concluded the young man had violently rung the bell. 'Sime,' he shouted to the servant, 'clear away this mess and lay the table again. Order more breakfast, all the breakfast you can get. Open the windows and get the tobacco smoke out of the air. Tidy up the place for there's a lady comin'. Quick, you juggins!'

He was on his feet now, and, with his arm in Dickson's, was heading for the door.

'My sainted aunt! And you topped off with pottin' at the factor. I've seen a few things in my day, but I'm blessed if I ever met a bird like you!'

ELEVEN

Gravity Out of Bed

IT is probable that Sir Archibald Roylance did not altogether believe Dickson's tale; it may be that he considered him an agreeable romancer, or a little mad, or no more than a relief to the tedium of a wet Sunday morning. But his incredulity did not survive one glance at Saskia as she stood in that bleak drawing-room among Victorian water-colours and faded chintzes. The young man's boyishness deserted him. He stopped short in his tracks, and made a profound and awkward bow. 'I am at your service, Mademoiselle,' he said, amazed at himself. The words seemed to have come out of a confused memory of plays and novels.

She inclined her head – a little on one side, and looked towards Dickson.

'Sir Archibald's going to do his best for us,' said that squire of dames. 'I was telling him that we had had our breakfast.'

'Let's get out of this sepulchre,' said their host, who was recovering himself. 'There's a roasting fire in my den. Of course you'll have something to eat – hot coffee, anyhow – I've trained my cook to make coffee like a Frenchwoman. The housekeeper will take charge of you, if you want to tidy up, and you must excuse our ramshackle ways, please. I don't believe there's ever been a lady in this house before, you know.'

He led her to the smoking-room and ensconced her in the great chair by the fire. Smilingly she refused a series of offers which ranged from a sheepskin mantle which he had got in the Pamirs and which he thought might fit her, to hot whisky and water as a specific against a chill. But she accepted a pair of slippers and deftly kicked off the brogues provided by Mrs Morran.

Also, while Dickson started rapaciously on a second breakfast, she allowed him to pour her out a cup of coffee.

'You are a soldier?' she asked.

'Two years infantry – 5th Battalion Lennox Highlanders, and then Flying Corps. Top-hole time I had too till the day before the Armistice, when my luck gave out and I took a nasty toss. Consequently I'm not as fast on my legs now as I'd like to be.'

'You were a friend of Captain Kennedy?'

'His oldest. We were at the same private school, and he was at m' tutor's, and we were never much separated till he went abroad to cram for the Diplomatic and I started east to shoot things.'

'Then I will tell you what I told Captain Kennedy.' Saskia, looking into the heart of the peats, began the story of which we have already heard a version, but she told it differently, for she was telling it to one who more or less belonged to her own world. She mentioned names at which the other nodded. She spoke of a certain Paul Abreskov. 'I heard of him at Bokhara in 1912,' said Sir Archie, and his face grew solemn. Sometimes she lapsed into French, and her hearer's brow wrinkled, but he appeared to follow. When she had finished he drew a long breath.

'My aunt! What a time you've been through! I've seen pluck in my day, but yours! It's not thinkable. D'you mind if I ask a question, Princess? Bolshevism we know all about, and I admit Trotsky and his friends are a pretty effective push; but how on earth have they got a world-wide graft going in the time so that they can stretch their net to an out-of-the-way spot like this? It looks as if they had struck a Napoleon somewhere.'

'You do not understand,' she said. 'I cannot make anyone understand – except a Russian. My country has been broken to pieces, and there is no law in it; therefore it is a nursery of crime. So would England be, or France, if you had suffered the same misfortunes. My people are not wickeder than others, but for the moment they are sick and have no strength. As for the government of the Bolsheviki it matters little, for it will pass.

Some parts of it may remain, but it is a government of the sick and fevered, and cannot endure in health. Lenin may be a good man – I do not think so, but I do not know – but if he were an archangel he could not alter things. Russia is mortally sick and therefore all evil is unchained, and the criminals have no one to check them. There is crime everywhere in the world, and the unfettered crime in Russia is so powerful that it stretches its hand to crime throughout the globe and there is a great mobilizing everywhere of wicked men. Once you boasted that law was international and that the police in one land worked with the police of all others. Today that is true about criminals. After a war evil passions are loosed, and, since Russia is broken, in her they can make their headquarters . . . It is not Bolshevism, the theory, you need fear, for that is a weak and dying thing. It is crime, which today finds its seat in my country, but is not only Russian. It has no fatherland. It is as old as human nature and as wide as the earth.'

'I see,' said Sir Archie. 'Gad, here have I been vegetatin' and thinkin' that all excitement had gone out of life with the war, and sometimes even regrettin' that the beastly old thing was over, and all the while the world fairly hummin' with interest. And Loudon too!'

'I would like your candid opinion on yon factor, Sir Archibald.' said Dickson.

'I can't say I ever liked him, and I've once or twice had a row with him, for he used to bring his pals to shoot over Dalquharter and he didn't quite play the game by me. But I know dashed little about him, for I've been a lot away. Bit hairy about the heels, of course. A great figure at local racemeetin's, and used to toady old Carforth and the huntin' crowd. He has a pretty big reputation as a sharp lawyer and some of the thick-headed lairds swear by him, but Quentin never could stick him. It's quite likely he's been gettin' into Queer Street, for he was always speculatin' in horseflesh, and I fancy he plunged a bit on the Turf. But I can't think how he got mixed up in this show.'

'I'm positive Dobson's his brother.'

'And put this business in his way. That would explain it all right . . . He must be runnin' for pretty big stakes, for that kind of lad don't dabble in crime for six-and-eightpence . . . Now for the layout. You've got three men shut up in Dalquharter House, who by this time have probably escaped. One of you – what's his name? – Heritage? – is in the old Tower, and you think that *they* think the Princess is still there and will sit round the place like terriers. Sometime today the Danish brig will arrive with reinforcements, and then there will be a hefty fight. Well, the first thing to be done is to get rid of Loudon's stymie with the authorities. Princess, I'm going to carry you off in my car to the Chief Constable. The second thing is for you after that to stay on here. It's a deadly place on a wet day, but it's safe enough.'

Saskia shook her head and Dickson spoke for her.

'You'll no' get her to stop here. I've done my best, but she's determined to be back at Dalquharter. You see she's expecting a friend, and besides, if there's going to be a battle she'd like to be in it. Is that so, Mem?'

Sir Archie looked helplessly around him, and the sight of the girl's face convinced him that argument would be fruitless. 'Anyhow she must come with me to the Chief Constable. Lethington's a slow bird on the wing, and I don't see myself convincin' him that he must get busy unless I can produce the Princess. Even then it may be a tough job, for it's Sunday, and in these parts people go to sleep till Monday mornin'.'

'That's just what I'm trying to get at,' said Dickson. 'By all means go to the Chief Constable, and tell him it's life or death. My lawyer in Glasgow, Mr Caw, will have been stirring him up yesterday, and you two should complete the job . . . But what I'm feared is that he'll not be in time. As you say, it's the Sabbath day, and the police are terrible slow. Now any moment that brig may be here, and the trouble will start. I'm wanting to save the Princess, but I'm wanting too to give these blagyirds the rough-est handling they ever got in their lives. Therefore I say there's no time to lose. We're far ower few to put up a fight, and we want every man you've got about this place to hold the fort till the police come.'

Sir Archibald looked upon the earnest flushed face of Dickson with admiration. 'I'm blessed if you're not the most whole-hearted brigand I've ever struck.'

'I'm not. I'm just a business man.'

'Do you realize that you're levying a private war and breaking every law of the land?'

'Hoots!' said Dickson. 'I don't care a docken about the law. I'm for seeing this job through. What force can you produce?'

'Only cripples, I'm afraid. There's Sime, my butler. He was a Fusilier Jock and, as you saw, has lost an arm. Then McGuffog the keeper is a good man, but he's still got a Turkish bullet in his thigh. The chauffeur, Carfrae, was in the Yeomanry, and lost half a foot; and there's myself, as lame as a duck. The herds on the home farm are no good, for one's seventy and the other is in bed with jaundice. The Mains can produce four men, but they're rather a job lot.'

'They'll do fine,' said Dickson heartily. 'All sodgers, and no doubt all good shots. Have you plenty guns?'

Sir Archie burst into uproarious laughter. 'Mr McCunn, you're a man after my own heart. I'm under your orders. If I had a boy I'd put him into the provision trade, for it's the place to see fightin'. Yes, we've no end of guns. I advise shotguns, for they've more stoppin' power in a rush than a rifle, and I take it it's a rough-and-tumble we're lookin' for.'

'Right,' said Dickson. 'I saw a bicycle in the hall. I want you to lend it me, for I must be getting back. You'll take the Princess and do the best you can with the Chief Constable.'

'And then?'

'Then you'll load up your car with your folk, and come down the hill to Dalquharter. There'll be a laddie, or maybe more than one, waiting for you on this side the village to give you instruc-tions. Take your orders from them. If it's a red-haired ruffian called Dougal you'll be wise to heed what he says, for he has a grand head for battles.'

Five minutes later Dickson was pursuing a quavering course like a snipe down the avenue. He was a miserable performer on a bicycle. Not for twenty years had he bestridden one, and he did not understand such new devices as free-wheels and change of gears. The mounting had been the worst part, and it had only been achieved by the help of a rockery. He had begun by cutting into two flower-beds, and missing a birch tree by inches. But he clung on desperately, well knowing that if he fell off it would be hard to remount, and at length he gained the avenue. When he passed the lodge gates he was riding fairly straight, and when he turned off the Ayr highway to the side road that led to Dalquharter he was more or less master of his machine.

He crossed the Garple by an ancient hunchbacked bridge, observing even in his absorption with the handle-bars that the stream was in roaring spate. He wrestled up the further hill with aching calf-muscles, and got to the top just before his strength gave out. Then as the road turned seaward he had the slope with him, and enjoyed some respite. It was no case for putting up his feet, for the gale was blowing hard on his right cheek, but the downward grade enabled him to keep his course with little exertion. His anxiety to get back to the scene of action was for the moment appeased, since he knew he was making as good speed as the weather allowed, so he had leisure for thought.

But the mind of this preposterous being was not on the business before him. He dallied with irrelevant things – with the problems of youth and love. He was beginning to be very nervous about Heritage, not as the solitary garrison of the old Tower, but as the lover of Saskia. That everybody should be in love with her appeared to him only proper, for he had never met her like, and assumed that it did not exist. The desire of the moth for the star seemed to him a reasonable thing, since hopeless loyalty and unrequited passion were the eternal stock-in-trade of romance. He wished he were twenty-five himself to have the chance of indulging in such sentimentality for such a lady. But Heritage was not like him and would never be content with a romantic folly . . . He had been in love with her for two years – a long time. He spoke about wanting to die for her, which was a flight beyond Dickson himself. 'I doubt it will be what they call a "grand passion",' he reflected with reverence. But it was hopeless; he saw quite clearly that it was hopeless.

Why, he could not have explained, for Dickson's instincts were subtler than his intelligence. He recognized that the two belonged to different circles of being, which nowhere intersected. That mysterious lady, whose eyes had looked through life to the other side, was no mate for the Poet. His faithful soul was agitated, for he had developed for Heritage a sincere affection. It would break his heart, poor man. There was he holding the fort alone and cheering himself with delightful fancies about one remoter than the moon. Dickson wanted happy endings, and here there was no hope of such. He hated to admit that life could be crooked, but the optimist in him was now fairly dashed.

Sir Archie might be the fortunate man, for of course he would soon be in love with her, if he were not so already. Dickson like all his class had a profound regard for the country gentry. The business Scot does not usually revere wealth, though he may pursue it earnestly, nor does he specially admire rank in the common sense. But for ancient race he has respect in his bones, though it may happen that in public he denies it, and the laird has for him a secular association with good family . . . Sir Archie might do. He was young, good-looking, obviously gallant . . . But no! He was not quite right either. Just a trifle too light in weight, too boyish and callow. The Princess must have youth, but it should be mighty youth, the youth of a Napoleon or a Caesar. He reflected that the Great Montrose, for whom he had a special veneration, might have filled the bill. Or young Harry with his beaver up? Or Claverhouse in the picture with the flush of temper on his cheek?

The meditations of the match-making Dickson came to an abrupt end. He had been riding negligently, his head bent against the wind, and his eyes vaguely fixed on the wet hill-gravel of the road. Of his immediate environs he was pretty well unconscious. Suddenly he was aware of figures on each side of him who advanced menacingly. Stung to activity he attempted to increase his pace, which was already good, for the road at this point descended steeply. Then, before he could prevent it, a stick was thrust into his front wheel, and the next second he was describing a curve through the air. His head took the ground, he felt a spasm of blinding pain, and then a sense of horrible suffocation before his wits left him.

'Are ye sure it's the richt man, Ecky?' said a voice which he did not hear.

'Sure. It's the Glesca body Dobson told us to look for yesterday. It's a pund note atween us for this job. We'll tie him up in the wud till we've time to attend to him.'

'Is he bad?'

'It doesna maitter,' said the one called Ecky. 'He'll be deid onyway long afore the morn.'

Mrs Morran all forenoon was in a state of unSabbatical disquiet. After she had seen Saskia and Dickson start she finished her housewifely duties, took Cousin Eugénie her breakfast, and made preparation for the midday dinner. The invalid in the bed in the parlour was not a repaying subject. Cousin Eugénie belonged to that type of elderly women who, having been spoiled in youth, find the rest of life fall far short of their expectations. Her voice had acquired a perpetual wail, and the corners of what had once been a pretty mouth drooped in an eternal peevishness. She found herself in a morass of misery and shabby discomfort, but had her days continued in an even tenor she would still have lamented. 'A dingy body,' was Mrs Morran's comment, but she laboured in kindness. Unhappily they had no common language, and it was only by signs that the hostess could discover her wants and show her goodwill. She fed her and bathed her face, saw to the fire and left her to sleep. 'I'm boilin' a hen to mak' broth for your denner, Mem. Try and get a bit sleep now.' The purport of the advice was clear, and Cousin Eugénie turned obediently on her pillow.

It was Mrs Morran's custom of a Sunday to spend the morning in devout meditation. Some years before she had given up tramping the five miles to kirk, on the ground that having been a regular attendant for fifty years she had got all the good out of it that was probable. Instead she read slowly aloud to herself the sermon printed in a certain religious weekly which reached her every Saturday, and concluded with a chapter or two of the Bible. But today something had gone wrong with her mind. She could not follow the thread of the Reverend Doctor MacMichael's discourse. She could not fix her attention on the wanderings and misdeeds of Israel as recorded in the Book of Exodus. She must always be getting up to look at the pot on the fire, or to open the back door and study the weather. For a little she fought against her unrest, and then she gave up the attempt at concentration. She took the big pot off the fire and allowed it to simmer, and presently she fetched her boots and umbrella, and kilted her petticoats. 'I'll be none the waur o' a breath o' caller air,' she decided.

The wind was blowing great guns but there was only the thinnest sprinkle of rain. Sitting on the hen-house roof and munching a raw turnip was a figure which she recognized as the smallest of the Die-Hards. Between bites he was singing dolefully to the tune of 'Annie Laurie' one of the ditties of his quondam Sunday school:

> *The Boorjoys' brays are bonnie,*
> *Too-roo-ra-roo-raloo,*
> *But the Worrkers o' the Worrld*
> *Wull gar them a' look blue,*
> *Wull gar them a' look blue,*
> *And droon them in the sea,*
> *And – for bonnie Annie Laurie*
> *I'll lay me down and dee.*

'Losh, laddie,' she cried, 'that's cauld food for the stamach. Come indoors about midday and I'll gie ye a plate o' broth!' The Die-Hard saluted and continued on the turnip.

She took the Auchenlochan road across the Garple bridge, for that was the best road to the Mains, and by it Dickson and the others might be returning. Her equanimity at all seasons was like a Turk's, and she would not have admitted that anything mortal had power to upset or excite her: nevertheless it was a fast-beating heart that she now bore beneath her Sunday jacket. Great events, she felt, were on the eve of happening, and of them she was a part. Dickson's anxiety was hers, to bring things to a business-like conclusion. The honour of Huntingtower was at stake and of the old Kennedys. She was carrying out Mr Quentin's commands, the dead boy who used to clamour for her treacle scones. And there was more than duty in it, for youth was not dead in her old heart, and adventure had still power to quicken it.

Mrs Morran walked well, with the steady long paces of the Scots countrywoman. She left the Auchenlochan road and took the side path along the tableland to the Mains. But for the surge of the gale and the far-borne boom of the furious sea there was little noise; not a bird cried in the uneasy air. With the wind behind her Mrs Morran breasted the ascent till she had on her right the moorland running south to the Lochan valley and on her left Garple chafing in its deep forested gorges. Her eyes were quick and she noted with interest a weasel creeping from a fern-clad cairn. A little way on she passed an old ewe in diffi-culties and assisted it to rise. 'But for me, my wumman, ye'd hae been braxy ere nicht,' she told it as it departed bleating. Then she realized that she had come a certain distance. 'Losh, I maun be gettin' back or the hen will be spiled,' she cried, and was on the verge of turning.

But something caught her eye a hundred yards farther on the road. It was something which moved with the wind like a wounded bird, fluttering from the roadside to a puddle and then back to the rushes. She advanced to it, missed it, and caught it.

It was an old dingy green felt hat, and she recognized it as Dickson's.

Mrs Morran's brain, after a second of confusion, worked fast and clearly. She examined the road and saw that a little way on the gravel had been violently agitated. She detected several prints of hobnailed boots. There were prints, too, on a patch of peat on the south side behind a tall bank of sods. 'That's where they were hidin',' she concluded. Then she explored on the other side in a thicket of hazels and wild raspberries, and presently her perseverance was rewarded. The scrub was all crushed and pressed as if several persons had been forcing a passage. In a hollow was a gleam of something white. She moved towards it with a quaking heart, and was relieved to find that it was only a new and expensive bicycle with the front wheel badly buckled.

Mrs Morran delayed no longer. If she had walked well on her out journey, she beat all records on the return. Sometimes she would run till her breath failed; then she would slow down till anxiety once more quickened her pace. To her joy, on the Dalquharter side of the Garple bridge she observed the figure of a Die-Hard. Breathless, flushed, with her bonnet awry and her umbrella held like a scimitar, she seized on the boy.

'Awfu' doin's! They've grippit Maister McCunn up the Mains road just afore the second milestone and forenent the auld bucht. I fund his hat, and a bicycle's lyin' broken in the wud. Haste ye, man, and get the rest and awa' and seek him. It'll be the tinklers frae the Dean. I'd gang mysel', but my legs are ower auld. Oh, laddie, dinna stop to speir questions. They'll hae him murdered or awa' to sea. And maybe the leddy was wi' him and they've got them baith. Wae's me! Wae's me!'

The Die-Hard, who was Wee Jaikie, did not delay. His eyes had filled with tears at her news, which we know to have been his habit. When Mrs Morran, after indulging in a moment of barbaric keening, looked back the road she had come, she saw a small figure trotting up the hill like a terrier who has been left behind. As he trotted he wept bitterly. Jaikie was getting dangerous.

TWELVE

How Mr McCunn Committed
an Assault upon an Ally

DICKSON always maintained that his senses did not leave him for more than a second or two, but he admitted that he did not remember very clearly the events of the next few hours. He was conscious of a bad pain above his eyes, and something wet trickling down his cheek. There was a perpetual sound of water in his ears and of men's voices. He found himself dropped roughly on the ground and forced to walk, and was aware that his legs were inclined to wobble. Somebody had a grip on each arm, so that he could not defend his face from the brambles, and that worried him, for his whole head seemed one aching bruise and he dreaded anything touching it. But all the time he did not open his mouth, for silence was the one duty that his muddled wits enforced. He felt that he was not the master of his mind, and he dreaded what he might disclose if he began to babble.

Presently there came a blank space of which he had no recollection at all. The movement had stopped, and he was allowed to sprawl on the ground. He thought that his head had got another whack from a bough, and that the pain put him into a stupor. When he awoke he was alone.

He discovered that he was strapped very tightly to a young Scotch fir. His arms were bent behind him and his wrists tied together with cords knotted at the back of the tree; his legs were shackled, and further cords fastened them to the bole. Also there was a halter round the trunk and just under his chin, so that while he breathed freely enough, he could not move his head. Before him was a tangle of bracken and scrub, and beyond that the gloom of dense pines; but as he could see only directly in front his prospect was strictly circumscribed.

Very slowly he began to take his bearings. The pain in his head was now dulled and quite bearable, and the flow of blood had stopped, for he felt the encrustation of it beginning on his cheeks. There was a tremendous noise all around him, and he traced this to the swaying of tree-tops in the gale. But there was an undercurrent of deeper sound – water surely, water churning among rocks. It was a stream – the Garple of course – and then he remembered where he was and what had happened.

I do not wish to portray Dickson as a hero, for nothing would annoy him more; but I am bound to say that his first clear thought was not of his own danger. It was intense exasperation at the miscarriage of his plans. Long ago he should have been with Dougal arranging operations, giving him news of Sir Archie, finding out how Heritage was faring, deciding how to use the coming reinforcements. Instead he was trussed up in a wood, a prisoner of the enemy, and utterly useless to his side. He tugged at his bonds, and nearly throttled himself. But they were of good tarry cord and did not give a fraction of an inch. Tears of bitter rage filled his eyes and made furrows on his encrusted cheeks. Idiot that he had been, he had wrecked everything! What would Saskia and Dougal and Sir Archie do without a business man by their side? There would be a muddle, and the little party would walk into a trap. He saw it all very clearly. The men from the sea would overpower them, there would be murder done, and an easy capture of the Princess; and the police would turn up at long last to find an empty headland.

He had also most comprehensively wrecked himself, and at the thought genuine panic seized him. There was no earthly chance of escape, for he was tucked away in this infernal jungle till such time as his enemies had time to deal with him. As to what that dealing would be like he had no doubts, for they knew that he had been their chief opponent. Those desperate ruffians would not scruple to put an end to him. His mind dwelt with horrible fascination upon throat-cutting, no doubt because of the presence of the cord below his chin. He had heard it was not a painful death; at any rate he remembered a clerk he had once had, a feeble, timid creature, who had twice attempted suicide that way. Surely it could not be very bad, and it would soon be over.

But another thought came to him. They would carry him off in the ship and settle with him at their leisure. No swift merciful death for him. He had read dreadful tales of the Bolsheviks' skill in torture, and now they all came back to him – stories of Chinese mercenaries, and men buried alive, and death by agonizing inches. He felt suddenly very cold and sick, and hung in his bonds, for he had no strength in his limbs. Then the pressure on his throat braced him, and also quickened his numb mind. The liveliest terror ran like quicksilver through his veins.

He endured some moments of this anguish, till after many despairing clutches at his wits he managed to attain a measure of self-control. He certainly wasn't going to allow himself to become mad. Death was death whatever form it took, and he had to face death as many better men had done before him. He had often thought about it and wondered how he should behave if the thing came to him. Respectably, he had hoped; heroically, he had sworn in his moments of confidence. But he had never for an instant dreamed of this cold, lonely, dreadful business. Last Sunday, he remembered, he had been basking in the afternoon sun in his little garden and reading about the end of Fergus MacIvor in *Waverley* and thrilling to the romance of it; and Tibby had come out and summoned him in to tea. Then he had rather wanted to be a Jacobite in the '45 and in peril of his neck, and now Providence had taken him most terribly at his word.

A week ago –! He groaned at the remembrance of that sunny garden. In seven days he had found a new world and tried a new life, and had come now to the end of it. He did not want to die, less now than ever with such wide horizons opening before him. But that was the worst of it, he reflected, for to have a great life great hazards must be taken, and there was always the risk of this sudden extinguisher ... Had he to choose again, far better the smooth sheltered bypath than this accursed romantic highway on to which he had blundered ... No, by Heaven, no! Confound it, if he had to choose he would do it all again. Something stiff and indomitable in his soul was bracing him to a manlier humour. There was no one to see the figure strapped to the fir, but had there been a witness he would have noted that at this stage Dickson shut his teeth and that his troubled eyes looked very steadily before him.

His business, he felt, was to keep from thinking, for if he thought at all there would be a flow of memories – of his wife, his home, his books, his friends – to unman him. So he steeled himself to blankness, like a sleepless man imagining white sheep in a gate ... He noted a robin below the hazels, strutting impudently. And there was a tit on a bracken frond, which made the thing sway like one of the see-saws he used to play with as a boy. There was no wind in that undergrowth, and any move-ment must be due to bird or beast. The tit flew off, and the oscillations of the bracken slowly died away. Then they began again, but more violently, and Dickson could not see the bird that caused them. It must be something down at the roots of the covert, a rabbit, perhaps, or a fox, or a weasel.

He watched for the first sign of the beast, and thought he caught a glimpse of tawny fur. Yes, there it was – pale dirty yellow, a weasel clearly. Then suddenly the patch grew larger, and to his amazement he looked at a human face – the face of a pallid small boy.

A head disentangled itself, followed by thin shoulders, and then by a pair of very dirty bare legs. The figure raised itself and looked sharply round to make certain that the coast was clear. Then it stood up and saluted, revealing the well-known linea-ments of Wee Jaikie.

At the sight Dickson knew that he was safe by that certainty of instinct which is independent of proof, like the man who prays for a sign and has his prayer answered. He observed that the boy was quietly sobbing. Jaikie surveyed the position for an instant with red-rimmed eyes and then unclasped a knife, feeling the edge of the blade on his thumb. He darted behind the fir, and a second later Dickson's wrists were free. Then he sawed at the legs, and cut the shackles which tied them together, and then – most circumspectly – assaulted the cord which bound Dickson's neck to the trunk. There now remained only the two bonds which fastened the legs and the body to the tree.

There was a sound in the wood different from the wind and stream. Jaikie listened like a startled hind.

'They're comin' back,' he gasped. 'Just you bide where ye are and let on ye're still tied up.'

He disappeared in the scrub as inconspicuously as a rat, while two of the tinklers came up the slope from the waterside. Dickson in a fever of impatience cursed Wee Jaikie for not cutting his remaining bonds so that he could at least have made a dash for freedom. And then he realized that the boy had been right. Feeble and cramped as he was, he would have stood no chance in a race.

One of the tinklers was the man called Ecky. He had been running hard, and was mopping his brow.

'Hob's seen the brig,' he said. 'It's droppin' anchor ayont the Dookits whaur there's a bield frae the wund and deep water. They'll be landit in half an 'oor. Awa' you up to the Hoose and tell Dobson, and me and Sim and Hob will meet the boats at the Garplefit.'

The other cast a glance towards Dickson.

'What about him?' he asked.

The two scrutinized their prisoner from a distance of a few paces. Dickson, well aware of his peril, held himself as stiff as if every bond had been in place. The thought flashed on him that if he were too immobile they might think he was dying or dead, and come close to examine him. If they only kept their distance, the dusk of the wood would prevent them detecting Jaikie's handiwork.

'What'll you take to let me go?' he asked plaintively.

'Naething that you could offer, my mannie,' said Ecky.

'I'll give you a five-pound note apiece.'

'Produce the siller,' said the other.

'It's in my pocket.'

'It's no that. We riped your pooches lang syne.'

'I'll take you to Glasgow with me and pay you there. Honour bright.'

Ecky spat. 'D'ye think we're gowks? Man, there's no siller ye could pay wad mak' it worth our while to lowse ye. Bide quiet there and ye'll see some queer things ere nicht. C'way, Davie.'

The two set off at a good pace down the stream, while Dickson's pulsing heart returned to its normal rhythm. As the sound of their feet died away Wee Jaikie crawled out from cover, dry-eyed now and very business-like. He slit the last thongs, and Dickson fell limply on his face.

'Losh, laddie, I'm awful stiff,' he groaned. 'Now, listen. Away all your pith to Dougal, and tell him that the brig's in and the men will be landing inside the hour. Tell him I'm coming as fast as my legs will let me. The Princess will likely be there already and Sir Archibald and his men, but if they're no', tell Dougal they're coming. Haste you, Jaikie. And see here, I'll never forget what you've done for me the day. You're a fine wee laddie!'

The obedient Die-Hard disappeared, and Dickson painfully and laboriously set himself to climb the slope. He decided that his quickest and safest route lay by the highroad, and he had also some hopes of recovering his bicycle. On examining his body he seemed to have sustained no very great damage, except a painful cramping of legs and arms and a certain dizziness in the head. His pockets had been thoroughly rifled, and he reflected with amusement that he, the well-to-do Mr McCunn, did not possess at the moment a single copper.

But his spirits were soaring, for somehow his escape had given him an assurance of ultimate success. Providence had directly interfered on his behalf by the hand of Wee Jaikie, and that surely meant that it would see him through. But his chief emotion was an ardour of impatience to get to the scene of action. He must be at Dalquharter before the men from the sea; he must find Dougal and discover his dispositions. Heritage would be on guard in the Tower, and in a very little the enemy would be round it. It would be just like the Princess to try and enter there, but at all costs that must be hindered. She and Sir Archie must not be cornered in stone walls, but must keep their communications open and fall on the enemy's flank. Oh, if the police would only come in time, what a rounding-up of miscreants that day would see!

As the trees thinned on the brow of the slope and he saw the sky, he realized that the afternoon was far advanced. It must be well on for five o'clock. The wind still blew furiously, and the oaks on the fringes of the wood were whipped like saplings. Ruefully he admitted that the gale would not defeat the enemy. If the brig found a sheltered anchorage on the south side of the headland beyond the Garple, it would be easy enough for boats to make the Garple mouth, though it might be a difficult job to get out again. The thought quickened his steps, and he came out of cover on to the public road without a prior reconnaissance.

Just in front of him stood a motor-bicycle. Something had gone wrong with it for its owner was tinkering at it, on the side farthest from Dickson. A wild hope seized him that this might be the vanguard of the police, and he went boldly towards it. The owner, who was kneeling, raised his face at the sound of footsteps and Dickson looked into his eyes.

He recognized them only too well. They belonged to the man he had seen in the inn at Kirkmichael, the man whom Heritage had decided to be an Australian, but whom they now knew to be their arch-enemy – the man called Paul who had persecuted the Princess for years and whom alone of all beings on earth she feared. He had been expected before, but had arrived now in the nick of time while the brig was casting anchor. Saskia had said that he had a devil's brain, and Dickson, as he stared at him, saw a fiendish cleverness in his straight brows and a remorseless cruelty in his stiff jaw and his pale eyes.

He achieved the bravest act of his life. Shaky and dizzy as he was, with freedom newly opened to him and the mental torments of his captivity still an awful recollection, he did not hesitate. He saw before him the villain of the drama, the one man that stood between the Princess and peace of mind. He regarded no consequences, gave no heed to his own fate, and thought only how to put his enemy out of action. There was a big spanner lying on the ground. He seized it and with all his strength smote at the man's face.

The motor-cyclist, kneeling and working hard at his machine, had raised his head at Dickson's approach and beheld a wild apparition – a short man in ragged tweeds, with a bloody brow and long smears of blood on his cheeks. The next second he observed the threat of attack, and ducked his head so that the spanner only grazed his scalp. The motor-bicycle toppled over, its owner sprang to his feet, and found the short man, very pale and gasping, about to renew the assault. In such a crisis there was no time for inquiry, and the cyclist was well trained in self-defence. He leaped the prostrate bicycle, and before his assailant could get in a blow brought his left fist into violent contact with his chin. Dickson tottered back a step or two and then subsided among the bracken.

He did not lose his senses, but he had no more strength in him. He felt horribly ill, and struggled in vain to get up. The cyclist, a gigantic figure, towered above him. 'Who the devil are you?' he was asking. 'What do you mean by it?'

Dickson had no breath for words, and knew that if he tried to speak he would be very sick. He could only stare up like a dog at the angry eyes. Angry beyond question they were, but surely not malevolent. Indeed, as they looked at the shameful figure on the ground, amusement filled them. The face relaxed into a smile.

'Who on earth are you?' the voice repeated. And then into it came recognition. 'I've seen you before. I believe you're the little man I saw last week at the Black Bull. Be so good as to explain why you want to murder me.'

Explanation was beyond Dickson, but his conviction was being woefully shaken. Saskia had said her enemy was as beautiful as a devil – he remembered the phrase, for he had thought it ridiculous. This man was magnificent, but there was nothing devilish in his lean grave face.

'What's your name?' the voice was asking.

'Tell me yours first,' Dickson essayed to stutter between spasms of nausea.

'My name is Alexander Nicholson,' was the answer.

'Then you're no' the man.' It was a cry of wrath and despair.

'You're a very desperate little chap. For whom had I the honour to be mistaken?'

Dickson had now wriggled into a sitting position and had clasped his hands above his aching head.

'I thought you were a Russian, name of Paul,' he groaned.

'Paul! Paul who?'

'Just Paul. A Bolshevik and an awful bad lot.'

Dickson could not see the change which his words wrought in the other's face. He found himself picked up in strong arms and carried to a bog-pool where his battered face was carefully washed, his throbbing brows laved, and a wet handkerchief bound over them. Then he was given brandy in the socket of a flask, which eased his nausea. The cyclist ran his bicycle to the roadside, and found a seat for Dickson behind the turf-dyke of the old bucht.

'Now you are going to tell me everything,' he said. 'If the Paul who is your enemy is the Paul I think him, then we are allies.'

But Dickson did not need this assurance. His mind had suddenly received a revelation. The Princess had expected an enemy, but also a friend. Might not this be the long-awaited friend, for whose sake she was rooted to Huntingtower with all its terrors?

'Are you sure your name's no' Alexis?' he asked.

'In my own country I was called Alexis Nicolaevitch, for I am a Russian. But for some years I have made my home with your folk, and I call myself Alexander Nicholson, which is the English form. Who told you about Alexis?'

'Give me your hand,' said Dickson shamefacedly. 'Man, she's been looking for you for weeks. You're terribly behind the fair.'

'She!' he cried. 'For God's sake, tell me what you mean.'

'Ay, she – the Princess. But what are we havering here for? I tell you at this moment she's somewhere down about the old Tower, and there's boat-loads of blagyirds landing from the sea. Help me up, man, for I must be off. The story will keep. Losh, it's very near the darkening. If you're Alexis, you're just about in time for a battle.'

But Dickson on his feet was but a frail creature. He was still deplorably giddy, and his legs showed an unpleasing tendency to crumple. 'I'm fair done,' he moaned. 'You see, I've been tied up all day to a tree and had two sore bashes on my head. Get you on that bicycle and hurry on, and I'll hirple after you the best I can. I'll direct you the road, and if you're lucky you'll find a Die-Hard about the village. Away with you, man, and never mind me.'

'We go together,' said the other quietly. 'You can sit behind me and hang on to my waist. Before you turned up I had pretty well got the thing in order.'

Dickson in a fever of impatience sat by while the Russian put the finishing touches to the machine, and as well as his anxiety allowed put him in possession of the main facts of the story. He told of how he and Heritage had come to Dalquharter, of the first meeting with Saskia, of the trip to Glasgow with the jewels, of the exposure of Loudon the factor, of last night's doings in the House, and of the journey that morning to the Mains of Garple. He sketched the figures on the scene – Heritage and Sir Archie, Dobson and his gang, the Gorbals Die-Hards. He told of the enemy's plans so far as he knew them.

'Looked at from a business point of view,' he said, 'the situation's like this. There's Heritage in the Tower, with Dobson, Léon, and Spidel sitting round him. Somewhere about the place there's the Princess and Sir Archibald and three men with guns from the Mains. Dougal and his five laddies are running loose in the policies. And there's four tinklers and God knows how many foreign ruffians pushing up from the Garplefoot, and a brig lying waiting to carry off the ladies. Likewise there's the police, somewhere on the road, though the dear kens when they'll turn up. It's awful the incompetence of our Government, and the rates and taxes that high! . . . And there's you and me by this roadside, and me no more use than a tattie-bogle . . . That's the situation, and the question is what's our plan to be? We must keep the blagyirds in play till the police come, and at the same time we must keep the Princess out of danger. That's why I'm wanting back, for they've sore need of a business head. Yon Sir Archibald's a fine fellow, but I doubt he'll be a bit rash, and the Princess is no' to hold or bind. Our first job is to find Dougal and get a grip of the facts.'

'I am going to the Princess,' said the Russian.

'Ay, that'll be best. You'll be maybe able to manage her, for you'll be well acquaint.'

'She is my kinswoman. She is also my affianced wife.'

'Keep us!' Dickson exclaimed, with a doleful thought of Heritage. 'What ailed you then no' to look after her better?'

'We have been long separated, because it was her will. She had work to do and disappeared from me, though I searched all Europe for her. Then she sent me word, when the danger became extreme, and summoned me to her aid. But she gave me poor directions, for she did not know her own plans very clearly. She spoke of a place called Darkwater, and I have been hunting half Scotland for it. It was only last night that I heard of Dalquharter and guessed that that might be the name. But I was far down in Galloway, and have ridden fifty miles today.'

'It's a queer thing, but I wouldn't take you for a Russian.'

Alexis finished his work and put away his tools. 'For the present,' he said, 'I am an Englishman, till my country comes again to her senses. Ten years ago I left Russia, for I was sick of the foolishness of my class and wanted a free life in a new world. I went to Australia and made good as an engineer. I am a partner in a firm which is pretty well known even in Britain. When war broke out I returned to fight for my people, and when Russia fell out of the war, I joined the Australians in France and fought with them till the Armistice. And now I have only one duty left, to save the Princess and take her with me to my new home till Russia is a nation once more.'

Dickson whistled joyfully. 'So Mr Heritage was right. He aye said you were an Australian ... And you're a business man! That's grand hearing and puts my mind at rest. You must take charge of the party at the House, for Sir Archibald's a daft young lad and Mr Heritage is a poet. I thought I would have to go myself, but I doubt I would just be a hindrance with my dwaibly legs. I'd be better outside, watching for the police ... Are you ready, sir?'

Dickson not without difficulty perched himself astride the luggage carrier, firmly grasping the rider round the middle. The machine started, but it was evidently in a bad way, for it made poor going till the descent towards the main Auchenlochan road. On the slope it warmed up and they crossed the Garple bridge at a fair pace. There was to be no pleasant April twilight, for the stormy sky had already made dusk, and in a very little the dark would fall. So sombre was the evening that Dickson did not notice a figure in the shadow of the roadside pines till it whistled shrilly on its fingers. He cried on Alexis to stop, and, this being accomplished with some suddenness, fell off at Dougal's feet.

'What's the news?' he demanded.

Dougal glanced at Alexis and seemed to approve his looks.

'Napoleon has just reported that three boat-loads, making either twenty-three or twenty-four men – they were gey ill to count – has landed at Garplefit and is makin' their way to the auld Tower. The tinklers warned Dobson and soon it'll be a' bye wi' Heritage.'

'The Princess is not there?' was Dickson's anxious inquiry.

'Na, na. Heritage is there his lone. They were for joinin' him, but I wouldn't let them. She came wi' a man they call Sir Erchibald and three gemkeepers wi' guns. I stoppit their cawr up the road and tell't them the lie o' the land. Yon Sir Erchibald has poor notions o' strawtegy. He was for bangin' into the auld Tower straight away and shootin' Dobson if he tried to stop them. "Havers," say I, "let them break their teeth on the Tower, thinkin' the leddy's inside, and that'll give us time, for Heritage is no' the lad to surrender in a hurry." '

'Where are they now?'

'In the Hoose o' Dalquharter, and a sore job I had gettin' them in. We've shifted our base again, without the enemy suspectin'.'

'Any word of the police?'

'The polis!' and Dougal spat cynically. 'It seems they're a dour crop to shift. Sir Erchibald was sayin' that him and the lassie had been to the Chief Constable, but the man was terrible auld and slow. They persuadit him, but he threepit that it would take a long time to collect his men and that there was no danger o' the brig landin' afore night. He's wrong there onyway, for they're landit.'

'Dougal,' said Dickson, 'you've heard the Princess speak of a friend she was expecting here called Alexis. This is him. You can address him as Mr Nicholson. Just arrived in the nick of time. You must get him into the House, for he's the best right to be beside the lady . . . Jaikie would tell you that I've been sore mishandled the day, and am no' very fit for a battle. But Mr Nicholson's a business man and he'll do as well. You're keeping the Die-Hards outside, I hope?'

'Ay. Thomas Yownie's in charge, and Jaikie will be in and out with orders. They've instructions to watch for the polis, and keep an eye on the Garplefit. It'a a mortal long front to hold, but there's no other way. I must be in the Hoose mysel'. Thomas Yownie's headquarters is the auld wife's hen-hoose.'

At that moment in a pause of the gale came the far-borne echo of a shot.

'Pistol,' said Alexis.

'Heritage,' said Dougal. 'Trade will be gettin' brisk with him. Start your machine and I'll hang on ahint. We'll try the road by the West Lodge.'

Presently the pair disappeared in the dusk, the noise of the engine was swallowed up in the wild orchestra of the wind, and Dickson hobbled towards the village in a state of excitement which made him oblivious of his wounds. That lonely pistol shot was, he felt, the bell to ring up the curtain on the last act of the play.

THIRTEEN

The Coming of the Danish Brig

MR JOHN HERITAGE, solitary in the old Tower, found much to occupy his mind. His giddiness was passing, though the dregs of a headache remained, and his spirits rose with his responsibilities. At daybreak he breakfasted out of the Mearns Street provision box, and made tea in one of the Die-Hards' camp kettles. Next he gave some attention to his toilet, necessary after the rough-and-tumble of the night. He made shift to bathe in icy water from the Tower well, shaved, tidied up his clothes, and found a clean shirt from his pack. He carefully brushed his hair, reminding himself that thus had the Spartans done before Thermopylae. The neat and somewhat pallid young man that emerged from these rites then ascended to the first floor to reconnoitre the landscape from the narrow unglazed windows.

If any one had told him a week ago that he would be in so strange a world he would have quarrelled violently with his informant. A week ago he was a cynical clear-sighted modern, a contemner of illusions, a swallower of formulas, a breaker of shams – one who had seen through the heroical and found it silly. Romance and such-like toys were playthings for fatted middle-age, not for strenuous and cold-eyed youth. But the truth was that now he was altogether spellbound by these toys. To think that he was serving his lady was rapture – ecstasy, that for her he was single-handed venturing all. He rejoiced to be alone with his private fancies. His one fear was that the part he had cast himself for might be needless, that the men from the sea would not come, or that reinforcements would arrive before he should be called upon. He hoped alone to make a stand against thousands. What the upshot might be he did not trouble to inquire. Of course the Princess would be saved, but first he must glut his appetite for the heroic.

He made a diary of events that day, just as he used to do at the front. At twenty minutes past eight he saw the first figure coming from the House. It was Spidel, who limped round the Tower, tried the door, and came to a halt below the window. Heritage stuck out his head and wished him good morning, getting in reply an amazed stare. The man was not disposed to talk, though Heritage made some interesting observations on the weather, but departed quicker than he came, in the direction of the West Lodge.

Just before nine o'clock he returned with Dobson and Léon. They made a very complete reconnaissance of the Tower, and for a moment Heritage thought that they were about to try to force an entrance. They tugged and hammered at the great oak door, which he had further strengthened by erecting behind it a pile of the heaviest lumber he could find in the place. It was imperative that they should not get in, and he got Dickson's pistol ready with the firm intention of shooting them if necessary. But they did nothing, except to hold a conference in the hazel clump a hundred yards to the north, when Dobson seemed to be laying down the law, and Léon spoke rapidly with a great fluttering of hands. They were obviously puzzled by the sight of Heritage, whom they believed to have left the neighbourhood. Then Dobson went off, leaving Léon and Spidel on guard, one at the edge of the shrubberies between the Tower and the House, the other on the side nearest the Laver glen. These were their posts, but they did sentry-go around the building, and passed so close to Heritage's window that he could have tossed a cigarette on their heads.

It occurred to him that he ought to get busy with camouflage. They must be convinced that the Princess was in the place, for he wanted their whole mind to be devoted to the siege. He rummaged among the ladies' baggage, and extracted a skirt and a coloured scarf. The latter he managed to flutter so that it could be seen at the window the next time one of the watchers came within sight. He also fixed up the skirt so that the fringe of it could be seen, and, when Léon appeared below, he was in the shadow talking rapid French in a very fair imitation of the tones of Cousin Eugénie. The ruse had its effect, for Léon promptly went off to tell Spidel, and when Dobson appeared he too was given the news. This seemed to settle their plans, for all three remained on guard, Dobson nearest to the Tower, seated on an outcrop of rock with his mackintosh collar turned up, and his eyes usually on the misty sea.

By this time it was eleven o'clock, and the next three hours passed slowly with Heritage. He fell to picturing the fortunes of his friends. Dickson and the Princess should by this time be far inland, out of danger and in the way of finding succour. He was confident that they would return, but he trusted not too soon, for he hoped for a run for his money as Horatius on the bridge. After that he was a little torn in his mind. He wanted the Princess to come back and to be somewhere near if there was a fight going, so that she might be a witness of his devotion. But she must not herself run any risk, and he became anxious when he remembered her terrible *sang-froid*. Dickson could no more restrain her than a child could hold a greyhound . . . But of course it would never come to that. The police would turn up long before the brig appeared – Dougal had thought that would not be till high tide, between four and five – and the only danger would be to the pirates. The three watchers would be put in the bag, and the men from the sea would walk into a neat trap. This reflexion seemed to take all the colour out of Heritage's prospect. Peril and heroism were not to be his lot – only boredom.

A little after twelve two of the tinklers appeared with some news which made Dobson laugh and pat them on the shoulder. He seemed to be giving them directions, pointing seaward and southward. He nodded to the Tower, where Heritage took the opportunity of again fluttering Saskia's scarf athwart the window. The tinklers departed at a trot, and Dobson lit his pipe as if well pleased. He had some trouble with it in the wind, which had risen to an uncanny violence. Even the solid Tower rocked with it, and the sea was a waste of spindrift and low scurrying cloud. Heritage discovered a new anxiety – this time about the possibility of the brig landing at all. He wanted a complete bag, and it would be tragic if they got only the three seedy ruffians now circumambulating his fortress.

About one o'clock he was greatly cheered by the sight of Dougal. At the moment Dobson was lunching off a hunk of bread and cheese directly between the Tower and the House, just short of the crest of the ridge on the other side of which lay the stables and the shrubberies; Léon was on the north side opposite the Tower door, and Spidel was at the south end near the edge of the Garple glen. Heritage, watching the ridge behind Dobson and the upper windows of the House which appeared over it, saw on the very crest something like a tuft of rusty bracken which he had not noticed before. Presently the tuft moved, and a hand shot up from it waving a rag of some sort. Dobson at the moment was engaged with a bottle of porter, and Heritage could safely wave a hand in reply. He could now make out clearly the red head of Dougal.

The Chieftain, having located the three watchers, proceeded to give an exhibition of his prowess for the benefit of the lonely inmate of the Tower. Using as cover a drift of bracken, he wormed his way down till he was not six yards from Dobson, and Heritage had the privilege of seeing his grinning countenance a very little way above the innkeeper's head. Then he crawled back and reached the neighbourhood of Léon, who was sitting on a fallen Scotch fir. At that moment it occurred to the Belgian to visit Dobson. Heritage's breath stopped, but Dougal was ready, and froze into a motionless blur in the shadow of a hazel bush. Then he crawled very fast into the hollow where Léon had been sitting, seized something which looked like a bottle, and scrambled back to the ridge. At the top he waved the object, whatever it was, but Heritage could not reply, for Dobson happened to be looking towards the window. That was the last he saw of the Chieftain, but presently he realized what was the booty he had annexed. It must be Léon's life-preserver, which the night before had broken Heritage's head.

After that cheering episode boredom again set in. He collected some food from the Mearns Street box, and indulged himself with a glass of liqueur brandy. He was beginning to feel miserably cold, so he carried up some broken wood and made a fire on the immense hearth in the upper chamber. Anxiety was clouding his mind again, for it was now two o'clock, and there was no sign of the reinforcements which Dickson and the Princess had gone to find. The minutes passed, and soon it was three o'clock, and from the window he saw only the top of the gaunt shuttered House, now and then hidden by squalls of sleet, and Dobson squatted like an Eskimo, and trees dancing like a witch-wood in the gale. All the vigour of the morning seemed to have gone out of his blood; he felt lonely and apprehensive and puzzled. He wished he had Dickson beside him, for that little man's cheerful voice and complacent triviality would be a comfort ... Also, he was abominably cold. He put on his waterproof, and turned his attention to the fire. It needed re-kindling, and he hunted in his pockets for paper, finding only the slim volume lettered *Whorls*.

I set it down as the most significant commentary on his state of mind. He regarded the book with intense disfavour, tore it in two, and used a handful of its fine deckle-edged leaves to get the fire going. They burned well, and presently the rest followed. Well for Dickson's peace of soul that he was not a witness of such vandalism.

A little warmer but in no way more cheerful, he resumed his watch near the window. The day was getting darker, and promised an early dusk. His watch told him that it was after four, and still nothing had happened. Where on earth were Dickson and the Princess? Where in the name of all that was holy were the police? Any minute now the brig might arrive and land its men, and he would be left there as a burnt-offering to their wrath. There must have been an infernal muddle somewhere ... Anyhow the Princess was out of the trouble, but where the Lord alone knew . . . Perhaps the reinforcements were lying in wait for the boats at the Garplefoot. That struck him as a likely explanation, and comforted him. Very soon he might hear the sound of an engagement to the south, and the next thing would be Dobson and his crew in flight. He was determined to be in the show somehow and would be very close on their heels. He felt a peculiar dislike to all three, but especially to Léon. The Belgian's small baby features had for four days set him clenching his fists when he thought of them.

The next thing he saw was one of the tinklers running hard towards the Tower. He cried something to Dobson, which Heritage could not catch, but which woke the latter to activity. The innkeeper shouted to Léon and Spidel, and the tinkler was excitedly questioned. Dobson laughed and slapped his thigh. He gave orders to the others, and himself joined the tinkler and hurried off in the direction of the Garplefoot. Something was happening there, something of ill omen, for the man's face and manner had been triumphant. Were the boats landing?

As Heritage puzzled over this event, another figure appeared on the scene. It was a big man in knickerbockers and mackintosh, who came round the end of the House from the direction of the South Lodge. At first he thought it was the advance-guard from his own side, the help which Dickson had gone to find, and he only restrained himself in time from shouting a welcome. But surely their supports would not advance so confidently in enemy country. The man strode over the slopes as if looking for somebody; then he caught sight of Léon and waved him to come. Léon must have known him, for he hastened to obey.

The two were about thirty yards from Heritage's window. Léon was telling some story volubly, pointing now to the Tower and now towards the sea. The big man nodded as if satisfied. Heritage noted that his right arm was tied up, and that the mackintosh sleeve was empty, and that brought him enlightenment. It was Loudon the factor, whom Dickson had winged the night before. The two of them passed out of view in the direction of Spidel.

The sight awoke Heritage to the supreme unpleasantness of his position. He was utterly alone on the headland, and his allies had vanished into space, while the enemy plans, moving like clockwork, were approaching their consummation. For a second he thought of leaving the Tower and hiding somewhere in the cliffs. He dismissed the notion unwillingly, for he remembered the task that had been set him. He was there to hold the fort to the last – to gain time, though he could not for the life of him see what use time was to be when all the strategy of his own side seemed to have miscarried. Anyhow, the blackguards would be sold, for they would not find the Princess. But he felt a horrid void in the pit of his stomach and a looseness about his knees.

The moments passed more quickly as he wrestled with his fears. The next he knew the empty space below his window was filling with figures. There was a great crowd of them, rough fellows with seamen's coats, still dripping as if they had had a wet landing. Dobson was with them, but for the rest they were strange figures.

Now that the expected had come at last Heritage's nerves grew calmer. He made out that the newcomers were trying the door, and he waited to hear it fall, for such a mob could soon force it. But instead a voice called from beneath.

'Will you please open to us?' it said.

He stuck his head out and saw a little group with one man at the head of it, a young man clad in oilskins whose face was dim in the murky evening. The voice was that of a gentleman.

'I have orders to open to no one,' Heritage replied.

'Then I fear we must force an entrance,' said the voice.

'You can go to the devil,' said Heritage.

That defiance was the screw which his nerves needed. His temper had risen, he had forgotten all about the Princess, he did not even remember his isolation. His job was to make a fight for it. He ran up the staircase which led to the attics of the Tower, for he recollected that there was a window there which looked over the space before the door. The place was ruinous, the floor filled with holes, and a part of the roof sagged down in a corner. The stones around the window were loose and crumbling, and he managed to pull several out so that the slit was enlarged. He found himself looking down on a crowd of men, who had lifted the fallen tree on which Léon had perched, and were about to use it as a battering ram.

'The first fellow who comes within six yards of the door I shoot,' he shouted.

There was a white wave below as every face was turned to him. He ducked back his head in time as a bullet chipped the side of the window.

But his position was a good one, for he had a hole in the broken wall through which he could see, and could shoot with his hand at the edge of the window while keeping his body in cover. The battering party resumed their task, and as the tree swung nearer, he fired at the foremost of them. He missed, but the shot for a moment suspended operations.

Again they came on, and again he fired. This time he damaged somebody, for the trunk was dropped.

A voice gave orders, a sharp authoritative voice. The battering squad dissolved, and there was a general withdrawal out of the line of fire from the window. Was it possible that he had intimidated them? He could hear the sound of voices, and then a single figure came into sight again, holding something in its hand.

He did not fire for he recognized the futility of his efforts. The baseball swing of the figure below could not be mistaken. There was a roar beneath, and a flash of fire, as the bomb exploded on the door. Then came a rush of men, and the Tower had fallen.

Heritage clambered through a hole in the roof and gained the topmost parapet. He had still a pocketful of cartridges, and there in a coign of the old battlements he would prove an ugly customer to the pursuit. Only one at a time could reach that siege perilous . . . They would not take long to search the lower rooms, and then would be hot on the trail of the man who had

fooled them. He had not a scrap of fear left or even of anger –
only triumph at the thought of how properly those ruffians had
been sold. 'Like schoolboys they who unaware' – instead of two
women they had found a man with a gun. And the Princess was
miles off and forever beyond their reach. When they had settled
with him they would no doubt burn the House down, but that
would serve them little. From his airy pinnacle he could see the
whole sea-front of Huntingtower, a blur in the dusk but for the
ghostly eyes of its white-shuttered windows.

Something was coming from it, running lightly over the
lawns, lost for an instant in the trees, and then appearing clear
on the crest of the ridge where some hours earlier Dougal had
lain. With horror he saw that it was a girl. She stood with the
wind plucking at her skirts and hair, and she cried in a high,
clear voice which pierced even the confusion of the gale. What
she cried he could not tell, for it was in a strange tongue . . .

But it reached the besiegers. There was a sudden silence in
the din below him and then a confusion of shouting. The men
seemed to be pouring out of the gap which had been the
doorway, and as he peered over the parapet first one and then
another entered his area of vision. The girl on the ridge, as soon
as she saw that she had attracted attention, turned and ran back,
and after her up the slopes went the pursuit bunched like
hounds on a good scent.

Mr John Heritage, swearing terribly, started to retrace his
steps.

FOURTEEN

The Second Battle of the Cruives

THE military historian must often make shift to write of battles with slender data, but he can pad out his deficiencies by learned parallels. If his were the talented pen describing this, the latest action fought on British soil against a foreign foe, he would no doubt be crippled by the absence of written orders and war diaries. But how eloquently he would descant on the resemblance between Dougal and Gouraud – how the plan of leaving the enemy to waste his strength upon a deserted position was that which on the 15th of July 1918 the French general had used with decisive effect in Champagne! But Dougal had never heard of Gouraud, and I cannot claim that, like the Happy Warrior, he

> through the heat of conflict kept the law
> In calmness made, and saw what he foresaw.

I have had the benefit of discussing the affair with him and his colleagues, but I should offend against historic truth if I represented the main action as anything but a scrimmage – a 'soldiers' battle', the historian would say, a Malplaquet, an Albuera.

Just after half-past three that afternoon the Commander-in-Chief was revealed in a very bad temper. He had intercepted Sir Archie's car, and, since Léon, was known to be fully occupied, had brought it in by the West Lodge, and hidden it behind a clump of laurels. There he had held a hoarse council of war. He had cast an appraising eye over Sime the butler, Carfrae the chauffeur, and McGuffog the gamekeeper, and his brows had lightened when he beheld Sir Archie with an armful of guns and two big cartridge-magazines. But they had darkened again at the first words of the leader of the reinforcements.

'Now for the Tower,' Sir Archie had observed cheerfully. 'We should be a match for the three watchers, my lad, and it's time that poor devil What's-his-name was relieved.'

'A bonny-like plan that would be,' said Dougal. 'Man, ye would be walkin' into the very trap they want. In an hour, or maybe two, the rest will turn up from the sea and they'd have ye tight by the neck. Na, na! It's time we're wantin', and the longer they think we're a' in the auld Tower the better for us. What news o' the polis?'

He listened to Sir Archie's report with a gloomy face.

'Not afore the darkenin'? They'll be ower late – the polis are aye ower late. It looks as if we had the job to do oursels. What's *your* notion?'

'God knows,' said the baronet, whose eyes were on Saskia. 'What's yours?'

The deference conciliated Dougal. 'There's just the one plan that's worth a docken. There's five o' us here, and there's plenty weapons. Besides there's five Die-Hards somewhere about, and though they've never tried it afore they can be trusted to loose off a gun. My advice is to hide at the Garplefoot and stop the boats landin'. We'd have the tinklers on our flank, no doubt, but I'm not muckle feared o' them. It wouldn't be easy for the boats to get in wi' this tearing' wind and us firin' volleys from the shore.'

Sir Archie stared at him with admiration. 'You're a hearty young fire-eater. But, Great Scott! we can't go pottin' at strangers before we find out their business. This is a lawabidin' country, and we're not entitled to start shootin' except in self-defence. You can wash that plan out, for it ain't feasible.'

Dougal spat cynically. 'For all that it's the right strawtegy. Man, we might sink the lot, and then turn and settle wi' Dobson, and all afore the first polisman showed his neb. It would be a grand performance. But I was feared ye wouldn't be for it ... Well, there's just the one other thing to do. We must get inside the Hoose and put it in a state of defence. Heritage has McCunn's pistol, and he'll keep them busy for a bit. When they've finished wi' him and find the place is empty, they'll try the Hoose and we'll give them a warm reception. That should keep us goin' till the polis arrive, unless they're comin' wi' the blind carrier.'

Sir Archie nodded. 'But why put ourselves in their power at all? They're at present barking up the wrong tree. Let them bark up another wrong 'un. Why shouldn't the House remain empty? I take it we're here to protect the Princess. Well, we'll have done that if they go off empty-handed.'

Dougal looked up to the heavens. 'I wish McCunn was here,' he sighed. 'Ay, we've got to protect the Princess, and there's just the one way to do it, and that's to put an end to this crowd o' blagyirds. If they gang empty-handed, they'll come again another day, either here or somewhere else, and it won't be long afore they get the lassie. But if we finish with them now she can sit down wi' an easy mind. That's why we've got to hang on to them till the polis comes. There's no way out o' this business but a battle.'

He found an ally. 'Dougal is right,' said Saskia. 'If I am to have peace, by some way or other the fangs of my enemies must be drawn for ever.'

He swung round and addressed her formally. 'Mem, I'm askin' ye for the last time. Will ye keep out of this business? Will ye gang back and sit doun aside Mrs Morran's fire and have your tea and wait till we come for ye. Ye can do no good, and ye're puttin' yourself terrible in the enemy's power. If we're beat and ye're no' there, they get very little satisfaction, but if they get *you* they get what they've come seekin'. I tell ye straight – ye're an encumbrance.'

She laughed mischievously. 'I can shoot better than you,' she said.

He ignored the taunt. 'Will ye listen to sense and fall to the rear?'

'I will not,' she said.

'Then gang your own gait. I'm ower wise to argy-bargy wi' women. The Hoose be it!'

It was a journey which sorely tried Dougal's temper. The only way in was by the veranda, but the door at the west end had been locked, and the ladder had disappeared. Now, of his party three were lame, one lacked an arm, and one was a girl; besides, there were the guns and cartridges to transport. Moreover, at more than one point before the veranda was reached the route was commanded by a point on the ridge near the old Tower, and that had been Spidel's position when Dougal made his last reconnaissance. It behoved to pass these points swiftly and unobtrusively, and his company was neither swift nor unobtrusive. McGuffog had a genius for tripping over obstacles, and Sir Archie was for ever proffering his aid to Saskia, who was in a position to give rather than to receive, being far the most active of the party. Once Dougal had to take the gamekeeper's head and force it down, a performance which would have led to an immediate assault but for Sir Archie's presence. Nor did the latter escape. 'Will ye stop heedin' the lassie, and attend to your own job,' the Chieftain growled. 'Ye're makin' as much noise as a road-roller.'

Arrived at the foot of the veranda wall there remained the problem of the escalade. Dougal clambered up like a squirrel by the help of cracks in the stones, and he could be heard trying the handle of the door into the House. He was absent for about five minutes, and then his head peeped over the edge accompanied by the hooks of an iron ladder. 'From the boiler-house,' he informed them as they stood clear for the thing to drop. It proved to be little more than half the height of the wall.

Saskia ascended first, and had no difficulty in pulling herself over the parapet. Then came the guns and ammunition, and then the one-armed Sime, who turned out to be an athlete. But it was no easy matter getting up the last three. Sir Archie anathematized his frailties. 'Nice old crock to go tiger-shootin' with,' he told the Princess. 'But set me to something where my confounded leg don't get in the way, and I'm still pretty useful!'

Dougal, mopping his brow with the rag he called his handker-chief, observed sourly that he objected to going scouting with a herd of elephants.

Once indoors his spirits rose. The party from the Mains had brought several electric torches, and the one lamp was presently found and lit. 'We can't count on the polis,' Dougal announced, 'and when the foreigners is finished wi' the Tower they'll come on here. If no', we must make them. What is it the sodgers call it? Forcin' a battle? Now see here! There's the two roads into this place, the back door and the verandy, leavin' out the front door which is chained and lockit. They'll try those two roads first, and we must get them well barricaded in time. But mind, if there's a good few o' them, it'll be an easy job to batter in the front door or the windies, so we maun be ready for that.'

He told off a fatigue party – the Princess, Sir Archie, and McGuffog – to help in moving furniture to the several doors. Sime and Carfrae attended to the kitchen entrance, while he himself made a tour of the ground-floor windows. For half an hour the empty house was loud with strange sounds. McGuffog, who was a giant in strength, filled the passage at the veranda end with an assortment of furniture ranging from a grand piano to a vast mahogany sofa, while Saskia and Sir Archie pillaged the bedrooms and packed up the interstices with mattresses in lieu of sandbags. Dougal on his turn saw fit to approve their work.

'That'll fickle the blagyirds. Down at the kitchen door we've got a mangle, five wash-tubs, and the best part of a ton o' coal. It's the windies I'm anxious about, for they're ower big to fill up. But I've gotten tubs o' water below them and a lot o' wire-nettin' I fund in the cellar.'

Sir Archie morosely wiped his brow. 'I can't say I ever hated a job more,' he told Saskia. 'It seems pretty cool to march into somebody else's house and make free with his furniture. I hope to goodness our friends from the sea do turn up, or we'll look pretty foolish. Loudon will have a score against me he won't forget.'

'Ye're no' weakenin'?' asked Dougal fiercely.

'Not a bit. Only hopin' somebody hasn't made a mighty big mistake.'

'Ye needn't be feared for that. Now you listen to your instructions. We're terrible few for such a big place, but we maun make up for shortness o' numbers by extra mobility. The gemkeeper will keep the windy that looks on the verandy, and fell any man that gets through. You'll hold the verandy door, and the ither lame man – is't Carfrae ye call him? – will keep the back door. I've told the one-armed man, who has some kind of a head on him, that he maun keep on the move, watchin' to see if they try the front door or any o' the other windies. If they do, he takes his station there. D'ye follow?'

Sir Archie nodded gloomily.

'What is my post?' Saskia asked.

'I've appointed ye my Chief of Staff,' was the answer. 'Ye see we've no reserves. If this door's the dangerous bit, it maun be reinforced from elsewhere; and that'll want savage thinkin'. Ye'll have to be aye on the move, Mem, and keep me informed. If they break in at two bits, we're beat, and there'll be nothing for it but to retire to our last position. Ye ken the room ayont the hall where they keep the coats. That's our last trench, and at the worst we fall back there and stick it out. It has a strong door and a wee windy, so they'll no' be able to get in on our rear. We should be able to put up a good defence there, unless they fire the place over our heads . . . Now, we'd better give out the guns.'

'We don't want any shootin' if we can avoid it,' said Sir Archie, who found his distaste for Dougal growing, though he was under the spell of the one being there who knew precisely his own mind.

'Just what I was goin' to say. My instructions is, reserve your fire, and don't loose off till you have a man up against the end o' your barrel.'

'Good Lord, we'll get into a horrible row. The whole thing may be a mistake, and we'll be had up for wholesale homicide. No man shall fire unless I give the word.'

The Commander-in-Chief looked at him darkly. Some bitter retort was on his tongue, but he restrained himself.

'It appears,' he said, 'that ye think I'm doin' all this for fun. I'll no' argy wi' ye. There can be just the one general in a battle, but I'll give ye permission to say the word when to fire . . . Macgreegor!' he muttered, a strange expletive only used in moments of deep emotion. 'I'll wager ye'll be for sayin' the word afore I'd say it mysel'.'

He turned to the Princess. 'I hand over to you, till I am back, for I maun be off and see to the Die-Hards. I wish I could bring them in here, but I daren't lose my communications. I'll likely get in by the boiler-house skylight when I come back, but it might be as well to keep a road open here unless ye're actually attacked.'

Dougal clambered over the mattresses and the grand piano; a flicker of waning daylight appeared for a second as he squeezed through the door, and Sir Archie was left staring at the wrathful countenance of McGuffog. He laughed ruefully.

'I've been in about forty battles, and here's that little devil rather worried about my pluck and talkin' to me like a corps commander to a newly joined second-lieutenant. All the same he's a remarkable child, and we'd better behave as if we were in for a real shindy. What do you think, Princess?'

'I think we are in for what you call a shindy. I am in command, remember, I order you to serve out the guns.'

This was done, a shotgun and a hundred cartridges to each, while McGuffog, who was a marksman, was also given a sporting Mannlicher, and two other rifles, a .303 and a small-bore Holland, were kept in reserve in the hall. Sir Archie, free from Dougal's compelling presence, gave the gamekeeper peremptory orders not to shoot till he was bidden, and Carfrae at the kitchen door was warned to the same effect. The shuttered house, where the only light apart from the garden-room was the feeble spark of the electric torches, had the most disastrous effect upon his spirits. The gale which roared in the chimney and eddied among the rafters of the hall seemed an infernal commotion in a tomb.

'Let's go upstairs,' he told Saskia; 'there must be a view from the upper windows.'

'You can see the top of the old Tower, and part of the sea,' she said. 'I know it well, for it was my only amusement to look at it. On clear days, too, one could see high mountains far in the west.' His depression seemed to have affected her, for she spoke listlessly, unlike the vivid creature who had led the way in.

In a gaunt west-looking bedroom, the one in which Heritage and Dickson had camped the night before, they opened a fold of the shutters and looked out into a world of grey wrack and driving rain. The Tower roof showed mistily beyond the ridge of down, but its environs were not in their prospect. The lower regions of the House had been gloomy enough, but this bleak place with its drab outlook struck a chill to Sir Archie's soul. He dolefully lit a cigarette.

'This is a pretty rotten show for you,' he told her. 'It strikes me as a rather unpleasant brand of nightmare.'

'I have been living with nightmares for three years,' she said wearily.

He cast his eyes round the room. 'I think the Kennedys were mad to build this confounded barrack. I've always disliked it, and old Quentin hadn't any use for it either. Cold, cheerless, raw monstrosity! It hasn't been a very giddy place for you, Princess.'

'It has been my prison, when I hoped it would be a sanctuary. But it may yet be my salvation.'

'I'm sure I hope so. I say, you must be jolly hungry. I don't suppose there's any chance of tea for you.'

She shook her head. She was looking fixedly at the Tower, as if she expected something to appear there, and he followed her eyes.

'Rum old shell, that. Quentin used to keep all kinds of live stock there, and when we were boys it was our castle where we played at bein' robber chiefs. It'll be dashed queer if the real thing should turn up this time. I suppose McCunn's Poet is roostin' there all by his lone. Can't say I envy him his job.'

Suddenly she caught his arm. 'I see a man,' she whispered. 'There! He is behind those far bushes. There is his head again!'

It was clearly a man, but he presently disappeared, for he had come round by the south end of the House, past the stables, and had now gone over the ridge.

'The cut of his jib is uncommonly like Loudon, the factor. I thought McCunn had stretched him on a bed of pain. Lord, if this thing should turn out a farce, I simply can't face Loudon . . . I say, Princess, you don't suppose by any chance that McCunn's a little bit wrong in the head?'

She turned her candid eyes on him. 'You are in a very doubting mood.'

'My feet are cold and I don't mind admittin' it. Hanged if I know what it is, but I don't feel this show a bit real. If it isn't, we're in a fair way to make howlin' idiots of ourselves, and get pretty well embroiled with the law. It's all right for the red-haired boy, for he can take everything seriously, even play. I could do the same thing myself when I was a kid. I don't mind runnin' some kinds of risk – I've had a few in my time – but this is so infernally outlandish, and I – I don't quite believe in it. That is to say, I believe in it right enough when I look at you or listen to McCunn, but as soon as my eyes are off you I begin to doubt again. I'm gettin' old and I've a stake in the country, and I dare say I'm gettin' a bit of a prig – anyway I don't want to make a jackass of myself. Besides, there's this foul weather and this beastly house to ice my feet.'

He broke off with an exclamation, for on the grey cloud-bounded stage in which the roof of the Tower was the central feature, actors had appeared. Dim hurrying shapes showed through the mist, dipping over the ridge, as if coming from the Garplefoot.

She seized his arm and he saw that her listlessness was gone. Her eyes were shining.

'It is they,' she cried. 'The nightmare is real at last. Do you doubt now?'

He could only stare, for these shapes arriving and vanishing like wisps of fog still seemed to him phantasmal. The girl held his arm tightly clutched, and craned towards the window space.

He tried to open the frame, and succeeded in smashing the glass. A swirl of wind drove inwards and blew a loose lock of Saskia's hair across his brow.

'I wish Dougal were back,' he muttered, and then came the crack of a shot.

The pressure on his arm slackened, and a pale face was turned to him. 'He is alone – Mr Heritage. He has no chance. They will kill him like a dog.'

'They'll never get in,' he assured her. 'Dougal said the place could hold out for hours.'

Another shot followed and presently a third. She twined her hands and her eyes were wild.

'We can't leave him to be killed,' she gasped.

'It's the only game. We're playin' for time, remember. Besides, he won't be killed. Great Scott!'

As he spoke, a sudden explosion cleft the drone of the wind and a patch of gloom flashed into yellow light.

'Bomb!' he cried. 'Lord, I might have thought of that.'

The girl had sprung back from the window. 'I cannot bear it. I will not see him murdered in sight of his friends. I am going to show myself, and when they see me they will leave him . . . No, you must stay here. Presently they will be round this house. Don't be afraid for me – I am very quick of foot.'

'For God's sake, don't! Here, Princess, stop,' and he clutched at her skirt. 'Look here, I'll go.'

'You can't. You have been wounded. I am in command, you know. Keep the door open till I come back.'

He hobbled after her, but she easily eluded him. She was smiling now, and blew a kiss to him. 'La, la, la,' she trilled, as she ran down the stairs. He heard her voice below, admonishing McGuffog. Then he pulled himself together and went back to the window. He had brought the little Holland with him, and he poked its barrel through the hole in the glass.

'Curse my game leg,' he said, almost cheerfully, for the situation was now becoming one with which he could cope. 'I ought to be able to hold up the pursuit a bit. My aunt! What a girl!'

With the rifle cuddled to his shoulder he watched a slim figure come into sight on the lawn, running towards the ridge. He reflected that she must have dropped from the high veranda wall. That reminded him that something must be done to make the wall climbable for her return, so he went down to McGuffog, and the two squeezed through the barricaded door to the veranda. The boiler-house ladder was still in position, but it did not reach half the height, so McGuffog was adjured to stand by to help, and in the meantime to wait on duty by the wall. Then he hurried upstairs to his watch-tower.

The girl was in sight, almost on the crest of the high ground. There she stood for a moment, one hand clutching at her errant hair, the other shielding her eyes from the sting of the rain. He heard her cry, as Heritage had heard her, but since the wind was blowing towards him the sound came louder and fuller. Again she cried, and then stood motionless with her hands above her head. It was only for an instant, for the next he saw she had turned and was racing down the slope, jumping the little scrogs of hazel like a deer. On the ridge appeared faces, and then over it swept a mob of men.

She had a start of some fifty yards, and laboured to increase it, having doubtless the veranda wall in mind. Sir Archie, sick with anxiety, nevertheless spared time to admire her prowess. 'Gad! she's a miler,' he ejaculated. 'She'll do it. I'm hanged if she don't do it.'

Against men in seamen's boots and heavy clothing she had a clear advantage. But two shook themselves loose from the pack and began to gain on her. At the main shrubbery they were not thirty yards behind, and in her passage through it her skirts must have delayed her, for when she emerged the pursuit had halved the distance. He got the sights of the rifle on the first man, but the lawns sloped up towards the house, and to his consternation he found that the girl was in the line of fire. Madly he ran to the other window of the room, tore back the shutters, shivered the glass, and flung his rifle to his shoulder. The fellow was within three yards of her, but, thank God! he had now a clear field. He fired low and just ahead of him, and had the satisfaction to see him drop like a rabbit, shot in the leg. His companion stumbled over him, and for a moment the girl was safe.

But her speed was failing. She passed out of sight on the veranda side of the house, and the rest of the pack had gained ominously over the easier ground of the lawn. He thought for a moment of trying to stop them by his fire, but realized that if every shot told there would still be enough of them left to make sure of her capture. The only chance was at the veranda, and he went downstairs at a pace undreamed of since the days when he had two whole legs.

McGuffog, Mannlicher in hand, was poking his neck over the wall. The pursuit had turned the corner and were about twenty yards off; the girl was at the foot of the ladder, breathless, drooping with fatigue. She tried to climb, limply and feebly, and very slowly, as if she were too giddy to see clear. Above were two cripples, and at her back the van of the now triumphant pack.

Sir Archie, game leg or no, was on the parapet preparing to drop down and hold off the pursuit were it only for seconds. But at that moment he was aware that the situation had changed.

At the foot of the ladder a tall man seemed to have sprung out of the ground. He caught the girl in his arms, climbed the ladder, and McGuffog's great hands reached down and seized her and swung her into safety. Up the wall, by means of cracks and tufts, was shinning a small boy.

The stranger coolly faced the pursuers, and at the sight of him they checked, those behind stumbling against those in front. He was speaking to them in a foreign tongue, and to Sir Archie's ear the words were like the crack of a lash. The hesitation was only for a moment, for a voice among them cried out, and the whole pack gave tongue shrilly and surged on again. But that instant of check had given the stranger his chance. He was up the ladder, and, gripping the parapet, found rest for his feet in a fissure. Then he bent down, drew up the ladder, handed it to McGuffog, and with a mighty heave pulled himself over the top.

He seemed to hope to defend the veranda, but the door at the west end was being assailed by a contingent of the enemy, and he saw that its thin woodwork was yielding.

'Into the House,' he cried, as he picked up the ladder and tossed it over the wall on the pack surging below. He was only just in time, for the west door yielded. In two steps he had followed McGuffog through the chink into the passage, and the concussion of the grand piano pushed hard against the veranda door from within coincided with the first battering on the said door from without.

In the garden-room the feeble lamp showed a strange grouping. Saskia had sunk into a chair to get her breath, and seemed too dazed to be aware of her surroundings. Dougal was manfully striving to appear at his ease, but his lip was quivering.

'A near thing that time,' he observed. 'It was the blame of that man's auld motor-bicycle.'

The stranger cast sharp eyes around the place and company.

'An awkward corner, gentlemen,' he said. 'How many are there of you? Four men and a boy? And you have placed guards at all the entrances?'

'They have bombs,' Sir Archie reminded him.

'No doubt. But I do not think they will use them here – or their guns, unless there is no other way. Their purpose is kidnapping, and they hope to do it secretly and slip off without leaving a trace. If they slaughter us, as they easily can, the cry will be out against them, and their vessel will be unpleasantly hunted. Half their purpose is already spoiled, for it is no longer secret . . . They may break us by sheer weight, and I fancy the first shooting will be done by us. It's the windows I'm afraid of.'

Some tone in his quiet voice reached the girl in the wicker chair. She looked up wildly, saw him, and with a cry of 'Alesha' ran to his arms. There she hung, while his hand fondled her hair, like a mother with a scared child. Sir Archie, watching the whole thing in some stupefaction, thought he had never in his days seen more nobly matched human creatures.

'It is my friend,' she cried triumphantly, 'the friend whom I appointed to meet me here. Oh, I did well to trust him. Now we need not fear anything.'

As if in ironical answer came a great crashing at the veranda door, and the twanging of chords cruelly mishandled.

The grand piano was suffering internally from the assaults of the boiler-house ladder.

'Wull I gie them a shot?' was McGuffog's hoarse inquiry.

'Action stations,' Alexis ordered, for the command seemed to have shifted to him from Dougal. 'The windows are the danger. The boy will patrol the ground floor, and give us warning, and I and this man,' pointing to Sime, 'will be ready at the threatened point. And, for God's sake, no shooting, unless I give the word. If we take them on at that game we haven't a chance.'

He said something to Saskia in Russian and she smiled assent and went to Sir Archie's side. 'You and I must keep this door,' she said.

Sir Archie was never very clear afterwards about the events of the next hour. The Princess was in the maddest spirits, as if the burden of three years had slipped from her and she was back in her first girlhood. She sang as she carried more lumber to the pile – perhaps the song which had once entranced Heritage, but Sir Archie had no ear for music. She mocked at the furious blows which rained at the other end, for the door had gone now, and in the windy gap could be seen a blur of dark faces. Oddly enough, he found his own spirits mounting to meet hers. It was real business at last, the qualms of the civilian had been forgotten, and there was rising in him that joy in a scrap which had once made him one of the most daring airmen on the Western Front. The only thing that worried him now was the coyness about shooting. What on earth were his rifles and shotguns for unless to be used? He had seen the enemy from the veranda wall, and a more ruffianly crew he had never dreamed of. They meant the uttermost business, and against such it was surely the duty of good citizens to wage whole-hearted war.

The Princess was humming to herself a nursery rhyme.

'*The King of Spain's daughter,*' she crooned, '*came to visit me, and all for the sake* – Oh, that poor piano!' In her clear voice she cried something in Russian, and the wind carried a laugh from the veranda. At the sound of it she stopped. 'I had forgotten,' she said. 'Paul is there. I had forgotten.' After that she was very quiet, but she redoubled her labours at the barricade.

To the man it seemed that the pressure from without was slackening. He called to McGuffog to ask about the garden-room window, and the reply was reassuring. The gamekeeper was gloomily contemplating Dougal's tubs of water and wire-netting, as he might have contemplated a vermin trap.

Sir Archie was growing acutely anxious – the anxiety of the defender of a straggling fortress which is vulnerable at a dozen points. It seemed to him that strange noises were coming from the rooms beyond the hall. Did the back door lie that way? And was not there a smell of smoke in the air? If they tried fire in such a gale the place would burn like matchwood.

He left his post and in the hall found Dougal.

'All quiet,' the Chieftain reported. 'Far ower quiet. I don't like it. The enemy's no' puttin' out his strength yet. The Russian says a' the west windies are terrible dangerous. Him and the chauffeur's doin' their best, but ye can't block thae muckle glass panes.'

He returned to the Princess, and found that the attack had indeed languished on that particular barricade. The withers of the grand piano were left unwrung, and only a faint scuffling informed him that the veranda was not empty. 'They're gathering for an attack elsewhere,' he told himself. But what if that attack were a feint? He and McGuffog must stick to their post, for in his belief the veranda door and the garden-room window were the easiest places where an entry in mass could be forced.

Suddenly Dougal's whistle blew, and with it came a most almighty crash somewhere towards the west side. With a shout of 'Hold tight, McGuffog,' Sir Archie bolted into the hall, and, led by the sound, reached what had once been the ladies' bedroom. A strange sight met his eyes, for the whole framework of one window seemed to have been thrust inward, and in the gap Alexis was swinging a fender. Three of the enemy were in the room – one senseless on the floor, one in the grip of Sime, whose single hand was tightly clenched on his throat, and one engaged with Dougal in a corner. The Die-Hard leader was sore pressed, and to his help Sir Archie went. The fresh assault made the seaman duck his head, and Dougal seized the occasion to smite him hard with something which caused him to roll over. It was Léon's life-preserver which he had annexed that afternoon.

Alexis at the window seemed to have for a moment daunted the attack. 'Bring that table,' he cried, and the thing was jammed into the gap. 'Now you' – this to Sime – 'get the man from the back door to hold this place with his gun. There's no attack there. It's about time for shooting now, or we'll have them in our rear. What in heaven is that?'

It was McGuffog whose great bellow resounded down the corridor. Sir Archie turned and shuffled back, to be met by a distressing spectacle. The lamp, burning as peacefully as it might have burned on an old lady's tea-table, revealed the window of the garden-room driven bodily inward, shutters and all, and now forming an inclined bridge over Dougal's ineffectual tubs. In front of it stood McGuffog, swinging his gun by the barrel and yelling curses, which, being mainly couched in the vernacular, were happily meaningless to Saskia. She herself stood at the hall door, plucking at something hidden in her breast. He saw that it was a little ivory-handled pistol.

The enemy's feint had succeeded, for even as Sir Archie looked three men leaped into the room. On the neck of one the butt of McGuffog's gun crashed, but two scrambled to their feet and made for the girl. Sir Archie met the first with his fist, a clean drive on the jaw, followed by a damaging hook with his left that put him out of action. The other hesitated for an instant and was lost, for McGuffog caught him by the waist from behind and sent him through the broken frame to join his comrades without.

'Up the stairs,' Dougal was shouting, for the little room beyond the hall was clearly impossible. 'Our flank's turned. They're pourin' through the other windy.' Out of a corner of his eye Sir Archie caught sight of Alexis, with Sime and Carfrae in support, being slowly forced towards them along the corridor. 'Upstairs,' he shouted. 'Come on, McGuffog. Lead on, Princess.' He dashed out the lamp, and the place was in darkness.

With this retreat from the forward trench line ended the opening phase of the battle. It was achieved in good order, and position was taken up on the first floor landing, dominating the main staircase and the passage that led to the back stairs. At their back was a short corridor ending in a window which gave on the north side of the House above the veranda, and from which an active man might descend to the veranda roof. It had been carefully reconnoitred beforehand by Dougal, and his were the dispositions.

The odd thing was that the retreating force were in good heart. The three men from the Mains were warming to their work, and McGuffog wore an air of genial ferocity. 'Dashed fine position I call this,' said Sir Archie. Only Alexis was silent and preoccupied. 'We are still at their mercy,' he said. 'Pray God your police come soon.' He forbade shooting yet awhile. 'The lady is our strong card,' he said. 'They won't use their guns while she is with us, but if it ever comes to shooting they can wipe us out in a couple of minutes. One of you watch that window, for Paul Abreskov is no fool.'

Their exhilaration was short-lived. Below in the hall it was black darkness save for a greyness at the entrance of the veranda passage; but the defence was soon aware that the place was thick with men. Presently there came a scuffling from Carfrae's post towards the back stairs, and a cry as of someone choking. And at the same moment a flare was lit below which brought the whole hall from floor to rafters into blinding light.

It revealed a crowd of figures, some still in the hall and some half-way up the stairs, and it revealed, too, more figures at the end of the upper landing where Carfrae had been stationed. The shapes were motionless like mannequins in a shop window.

'They've got us treed all right,' Sir Archie groaned. 'What the devil are they waiting for?'

'They wait for their leader,' said Alexis.

No one of the party will ever forget the ensuing minutes. After the hubbub of the barricades the ominous silence was like icy water, chilling and petrifying with an indefinable fear. There was no sound but the wind, but presently mingled with it came odd wild voices.

'Hear to the whaups,' McGuffog whispered.

Sir Archie, who found the tension unbearable, sought relief in contradiction. 'You're an unscientific brute, McGuffog,' he told his henchman. 'It's a disgrace that a gamekeeper should be such a rotten naturalist. What would whaups be doin' on the shore at this time of year?'

'A' the same, I could swear it's whaups, Sir Erchibald.'

Then Dougal broke in and his voice was excited. 'It's no whaups. That's our patrol signal. Man, there's hope for us yet. I believe it's the polis.'

His words were unheeded, for the figures below drew apart and a young man came through them. His beautifully-shaped dark head was bare, and as he moved he unbuttoned his oilskins and showed the trim dark-blue garb of the yachtsman. He walked confidently up the stairs, an odd elegant figure among his heavy companions.

'Good afternoon, Alexis,' he said in English. 'I think we may now regard this interesting episode as closed. I take it that you surrender. Saskia, dear, you are coming with me on a little journey. Will you tell my men where to find your baggage?'

The reply was in Russian. Alexis' voice was as cool as the other's, and it seemed to wake him to anger. He replied in a rapid torrent of words, and appealed to the men below, who shouted back. The flare was dying down, and shadows again hid most of the hall.

Dougal crept up behind Sir Archie. 'Here, I think it's the polis. They're whistlin' outbye, and I hear folk cryin' to each other – no' the foreigners.'

Again Alexis spoke, and then Saskia joined in. What she said rang sharp with contempt, and her fingers played with her little pistol.

Suddenly, before the young man could answer, Dobson bustled towards him. The innkeeper was labouring under some strong emotion, for he seemed to be pleading and pointing urgently towards the door.

'I tell ye it's the polis,' whispered Dougal. 'They're nickit.'

There was a swaying in the crowd and anxious faces. Men surged in, whispered, and went out, and a clamour arose which the leader stilled with a fierce gesture.

'You there,' he cried, looking up, 'you English. We mean you no ill, but I require you to hand over to me the lady and the Russian who is with her. I give you a minute by my watch to decide. If you refuse, my men are behind you and around you, and you go with me to be punished at my leisure.'

'I warn you,' cried Sir Archie. 'We are armed, and will shoot down anyone who dares to lay a hand on us.'

'You fool,' came the answer. 'I can send you all to eternity before you touch a trigger.'

Léon was by his side now – Léon and Spidel, imploring him to do something which he angrily refused. Outside there was a new clamour, faces showing at the door and then vanishing, and an anxious hum filled the hall . . . Dobson appeared again and this time he was a figure of fury.

'Are ye daft, man?' he cried. 'I tell ye the polis are closin' round us, and there's no' a moment to lose if we would get back to the boats. If ye'll no' think o' your own neck, I'm thinkin' o' mine. The whole thing's a bloody misfire. Come on, lads, if ye're no besotted on destruction.'

Léon laid a hand on the leader's arm and was roughly shaken off. Spidel fared no better, and the little group on the upper landing saw the two shrug their shoulders and make for the door. The hall was emptying fast and the watchers had gone from the back stairs. The young man's voice rose to a scream; he commanded, threatened, cursed; but panic was in the air and he had lost his mastery.

'Quick,' croaked Dougal, 'now's the time for the counter-attack.'

But the figure on the stairs held them motionless. They could not see his face, but by instinct they knew that it was distraught with fury and defeat. The flare blazed up again as the flame caught a knot of fresh powder, and once more the place was bright with the uncanny light . . . The hall was empty save for the pale man who was in the act of turning.

He looked back. 'If I go now, I will return. The world is not wide enough to hide you from me, Saskia.'

'You will never get her,' said Alexis.

A sudden devil flamed into his eyes, the devil of some ancestral savagery, which would destroy what is desired but unattainable. He swung round, his hand went to his pocket, something clicked, and his arm shot out like a baseball pitcher's.

So intent was the gaze of the others on him, that they did not see a second figure ascending the stairs. Just as Alexis flung himself before the Princess, the newcomer caught the young man's outstretched arm and wrenched something from his hand. The next second he had hurled it into a far corner where stood the great fireplace. There was a blinding sheet of flame, a dull roar, and then billow upon billow of acrid smoke. As it cleared they saw that the fine Italian chimneypiece, the pride of the builder of the House, was a mass of splinters, and that a great hole had been blown through the wall into what had been the dining-room . . . A figure was sitting on the bottom step feeling its bruises. The last enemy had gone.

When Mr John Heritage raised his eyes he saw the Princess with a very pale face in the arms of a tall man whom he had never seen before. If he was surprised at the sight, he did not show it. 'Nasty little bomb that. I remember we struck the brand first in July '18.'

'Are they rounded up?' Sir Archie asked.

'They've bolted. Whether they'll get away is another matter. I left half the mounted police a minute ago at the top of the West Lodge avenue. The other lot went to the Garplefoot to cut off the boats.'

'Good Lord, man,' Sir Archie cried, 'the police have been here for the last ten minutes.'

'You're wrong. They came with me.'

'Then what on earth –' began the astonished baronet. He stopped short, for he suddenly got his answer. Into the hall from the veranda limped a boy. Never was there seen so ruinous a child. He was dripping wet, his shirt was all but torn off his back, his bleeding nose was poorly staunched by a wisp of hand-kerchief, his breeches were in ribbons, and his poor bare legs looked as if they had been comprehensively kicked and scratched. Limpingly he entered, yet with a kind of pride, like some small cock-sparrow who has lost most of his plumage but has vanquished his adversary.

With a yell Dougal went down the stairs. The boy saluted him, and they gravely shook hands. It was the meeting of Wellington and Blücher.

The Chieftain's voice shrilled in triumph, but there was a break in it. The glory was almost too great to be borne.

'I kenned it,' he cried. 'It was the Gorbals Die-Hards. There stands the man that done it . . . Ye'll no' fickle Thomas Yownie.'

FIFTEEN

The Gorbals Die-Hards Go into Action

WE left Mr McCunn, full of aches but desperately resolute in spirit, hobbling by the Auchenlochan road into the village of Dalquharter. His goal was Mrs Morran's hen-house, which was Thomas Yownie's *poste de commandement*. The rain had come on again, and, though in other weather there would have been a slow twilight, already the shadow of night had the world in its grip. The sea even from the high ground was invisible, and all to westward and windward was a ragged screen of dark cloud. It was foul weather for foul deeds.

Thomas Yownie was not in the hen-house, but in Mrs Morran's kitchen, and with him were the pug-faced boy known as Old Bill, and the sturdy figure of Peter Paterson. But the floor was held by the hostess. She still wore her big boots, her petti-coats were still kilted, and round her venerable head in lieu of a bonnet was drawn a tartan shawl.

'Eh, Dickson, but I'm blithe to see ye. And, puir man, ye've been sair mishandled. This is the awfu'est Sabbath day that ever you and me pit in. I hope it'll be forgiven us . . . Whaur's the young leddy?'

'Dougal was saying she was in the House with Sir Archibald and the men from the Mains.'

'Wae's me!' Mrs Morran keened. 'And what kind o' place is yon for her? Thae laddies tell me there's boatfu's o' scoondrels landit at the Garplefit. They'll try the auld Tower, but they'll no' wait there when they find it toom, and they'll be inside the Hoose in a jiffy and awa' wi' the puir lassie. Sirs, it maunna be. Ye're lippenin' to the polis, but in a' my days I never kenned the polis in time. We maun be up and daein' oorsels. Oh, if I could get a haud o' that red-heided Dougal . . .'

As she spoke there came on the wind the dull reverberation of an explosion.

'Keep us, what's that?' she cried.

'It's dinnymite,' said Peter Paterson.

'That's the end o' the auld Tower,' observed Thomas Yownie in his quiet, even voice. 'And it's likely the end o' the man Heritage.'

'Lord peety us!' the old woman wailed. 'And us standin' here like stookies and no' liftin' a hand. Awa' wi ye, laddies, and dae something. Awa' you too, Dickson, or I'll tak' the road mysel'.'

'I've got orders,' said the Chief of Staff, 'no' to move till the sityation's clear. Napoleon's up at the Tower and Jaikie's in the policies. I maun wait on their reports.'

For a moment Mrs Morran's attention was distracted by Dickson, who suddenly felt very faint and sat down heavily on a kitchen chair. 'Man, ye're as white as a dish-clout,' she exclaimed with compunction. 'Ye're fair wore out, and ye'll have had nae meat sin' your breakfast. See, and I'll get ye a cup o' tea.'

She proved to be in the right, for as soon as Dickson had swallowed some mouthfuls of her strong scalding brew the colour came back to his cheeks, and he announced that he felt better. 'Ye'll fortify it wi' a dram,' she told him, and produced a black bottle from her cupboard. 'My father aye said that guid whisky and het tea keepit the doctor's gig oot o' the close.'

The back door opened and Napoleon entered, his thin shanks blue with cold. He saluted and made his report in a voice shrill with excitement.

'The Tower has fallen. They've blown in the big door, and the feck o' them's inside.'

'And Mr Heritage?' was Dickson's anxious inquiry.

'When I last saw him he was up at a windy, shootin'. I think he's gotten on to the roof. I wouldna wonder but the place is on fire.'

'Here, this is awful,' Dickson groaned. 'We can't let Mr Heritage be killed that way. What strength is the enemy?'

'I counted twenty-seven, and there's stragglers comin' up from the boats.'

'And there's me and you five laddies here, and Dougal and the others shut up in the House.' He stopped in sheer despair. It was a fix from which the most enlightened business mind showed no escape. Prudence, inventiveness, were no longer in question; only some desperate course of violence.

'We must create a diversion,' he said. 'I'm for the Tower, and you laddies must come with me. We'll maybe see a chance. Oh, but I wish I had my wee pistol.'

'If ye're gaun there, Dickson, I'm comin' wi' ye,' Mrs Morran announced.

Her words revealed to Dickson the preposterousness of the whole situation, and for all his anxiety he laughed. 'Five laddies, a middle-aged man, and an auld wife,' he cried. 'Dod, it's pretty hopeless. It's like the thing in the Bible about the weak things of the world trying to confound the strong.'

'The Bible's whiles richt,' Mrs Morran answered drily. 'Come on, for there's no time to lose.'

The door opened again to admit the figure of Wee Jaikie. There were no tears in his eyes, and his face was very white.

'They're a' round the Hoose,' he croaked. 'I was up a tree forenent the verandy and seen them. The lassie ran oot and cried on them from the top o' the brae, and they a' turned and hunted her back. Gosh, but it was a near thing. I seen the Captain sklimmin' the wall, and a muckle man took the lassie and flung her up the ladder. They got inside just in time and steekit the door, and now the whole pack is roarin' round the Hoose seekin' a road in. They'll no' be long over the job, neither.'

'What about Mr Heritage?'

'They're no' heedin' about him any more. The auld Tower's bleezin'.'

'Worse and worse,' said Dickson. 'If the police don't come in the next ten minutes, they'll be away with the Princess. They've beaten all Dougal's plans, and it's a straight fight with odds of six to one. It's not possible.'

Mrs Morran for the first time seemed to lose hope. 'Eh, the puir lassie!' she wailed, and sinking on a chair covered her face with her shawl.

'Laddies, can you no' think of a plan?' asked Dickson, his voice flat with despair.

Then Thomas Yownie spoke. So far he had been silent, but under his tangled thatch of hair his mind had been busy. Jaikie's report seemed to bring him to a decision.

'It's gey dark,' he said, 'and it's gettin' darker.'

There was that in his voice which promised something, and Dickson listened.

'The enemy's mostly foreigners, but Dobson's there and I think he's a kind of guide to them. Dobson's feared of the polis, and if we can terrify Dobson he'll terrify the rest.'

'Ay, but where are the police?'

'They're no' here yet, but they're comin'. The fear o' them is aye in Dobson's mind. If he thinks the polis has arrived, he'll put the wind up the lot . . . *We* maun be the polis.'

Dickson could only stare while the Chief of Staff unfolded his scheme. I do not know to whom the Muse of History will give the credit of the tactics of 'infiltration', whether to Ludendorff or von Hutier or some other proud captain of Germany, or to Foch, who revised and perfected them. But I know that the same notion was at this moment of crisis conceived by Thomas Yownie, whom no parents acknowledged, who slept usually in a coal cellar, and who had picked up his education among Gorbals closes and along the wharves of Clyde.

'It's gettin' dark,' he said, 'and the enemy are that busy tryin' to break into the Hoose that they'll no' be thinkin' o' their rear. The five o' us Die-Hards is grand at dodgin' and keepin' out of sight, and what hinders us to get in among them, so that they'll hear us but never see us. We're used to the ways o' the polis, and can imitate them fine. Forbye we've all got our whistles, which are the same as a bobbie's birl, and Old Bill and Peter are grand at copyin' a man's voice. Since the Captain is shut up in the Hoose, the command falls to me, and that's my plan.'

With a piece of chalk he drew on the kitchen floor a rough sketch of the environs of Huntingtower. Peter Paterson was to move from the shrubberies beyond the veranda, Napoleon from the stables, Old Bill from the Tower, while Wee Jaikie and Thomas himself were to advance as if from the Garplefoot, so that the enemy might fear for his communications. 'As soon as one o' ye gets into position he's to gie the patrol cry, and when each o' ye has heard five cries, he's to advance. Begin birlin' and roarin' afore ye get among them, and keep it up till ye're at the Hoose wall. If they've gotten inside, in ye go after them. I trust each Die-Hard to use his judgement, and above all to keep out o' sight and no let himsel' be grippit.'

The plan, like all great tactics, was simple, and no sooner was it expounded than it was put into action. The Die-Hards faded out of the kitchen like fog-wreaths, and Dickson and Mrs Morran were left looking at each other. They did not look long. The bare feet of Wee Jaikie had not crossed the threshold fifty seconds, before they were followed by Mrs Morran's out-of-doors boots and Dickson's tackets. Arm in arm the two hobbled down the back path behind the village which led to the South Lodge. The gate was unlocked, for the warder was busy elsewhere, and they hastened up the avenue. Far off Dickson thought he saw shapes fleeting across the park, which he took to be the shock-troops of his own side, and he seemed to hear snatches of song. Jaikie was giving tongue, and this was what he sang:

> *Proley Tarians, arise!*
> *Wave the Red Flag to the skies,*
> *Heed nae mair the Fat Man's lees,*
> *   Stap them doun his throat!*
> *Nocht to loss except our chains –*

But he tripped over a rabbit wire and thereafter conserved his breath.

The wind was so loud that no sound reached them from the House, which, blank and immense, now loomed before them.

Dickson's ears were alert for the noise of shots or the dull crash of bombs; hearing nothing, he feared the worst, and hurried Mrs Morran at a pace which endangered her life. He had no fear for himself, arguing that his foes were seeking higher game, and judging, too, that the main battle must be round the veranda at the other end. The two passed the shrubbery where the road forked, one path running to the back door and one to the stables. They took the latter and presently came out on the downs, with the ravine of the Garple on their left, the stables in front, and on the right the hollow of a formal garden running along the west side of the House.

The gale was so fierce, now that they had no wind-break between them and the ocean, that Mrs Morran could wrestle with it no longer, and found shelter in the lee of a clump of rhododendrons. Darkness had all but fallen, and the House was a black shadow against the dusky sky, while a confused greyness marked the sea. The old Tower showed a tooth of masonry; there was no glow from it, so the fire, which Jaikie had reported, must have died down. A whaup cried loudly, and very eerily: then another.

The birds stirred up Mrs Morran. 'That's the laddies' patrol,' she gasped. 'Count the cries, Dickson.'

Another bird wailed, this time very near. Then there was perhaps three minutes' silence till a fainter wheeple came from the direction of the Tower. 'Four,' said Dickson, but he waited in vain on the fifth. He had not the acute hearing of the boys, and could not catch the faint echo of Peter Paterson's signal beyond the veranda. The next he heard was a shrill whistle cutting into the wind, and then others in rapid succession from different quarters, and something which might have been the hoarse shouting of angry men.

The Gorbals Die-Hards had gone into action.

Dull prose is no medium to tell of that wild adventure. The sober sequence of the military historian is out of place in recording deeds that knew not sequence or sobriety. Were I a bard, I would cast this tale in excited verse, with a lilt which would

catch the speed of the reality. I would sing of Napoleon, not
unworthy of his great namesake, who penetrated to the very
window of the ladies' bedroom, where the framework had been
driven in and men were pouring through; of how there he made
such pandemonium with his whistle that men tumbled back
and ran about blindly seeking for guidance; of how in the long
run his pugnacity mastered him, so that he engaged in combat
with an unknown figure and the two rolled into what had once
been a fountain. I would hymn Peter Paterson, who across
tracts of darkness engaged Old Bill in a conversation which
would have done no discredit to a Gallowgate policeman. He
pretended to be making reports and seeking orders. 'We've
gotten three o' the deevils, sir. What'll we dae wi' them?' he
shouted; and back would come the reply in a slightly more
genteel voice: 'Fall them to the rear. Tamson has charge of the
prisoners.' Or it would be: 'They've gotten pistols, sir. What's
the orders?' and the answer would be: 'Stick to your batons. The
guns are posted on the knowe, so we needn't hurry.' And over all
the din there would be a perpetual whistling and a yelling of
'Hands up!'

I would sing, too, of Wee Jaikie, who was having the red-letter
hour of his life. His fragile form moved like a lizard in places
where no mortal could be expected, and he varied his duties
with impish assaults upon the persons of such as came in his
way. His whistle blew in a man's ear one second and the next
yards away. Sometimes he was moved to song, and unearthly
fragments of 'Class-conscious we are' or 'Proley Tarians, arise!'
mingled with the din, like the cry of seagulls in a storm. He saw
a bright light flare up within the House which warned him not
to enter, but he got as far as the garden-room, in whose dark
corners he made havoc. Indeed he was almost too successful,
for he created panic where he went, and one or two fired blindly
at the quarter where he had last been heard. These shots were
followed by frenzied prohibitions from Spidel and were not
repeated. Presently he felt that aimless surge of men that is the
prelude to flight, and heard Dobson's great voice roaring in the

hall. Convinced that the crisis had come, he made his way outside, prepared to harass the rear of any retirement. Tears now flowed down his face, and he could not have spoken for sobs, but he had never been so happy.

But chiefly would I celebrate Thomas Yownie, for it was he who brought fear into the heart of Dobson. He had a voice of singular compass, and from the veranda he made it echo round the House. The efforts of Old Bill and Peter Paterson had been skilful indeed, but those of Thomas Yownie were deadly. To some leader beyond he shouted news: 'Robison's just about finished wi' his lot, and then he'll get the boats.' A furious charge upset him, and for a moment he thought he had been discovered. But it was only Dobson rushing to Léon, who was leading the men in the doorway. Thomas fled to the far end of the veranda, and again lifted up his voice. 'All foreigners,' he shouted, 'except the man Dobson. Ay. Ay. Ye've got Loudon? Well done!'

It must have been this last performance which broke Dobson's nerve and convinced him that the one hope lay in a rapid retreat to the Garplefoot. There was a tumbling of men in the doorway, a muttering of strange tongues, and the vision of the innkeeper shouting to Léon and Spidel. For a second he was seen in the faint reflexion that the light in the hall cast as far as the veranda, a wild figure urging the retreat with a pistol clapped to the head of those who were too confused by the hurricane of events to grasp the situation. Some of them dropped over the wall, but most huddled like sheep through the door on the west side, a jumble of struggling, blasphemous mortality. Thomas Yownie, staggered at the success of his tactics, yet kept his head and did his utmost to confuse the retreat, and the triumphant shouts and whistles of the other Die-Hards showed that they were not unmindful of this final duty . . .

The veranda was empty, and he was just about to enter the House, when through the west door came a figure, breathing hard and bent apparently on the same errand. Thomas prepared for battle, determined that no straggler of the enemy should now wrest from him victory, but, as the figure came into the faint glow at the doorway, he recognized it as Heritage. And at the same moment he heard something which made his tense nerves relax. Away on the right came sounds, a thud of galloping horses on grass and the jingle of bridle reins and the voices of men. It was the real thing at last. It is a sad commentary on his career, but now for the first time in his brief existence Thomas Yownie felt charitably disposed towards the police.

The Poet, since we left him blaspheming on the roof of the Tower, had been having a crowded hour of most inglorious life. He had started to descend at a furious pace, and his first misadventure was that he stumbled and dropped Dickson's pistol over the parapet. He tried to mark where it might have fallen in the gloom below, and this lost him precious minutes. When he slithered through the trap into the attic room, where he had tried to hold up the attack, he discovered that it was full of smoke which sought in vain to escape by the narrow window. Volumes of it were pouring up the stairs, and when he attempted to descend, he found himself choked and blinded. He rushed gasping to the window, filled his lungs with fresh air, and tried again, but he got no farther than the first turn, from which he could see through the cloud red tongues of flame in the ground room. This was solemn indeed, so he sought another way out. He got on the roof, for he remembered a chimney-stack, cloaked with ivy, which was built straight from the ground, and he thought he might climb down it.

He found the chimney and began the descent confidently, for he had once borne a good reputation at the Montervers and Cortina. At first all went well, for stones stuck out at decent intervals like the rungs of a ladder, and roots of ivy supplemented their deficiencies. But presently he came to a place where the masonry had crumbled into a cave, and left a gap some twenty feet high. Below it he could dimly see a thick mass of ivy which would enable him to cover the further forty feet to the ground, but at that cave he stuck most finally. All around the lime and stone had lapsed into *débris*, and he could find no safe foothold. Worse still, the block on which he relied proved loose, and only by a dangerous traverse did he avert disaster.

There he hung for a minute or two, with a cold void in his stomach. He had always distrusted the handiwork of man as a place to scramble on, and now he was planted in the dark on a decomposing wall, with an excellent chance of breaking his neck, and with the most urgent need for haste. He could see the windows of the House, and, since he was sheltered from the gale, he could hear the faint sound of blows on woodwork. There was clearly the devil to pay there, and yet here he was helplessly stuck . . . Setting his teeth, he started to ascend again. Better the fire than this cold breakneck emptiness.

It took him the better part of half an hour to get back, and he passed through many moments of acute fear. Footholds which had seemed secure enough in the descent now proved impossible, and more than once he had his heart in his mouth when a rotten ivy stump or a wedge of stone gave in his hands, and dropped dully into the pit of night, leaving him crazily spread-eagled. When at last he reached the top he rolled on his back and felt very sick. Then, as he realized his safety, his impatience revived. At all costs he would force his way out though he should be grilled like a herring.

The smoke was less thick in the attic, and with his handkerchief wet with the rain and bound across his mouth he made a dash for the ground room. It was as hot as a furnace, for everything inflammable in it seemed to have caught fire, and the lumber glowed in piles of hot ashes. But the floor and walls were stone, and only the blazing jambs of the door stood between him and the outer air. He had burned himself considerably as he stumbled downwards, and the pain drove him to a wild leap through the broken arch, where he miscalculated the distance, charred his shins, and brought down a red-hot fragment of the lintel on his head. But the thing was done, and a minute later he was rolling like a dog in the wet bracken to cool his burns and put out various smouldering patches on his raiment.

Then he started running for the House, but, confused by the darkness, he bore too much to the north, and came out in the side avenue from which he and Dickson had reconnoitred on the first evening. He saw on the right a glow in the veranda which, as we know, was the reflexion of the flare in the hall, and he heard a babble of voices. But he heard something more, for away on his left was the sound which Thomas Yownie was soon to hear – the trampling of horses. It was the police at last, and his task was to guide them at once to the critical point of action ... Three minutes later a figure like a scarecrow was admonishing a bewildered sergeant, while his hands plucked feverishly at a horse's bridle.

It is time to return to Dickson in his clump of rhododendrons. Tragically aware of his impotence he listened to the tumult of the Die-Hards, hopeful when it was loud, despairing when there came a moment's lull, while Mrs Morran like a Greek chorus drew loudly upon her store of proverbial philosophy and her memory of Scripture texts. Twice he tried to reconnoitre towards the scene of battle, but only blundered into sunken plots and pits in the Dutch garden. Finally he squatted beside Mrs Morran, lit his pipe, and took a firm hold on his patience.

It was not tested for long. Presently he was aware that a change had come over the scene – that the Die-Hards' whistles and shouts were being drowned in another sound, the cries of panicky men. Dobson's bellow was wafted to him. 'Auntie Phemie,' he shouted, 'the innkeeper's getting rattled. Dod, I believe they're running.' For at that moment twenty paces on his left the van of the retreat crashed through the creepers on the garden's edge and leaped the wall that separated it from the cliffs of the Garplefoot.

The old woman was on her feet.

'God be thankit, is't the polis?'

'Maybe. Maybe no'. But they're running.'

Another bunch of men raced past, and he heard Dobson's voice.

'I tell you, they're broke. Listen, it's horses. Ay, it's the police, but it was the Die-Hards that did the job . . . Here! They mustn't escape. Have the police had the sense to send men to the Garplefoot?'

Mrs Morran, a figure like an ancient prophetess, with her tartan shawl lashing in the gale, clutched him by the shoulder.

'Doun to the waterside and stop them. Ye'll no' be beat by wee laddies! On wi' ye and I'll follow! There's gaun to be a juidgment on evil-doers this nicht.'

Dickson needed no urging. His heart was hot within him, and the weariness and stiffness had gone from his limbs. He, too, tumbled over the wall, and made for what he thought was the route by which he had originally ascended from the stream. As he ran he made ridiculous efforts to cry like a whaup in the hope of summoning the Die-Hards. One, indeed, he found – Napoleon, who had suffered a grievous pounding in the fountain, and had only escaped by an eel-like agility which had aforetime served him in good stead with the law of his native city. Lucky for Dickson was the meeting, for he had forgotten the road and would certainly have broken his neck. Led by the Die-Hard he slid forty feet over screes and boiler-plates, with the gale plucking at him, found a path, lost it, and then tumbled down a raw bank of earth to the flat ground beside the harbour. During all this performance, he has told me, he had no thought of fear, nor any clear notion what he meant to do. He just wanted to be in at the finish of the job.

Through the narrow entrance the gale blew as through a funnel, and the usually placid waters of the harbour were a froth of angry waves. Two boats had been launched and were plunging furiously, and on one of them a lantern dipped and fell. By its light he could see men holding a further boat by the shore. There was no sign of the police; he reflected that probably they had become tangled in the Garple Dean. The third boat was waiting for someone.

Dickson – a new Ajax by the ships – divined who this someone must be and realized his duty. It was the leader, the archenemy, the man whose escape must at all costs be stopped. Perhaps he had the Princess with him, thus snatching victory from apparent defeat. In any case he must be tackled, and a fierce anxiety gripped his heart. 'Aye finish a job,' he told himself, and peered up into the darkness of the cliffs, wondering just how he should set about it, for except in the last few days he had never engaged in combat with a fellow-creature.

'When he comes, you grip his legs,' he told Napoleon, 'and get him down. He'll have a pistol, and we're done if he's on his feet.'

There was a cry from the boats, a shout of guidance, and the light on the water was waved madly. 'They must have good eyesight, thought Dickson, for he could see nothing. And then suddenly he was aware of steps in front of him, and a shape like a man rising out of the void at his left hand.

In the darkness Napoleon missed his tackle, and the full shock came on Dickson. He aimed at what he thought was the enemy's throat, found only an arm, and was shaken off as a mastiff might shake off a toy terrier. He made another clutch, fell, and in falling caught his opponent's leg so that he brought him down. The man was immensely agile, for he was up in a second and something hot and bright blew into Dickson's face. The pistol bullet had passed through the collar of his faithful waterproof, slightly singeing his neck. But it served its purpose, for Dickson paused, gasping, to consider where he had been hit, and before he could resume the chase the last boat had pushed off into deep water.

To be shot at from close quarters is always irritating, and the novelty of the experience increased Dickson's natural wrath. He fumed on the shore like a deerhound when the stag has taken to the sea. So hot was his blood that he would have cheerfully assaulted the whole crew had they been within his reach. Napoleon, who had been incapacitated for speed by having his stomach and bare shanks savagely trampled upon, joined him, and together they watched the bobbing black specks as they crawled out of the estuary into the grey spindrift which marked the harbour mouth.

But as he looked the wrath died out of Dickson's soul. For he saw that the boats had indeed sailed on a desperate venture, and that a pursuer was on their track more potent than his breathless middle-age. The tide was on the ebb, and the gale was driving the Atlantic breakers shoreward, and in the jaws of the entrance the two waters met in an unearthly turmoil. Above the noise of the wind came the roar of the flooded Garple and the fret of the harbour, and far beyond all the crashing thunder of the conflict at the harbour mouth. Even in the darkness, against the still faintly grey western sky, the spume could be seen rising like waterspouts. But it was the ear rather than the eye which made certain presage of disaster. No boat could face the challenge of that loud portal.

As Dickson struggled against the wind and stared, his heart melted and a great awe fell upon him. He may have wept; it is certain that he prayed. 'Poor souls, poor souls!' he repeated. 'I doubt the last hour or two has been a poor preparation for eternity.'

The tide next day brought the dead ashore. Among them was a young man, different in dress and appearance from the rest – a young man with a noble head and a finely-cut classic face, which was not marred like the others from pounding among the Garple rocks. His dark hair was washed back from his brow, and the mouth, which had been hard in life, was now relaxed in the strange innocence of death.

Dickson gazed at the body and observed that there was a slight deformation between the shoulders.

'Poor fellow,' he said. 'That explains a lot . . . As my father used to say, cripples have a right to be cankered.'

SIXTEEN

In which a Princess Leaves a Dark Tower and a Provision Merchant Returns to his Family

THE three days of storm ended in the night, and with the wild weather there departed from the Cruives something which had weighed on Dickson's spirits since he first saw the place. Monday – only a week from the morning when he had conceived his plan of holiday – saw the return of the sun and the bland airs of spring. Beyond the blue of the yet restless waters rose dim mountains tipped with snow, like some Mediterranean seascape. Nesting birds were busy on the Laver banks and in the Huntingtower thickets; the village smoked peacefully to the clear skies; even the House looked cheerful if dishevelled. The Garple Dean was a garden of swaying larches, linnets, and wild anemones. Assuredly, thought Dickson, there had come a mighty change in the countryside, and he meditated a future discourse to the Literary Society of the Guthrie Memorial Kirk on 'Natural Beauty in Relation to the Mind of Man'.

It remains for the chronicler to gather up the loose ends of his tale. There was no newspaper story with bold headlines of this the most recent assault on the shores of Britain. Alexis Nicolaevitch, once a Prince of Muscovy and now Mr Alexander Nicholson of the rising firm of Sprot and Nicholson of Melbourne, had interest enough to prevent it. For it was clear that if Saskia was to be saved from persecution, her enemies must disappear without trace from the world, and no story be told of the wild venture which was their undoing. The constabulary of Carrick and Scotland Yard were indisposed to ask questions, under a hint from their superiors, the more so as no serious damage had been done to the persons of His Majesty's lieges, and no lives had been lost except by the violence of Nature. The Procurator-Fiscal investigated the case of the drowned men, and reported that so many foreign sailors, names and origins unknown, had perished in attempting to return to their ship at the Garplefoot. The Danish brig had vanished into the mist of the northern seas. But one signal calamity the Procurator-Fiscal had to record. The body of Loudon the factor was found on the Monday morning below the cliffs, his neck broken by a fall. In the darkness and confusion he must have tried to escape in that direction, and he had chosen an impracticable road or had slipped on the edge. It was returned as 'death by misadventure', and the *Carrick Herald* and the *Auchenlochan Advertiser* excelled themselves in eulogy. Mr Loudon, they said, had been widely known in the south-west of Scotland as an able and trusted lawyer, an assiduous public servant, and not least as a good sportsman. It was the last trait which had led to his death, for, in his enthusiasm for wild nature, he had been studying bird life on the cliffs of the Cruives during the storm, and had made that fatal slip which had deprived the shire of a wise counsellor and the best of good fellows.

The tinklers of the Garplefoot took themselves off, and where they may now be pursuing their devious courses is unknown to the chronicler. Dobson, too, disappeared, for he was not among the dead from the boats. He knew the neighbourhood, and probably made his way to some port from which he took passage to one or other of those foreign lands which had formerly been honoured by his patronage. Nor did all the Russians perish. Three were found skulking next morning in the woods, starving and ignorant of any tongue but their own, and five more came ashore much battered but alive. Alexis took charge of the eight survivors, and arranged to pay their passage to one of the British Dominions and to give them a start in a new life. They were broken creatures, with the dazed look of lost animals, and four of them had been peasants on Saskia's estates. Alexis spoke to them in their own language. 'In my grandfather's time,' he said, 'you were serfs. Then there came a change, and for some time you were free men. Now you have slipped back into being slaves again – the worst of slaveries, for you have been the serfs of fools and scoundrels and the black passion of your own hearts. I give you a chance of becoming free men once more. You have the task before you of working out your own salvation. Go, and God be with you.'

Before we take leave of these companions of a single week I would present them to you again as they appeared on a certain sunny afternoon when the episode of Huntingtower was on the eve of closing. First we see Saskia and Alexis walking on the thymy sward of the cliff-top, looking out to the fretted blue of the sea. It is a fitting place for lovers – above all for lovers who have turned the page on a dark preface, and have before them still the long bright volume of life. The girl has her arm linked in the man's, but as they walk she breaks often away from him, to dart into copses, to gather flowers, or to peer over the brink where the gulls wheel and oystercatchers pipe among the shingle. She is no more the tragic muse of the past week, but a laughing child again, full of snatches of song, her eyes bright with expectation. They talk of the new world which lies before them, and her voice is happy. Then her brows contract, and, as she flings herself down on a patch of young heather, her air is thoughtful.

'I have been back among fairy tales,' she says. 'I do not quite understand, Alesha. Those gallant little boys! They are youth, and youth is always full of strangeness. Mr Heritage! He is youth, too, and poetry, perhaps, and a soldier's tradition. I think I know him ... But what about Dickson? He is the *petit bourgeois*, the *épicier*, the class which the world ridicules. He is unbelievable. The others with good fortune I might find elsewhere – in Russia perhaps. But not Dickson.'

'No,' is the answer. 'You will not find him in Russia. He is what they call the middle-class, which we who were foolish used to laugh at. But he is the stuff which above all others makes a great people. He will endure when aristocracies crack and proletariats crumble. In our own land we have never known him, but till we create him our land will not be a nation.'

Half a mile away on the edge of the Laver glen Dickson and Heritage are together, Dickson placidly smoking on a tree-stump and Heritage walking excitedly about and cutting with his stick at the bracken. Sundry bandages and strips of sticking plaster still adorn the Poet, but his clothes have been tidied up by Mrs Morran, and he has recovered something of his old precision of garb. The eyes of both are fixed on the two figures on the cliff-top. Dickson feels acutely uneasy. It is the first time that he has been alone with Heritage since the arrival of Alexis shivered the Poet's dream. He looks to see a tragic grief; to his amazement he beholds something very like exultation.

'The trouble about you, Dogson,' says Heritage, 'is that you're a bit of an anarchist. All you false romantics are. You don't see the extraordinary beauty of the conventions which time has consecrated. You always want novelty, you know, and the novel is usually the ugly and rarely the true. I am for romance, but upon the old, noble classic lines.'

Dickson is scarcely listening. His eyes are on the distant lovers, and he longs to say something which will gently and graciously express his sympathy with his friend.

'I'm afraid,' he begins hesitatingly, 'I'm afraid you've had a bad blow, Mr Heritage. You're taking it awful well, and I honour you for it.'

The Poet flings back his head. 'I am reconciled,' he says. 'After all " 'tis better to have loved and lost," you know. It has been a great experience and has shown me my own heart. I love her, I shall always love her, but I realize that she was never meant for me. Thank God I've been able to serve her – that is all a moth can ask of a star. I'm a better man for it, Dogson. She will be a glorious memory, and Lord! what poetry I shall write! I give her up joyfully, for she has found her mate. "Let us not to the marriage of true minds admit impediments!" The thing's too perfect to grieve about … Look! There is romance incarnate.'

He points to the figures now silhouetted against the farther sea. 'How does it do, Dogson?' he cries. ' "And on her lover's arm she leant" – what next? You know the thing.'

Dickson assists and Heritage declaims:

> *And on her lover's arm she leant*
> *And round her waist she felt it fold,*
> *And far across the hills they went*
> *In that new world which is the old:*
> *Across the hills and far away*
> *Beyond their utmost purple rim,*
> *And deep into the dying day*
> *The happy princess followed him.*

He repeats the last two lines twice and draws a deep breath. 'How right!' he cries. 'How absolutely right! Lord! It's astonishing how that old bird Tennyson got the goods!'

After that Dickson leaves him and wanders among the thickets on the edge of the Huntingtower policies above the Laver glen. He feels childishly happy, wonderfully young, and at the same time supernaturally wise. Sometimes he thinks the past week has been a dream, till he touches the sticking-plaster on his brow, and finds that his left thigh is still a mass of bruises and that his right leg is woefully stiff. With that the past becomes very real again, and he sees the Garple Dean in that stormy afternoon, he wrestles again at midnight in the dark House, he stands with quaking heart by the boats to cut off the retreat. He sees it all, but without terror in the recollection, rather with gusto and a modest pride. 'I've surely had a remarkable time,' he tells himself, and then Romance, the goddess whom he has worshipped so long, marries that furious week with the idyllic. He is supremely content, for he knows that in his humble way he has not been found wanting. Once more for him the

Chavender or Chub, and long dreams among summer hills. His mind flies to the days ahead of him, when he will go wandering with his pack in many green places. Happy days they will be, the prospect with which he has always charmed his mind. Yes, but they will be different from what he had fancied, for he is another man than the complacent little fellow who set out a week ago on his travels. He has now assurance of himself, assurance of his faith. Romance, he sees, is one and indivisible . . .

Below him by the edge of the stream he sees the encampment of the Gorbals Die-Hards. He calls and waves a hand, and his signal is answered. It seems to be washing day, for some scanty and tattered raiment is drying on the sward. The band is evidently in session, for it is sitting in a circle, deep in talk.

As he looks at the ancient tents, the humble equipment, the ring of small shockheads, a great tenderness comes over him. The Die-Hards are so tiny, so poor, so pitifully handicapped, and yet so bold in their meagreness. Not one of them has had anything that might be called a chance. Their few years have been spent in kennels and closes, always hungry and hunted, with none to care for them; their childish ears have been habituated to every coarseness, their small minds filled with the desperate shifts of living . . . And yet, what a heavenly spark was in them! He had always thought nobly of the soul; now he wants to get on his knees before the queer greatness of humanity.

A figure disengages itself from the group, and Dougal makes his way up the hill towards him. The Chieftain is not more reputable in garb than when we first saw him, nor is he more cheerful of countenance. He has one arm in a sling made out of his neckerchief, and his scraggy little throat rises bare from his voluminous shirt. All that can be said for him is that he is appreciably cleaner. He comes to a standstill and salutes with a special formality.

'Dougal,' says Dickson, 'I've been thinking. You're the grandest lot of wee laddies I ever heard tell of, and, forbye, you've saved my life. Now, I'm getting on in years, though you'll admit that I'm not that dead old, and I'm not a poor man, and I haven't chick or child to look after. None of you has ever had a proper chance or been right fed or educated or taken care of. I've just the one thing to say to you. From now on you're *my* bairns, every one of you. You're fine laddies, and I'm going to see that you turn into fine men. There's the stuff in you to make Generals and Provosts – ay, and Prime Ministers, and Dod! it'll not be my blame if it doesn't get out.'

Dougal listens gravely and again salutes.

'I've brought ye a message,' he says. 'We've just had a meetin' and I've to report that ye've been unanimously eleckit Chief Die-Hard. We're a' hopin' ye'll accept.'

'I accept,' Dickson replies. 'Proudly and gratefully I accept.'

The last scene is some days later, in a certain southern suburb of Glasgow. Ulysses has come back to Ithaca, and is sitting by his fireside, waiting for the return of Penelope from the Neuk Hydropathic. There is a chill in the air, so a fire is burning in the grate, but the laden tea-table is bright with the first blooms of lilac. Dickson, in a new suit with a flower in his buttonhole, looks none the worse for his travels, save that there is still sticking-plaster on his deeply sunburnt brow. He waits impatiently with his eye on the black marble timepiece, and he fingers something in his pocket.

Presently the sound of wheels is heard, and the pea-hen voice of Tibby announces the arrival of Penelope. Dickson rushes to the door, and at the threshold welcomes his wife with a resounding kiss. He leads her into the parlour and settles her in her own chair.

'My! but it's nice to be home again!' she says. 'And everything that comfortable. I've had a fine time, but there's no place like your own fireside. You're looking awful well, Dickson. But losh! What have you been doing to your head?'

'Just a small tumble. It's very near mended already. Ay, I've had a grand walking tour, but the weather was a wee bit thrawn. It's nice to see you back again, Mamma. Now that I'm an idle man you and me must take a lot of jaunts together.'

She beams on him as she stays herself with Tibby's scones, and when the meal is ended, Dickson draws from his pocket a slim case. The jewels have been restored to Saskia, but this is one of her own which she has bestowed upon Dickson as a parting memento. He opens the case and reveals a necklet of emeralds, any one of which is worth half the street.

'This is a present for you,' he says bashfully.

Mrs McCunn's eyes open wide. 'You're far too kind,' she gasps. 'It must have cost an awful lot of money.'

'It didn't cost me that much,' is the truthful answer.

She fingers the trinket and then clasps it round her neck, where the green depths of the stones glow against the black satin of her bodice. Her eyes are moist as she looks at him. 'You've been a kind man to me,' she says, and she kisses him as she has not done since Janet's death.

She stands up and admires the necklet in the mirror. Romance once more, thinks Dickson. That which has graced the slim throats of princesses in far-away courts now adorns an elderly matron in a semi-detached villa; the jewels of the wild Nausicaa have fallen to the housewife Penelope.

Mrs McCunn preens herself before the glass. 'I call it very genteel,' she says. 'Real stylish. It might be worn by a queen.'

'I wouldn't say but it has,' says Dickson.